OUR TAINTED SOULS

A Novel

By:

Minaal Maan

Chapter 1

Ahmed

He was a monster. Today was one of those days when he felt as if he was corrupting the very air around him, and it had nothing to do with the acrid smoke that he was expelling through his lips. He felt like he was destroying everything around him because of the thoughts that were running through his head, and the opinions he held about the world after twenty three years of being stuck in the battle that was his life.

    Ahmed's attention was soon drawn towards a little girl sitting on a swing a few yards away, her dark brown hair blowing around her face as she pumped her legs back and forth. She would squeal in joy as she swung forward, her face lighting up with one of those smiles that could only be seen on a child, hopeful and genuinely happy with the world around her. He forced his gaze away then, hating himself because he had been staring at a five or six year old, something he judged those disgusting child predators for with a passion. It shocked him how they could live with themselves, but here he was doing the same thing.

But then as his eyes landed on the girl's mother who was sitting a few meters away, he reminded himself that he, unlike the predators felt no desire to be intimate with that little girl; in fact he envied her. He could feel a faint hatred towards her simmering in his veins at that very moment. Why was it that that little girl got to live her life so freely? Judging by the light in her eyes and the colour in her plump cheeks, she was happy and had a family that cared about her. Yeah, he thought incredulously. They must love her to bits, and the little brat probably took it all for granted.

His thoughts were confirmed when the mother came over to tell her it was time to go home and he watched as she threw a tantrum about how, her life was unfair and everyone was out to get her because she wanted to go on the slide before going home. Her mother had shaken her head and told her that the smog was about to set in, and she didn't want to get sick, did she? But the child had scrunched her eyebrows together and crossed her arms. In the end, her mother had carried her out while she had bawled her heart out for the whole park to hear. He scoffed, thinking about the countless other miserable brats who had no idea what they had, and just how much others craved it, or had craved at some point. It was too late now anyway.

Suddenly, he was ten years old again, waiting for his father to come home from his trip to Dubai. It was his birthday, and he sat alone on his bed with an Enid Blyton book open in his lap. His mother had one of her society brunches that day and he had pretended to be sick in order to stay home from school because all the other kids had been expecting a cake in class and then a birthday party at his house. Of course nobody knew that the strange boy who appeared to be enjoying every luxury that life had to offer because of his well-connected parents, was really just a kid who longed for some love and attention.

That was how almost all his birthdays had been. Dubai was sometimes substituted for London or New York and society brunches were replaced by fundraisers for NGO's, but the loneliness and depravity had remained a constant in Ahmed's life, and adulthood had only brought higher expectations and deprecating remarks with it.

He sighed, taking one last drag from his cigarette. God, he needed to buy another pack, he thought with a sigh. He would have to stop by the small shop on the corner of the road, and then meekly smile when the old man who had a fruit shop next to it looked at him through his round spectacles and told him how he was slowly killing himself, and ask him if his parents knew. He almost laughed out loud every time he asked that question.

Ahmed watched as the park slowly cleared and parents, or in some cases, maids and manservants tugged the children away from the swings and slides as the smog really began to set in. It always started out slowly, but then it was only a matter of minutes before everything seemed to be lost beneath it. Lost, he thought with a pang of despair. That was what he felt most of the time now. But he pushed that thought aside as soon as it surfaced, dismissing it as pointless.

His phone buzzed in his lap and he glanced down to realise that he had missed three calls in the past hour. A single name flashed across the screen, taunting him, reminding him of a life he had shared with someone who had left a long time ago. *Fahad.* If he paused and thought about it, he knew he would be taken back to those days and nights that were a mere memory now. He chose to ignore the calls instead.

Sighing, he got to his feet and started to make his way outside. His motorcycle was parked where he had left it, and he could feel that familiar, momentary burst of joy as his gaze landed on it. That Harley was the only thing that had some power to bring a smile to his lips, even if it was only for a moment. It was not just the thrill of the ride that elated him, but a lot more. He had bought it himself; with money that he had actually earned and not gotten from his father. He had worked day and night for it and for once, his parents had given him credit for something.

And that was it. The momentary smile dropped from his lips as thoughts of his parents entered his mind. He could almost picture them now, getting ready for the event tonight, going over "safe" conversation topics, and coordinating the lies that they were about to spin. It made him sick. He could feel the familiar rage burning inside him, coursing through his blood as the wind whipped his face and tousled his hair.

He could imagine the disapproving glare that his father would send his way when he saw him walking in with his windswept hair, leather jacket and his breath reeking of tobacco. But he would not be angry because of reasons a normal parent would. He would be angry because if anyone saw his son like that, it would raise questions and that could potentially ruin the image he had worked so hard to construct in the minds of these people, just so they would help him in the upcoming elections. A son who acted out was not something he needed right now.

He stopped at a red light and glanced around him, knowing that the city was far from what it appeared to be. While the towering buildings, luxurious restaurants, and illuminated billboards with their bright and colorful advertisements were enough to make an outsider believe that Lahore was not unlike any other city where people knew how to have a good time and the corporate industry was clearly doing well, he knew the city better than that. After all, while most people from his background had spent their teenage years attending the schools that were supposedly meant for the elite and labeled you as someone from a respectable background, his years had been spent wandering the streets as well. He had seen every nook and cranny of this city: seen what went on in its underbelly and had had experiences that would put the night life in Vegas to shame.

Ahmed winced, remembering the time he had failed ninth grade, and had gone home thinking his mother at least would want to know why he had been skipping classes, only to find that both his parents had expected nothing more from him, had assumed it was because "that was just the kind of person he was," and had already paid his fee for the next year along with something extra so that "people wouldn't talk." The truth that they had chosen not to find out was that he had been spending the days at the hospital with the librarian who was on her deathbed at that time. She had been a close confidant ever since he had started seeking solace in the four walls of the library in sixth grade, and had never uttered one comment that had made him feel like she was judging him. She had died at the end of that year.

That night had been the first time he had smoked marijuana, and the only thing he remembered about it was the discomfort, the numbness and then the high. It had been one of the best nights of his life. Money got you anything in this city, he thought with a stab of disgust. It did not matter if you were fifteen or twenty five as long as you had money and knew the right people.

The light turned green and traffic began moving, speeding forward as if everyone was in a hurry to get somewhere, which made sense once he thought about it. Why wouldn't anyone be in a hurry to get home? Just because he had a messed up family did not mean everyone else did too. But then he cringed as he passed a man sitting on the sidewalk, his head bent and hands clasped around his knees. As he turned the corner, the man raised his face and he saw that his eyes were bloodshot and swollen. He had expected it if he was being honest. That man probably had a family waiting at home, and here he was, wasted at the side of a road when he could be doing something for them. Poverty and despair sure drove you to do crazy things; he thought with another sigh as he neared his house. Oddly enough, he was glad he was not the only one with problems, that someone else was going through a hard time as well.

Yet at the same time, it sickened him how men like his father had the power and resources to make a difference in people's lives, and they still focused all of that on petty things, things that only brought momentary benefits. Of course he had tried to get his father to help people like the old man, but his opinion had, like always, been dismissed on the grounds of it being "near sighted" and "an inexperienced boy's ideas that had no place or potential if one wanted to succeed in the real world." He ground his teeth at the thought and continued to look ahead. He was pretty sure he would see plenty of other things tonight that would be worth criticizing.

  He almost cursed out loud when a little way further down, he was met with packed traffic and barely any room to pass. Street sellers and beggars were making full use of the opportunity, going from one car to the next, but were being driven away by the over-privileged people of the upper-class. He watched with disgust raging inside him as a man in a white Mercedes sneered out of his window at the boy asking him if he would buy a flower from him because he had three sisters to earn money for, The boy walked away after the man condescendingly told him to get an actual job.

  Ahmed could not help the wave of loathing that washed over him, not just for that man, but for the entire "elite" class of Lahore. They breezed through life in their BMW's and Mercedes, throwing their parties with money that was supposed to go elsewhere, not giving a damn about just how many people they were hurting, and he hated being a part of that class. You did not control what family you were born into, but you did have a say in what you believed in and stood for; he stood for everything that his parents did not.

A whole lot of good that had done him too, he thought sarcastically as he stopped by the small shop for his pack of Marlboros. Just as he had expected, the old man selling fruit was there. He could practically feel the judgmental comments rolling off him in waves, and almost snapped at him. He almost told him to mind his own business and not get in his. It was his life, was it not? He had every right to live it however he wanted.

When he had paid and had tucked the pack inside his jacket pocket, he moved on, not looking back at the shop or the old man, who had thankfully not said anything that day. Maybe he had finally realized that what he said would not change anything, and that he needed to focus on selling his fruit instead.

His phone rang for the fourth time in two hours then, and he took it out to see if it was the same number as before, but he was surprised when he saw the word, "Mom" flash across the screen. He had barely registered the fact that his mother was calling to check on him after who knew how long when the call ended. He had missed it. Clenching his other hand tighter around the handlebar, he breathed in sharply. Now was not the time to dwell on the fact that his mother had not called to check on him in what seemed like forever, that after months of her leaving him to his own devices when he went out, she had finally called. He was twenty three, a grown man. It was a little too late for all the sentimentality now anyway.

His phone vibrated again, and he reached in his pocket, his heart clenching. *If anyone asks, we went to Switzerland last week because your father wanted to take the family on vacation.* The text flashed before his eyes and he could feel the familiar heat of anger in his whole body. His heart was hammering inside his ribcage, and he felt the heat seep into his very bones. He could feel wetness behind his eyelids but he blinked, because as his father always said, "Men did not cry."

Of course the call had been because of a personal agenda. Of course it had not been to ask if he was doing alright, and yet again, he directed his hatred towards that little girl in the park who had taken her mother's concern for granted. Kids like that did not deserve love. They were the ones who deserved the life he was living. They deserved this Hell on Earth, and then perhaps they would know what they had.

He shook his head at the thoughts. Now he was just as bad as the others, judging everyone based on how they appeared on the outside. He had hated this quality in people for so long now; ever since the kids at school had automatically assumed that he had everything and was happy just because his father had money and power. The anger he had been feeling a moment ago turned to intense hatred, hatred aimed at nobody except himself. He did not want the negative thoughts that constantly flooded his mind, and he did not want to judge people from afar. He tightened his grip on the handlebars of his motorcycle again and blinked. He had missed a turn. Of course he had.

    Cursing his stupidity, he stared ahead of him. The road appeared to be a service lane and was deserted. He could see his own breath in white puffs in front of his mouth as he exhaled, and the firm cover of smog did not help his visibility either. Smog; it was another term that had found a place in his heart. Lahore, with all its shallow, rule-breaking citizens could not even get normal fog. No, here the water vapor in the air was absorbed by various poisonous gases in the air and thus became deadly. It could kill people with heart problems, he realized. The poisonous gases were of course released into the atmosphere by the countless factories, most of which did not even have licenses, and by motor vehicles, but recently he had come up with another theory that he found quite amusing. All that venom in people's hearts and minds had to go somewhere, right?

He was just contemplating this fact when he heard it, a soft rustling sound from under a tree that was not far off. He stopped, and his jaw dropped when his gaze fell on her.

Her hair was a tangled mess around her narrow shoulders and her eyes were wide with shock or anguish, he could not tell which. Ahmed could practically see her story reflected in her eyes. It was dark, but he could make out the intensity of her suffering from ten yards away. Her clothes hung in tatters over her thin frame, and he could see her left breast, limp and poking out as she tried to control her sobs. She was pressing a hand to her crotch area and he could see that she was trembling from head to toe. He almost turned his motorcycle to go over to her. He almost asked if she needed him to call someone.

But he did not, and he despised his parents with every fibre in his being for it. He could almost hear his father's voice ringing in his head when he found out that he had stopped and helped a girl who had just been raped. "Do you know what this could do to my career? Do you know the bad publicity I could get if my son is ever mixed up in a rape scandal? I have been working day and night for these elections, and you just ruined any shot I might have had at winning." He could also feel his mother's disappointed gaze as she looked him over and sighed, probably wondering why she was stuck with a son who refused to cooperate.

The girl shuddered and he could feel his heart sink as their eyes met across the empty road. Hers held nothing but despair and hopelessness, and in a way he could relate to that feeling as well. But then she blinked, and he was surprised to see a glint of steel in them. She had just been through hell, but she looked at him with grim determination, as if daring him to drive past. He envied her for her courage at that moment.

    Ahmed felt the guilt eating away at his insides, almost as if it were an actual beast living inside him, as he finally shifted his gaze to the road ahead and eased his bike forward before speeding off as if he were being chased by demons. As he spotted a turn up ahead that would take him back to the main road, he realized he actually was running away from demons, and maybe they were not visible but they were there nonetheless. He had been running almost his whole life and he loathed himself even more when he realized that that was how it was always going to be. He was a coward to the very core of his being.

    He could see his house looming in the distance now. They had blocked off the main road for ordinary citizens because "there was an important political gathering at an important politician's house up ahead." He felt the familiar pang of guilt as he saw cars turning around when they came to the barriers that had been put in place. He barely registered the drive up to his house from that point; it was as if his mind had drifted off to another place, somewhere he was free to help others without feeling guilty about it, and every move he made was not criticized.

He took the familiar path to the side entrance of the kitchen and then to his room, not really hearing the laughter and chatter coming from the adjacent rooms. It was all staged anyway, he told himself. It was just a bunch of people performing the social and political obligations that they had set upon themselves. "Contacts are everything these days," was something that he heard on a regular basis.

He barely felt anything when people patted him on the back or shook his hand as he came down after changing into what was considered the "proper attire" for the event, and tried not to chuckle when he saw a young woman, sporting more jewels then he could count talking to a man in a designer suit. To anyone else, the sight might have looked reasonably normal, but he knew better. That woman would soon be with that man in one of the many bedrooms upstairs, and that man would feel no guilt whatsoever as he touched another man's wife, all for a political alliance not many people knew about.

He tried to ignore the urge to scan the room for his parents, but could not help running his gaze over each unfamiliar and familiar face as he sipped from a glass of sparkling water. He spotted his mother first; she was standing in the middle of a group of important-looking men and women who seemed to be hanging on to her every word. She was the center of attention which was just how she liked it. When their eyes met across the room, she discreetly nodded towards his front pocket where she knew his phone was. "Don't forget what you are supposed to say if anyone asks why we were in Switzerland," she seemed to be telling him.

His father was talking to a woman in a pale pink *saree* a few yards away. He would occasionally touch her shoulder or brush his fingers along her arm, and she would look at him from under her heavily made-up lashes as she continued to listen to him go on about whatever they were talking about. He did not even feel the usual burst of disgust at that moment. He was numb to it all now.

"Ahmed!" He turned to see a man who looked like he was in his mid-forties with a receding hairline and curious, hazel eyes that seemed to promise that they would notice the vaguest of details, standing behind him. He knew who he was of course: this man was the reason his father had lost the elections last year. He reluctantly turned and shook the man's hand enthusiastically, with a practiced smile that was so well done he almost convinced himself it was real. Ahmed zoned out as he made small talk; talking about his recent trip to Paris and how his son wanted to come today but had not been able to make it.

"He probably doesn't know that you're back from Switzerland," he laughed, and that was when Ahmed forced himself to actually focus on the conversation. "But your father plans these trips so suddenly it's hard to keep track of when you leave and when you get back!"

"Yes," he heard himself say. "He doesn't even tell us until the day before we're supposed to leave."

"Your father is a very good man though," he paused. "Springing these surprises on you must be his way of showing affection!" He laughed as if he had just said the funniest thing in the world. "So what was this trip about?"

He could feel a lump in his throat and tried to swallow past it, picturing the girl he had seen mere minutes ago, and the man sitting on the sidewalk. He also imagined the girl from the park earlier and then, with venom practically dripping with every word and pure hatred coursing through him, he said. "Oh, he wanted to take the family on a vacation to celebrate my mother's birthday."

Chapter 2

Seher

Her breaths came in shallow pants, and she was finding it impossible to swallow past the lump in her throat. The small room that she shared with her parents, brother and sister was dark, the only source of light being the occasional clap of lightning outside. She watched, almost dazedly as the makeshift curtain that marked the entrance swayed back and forth as if propelled by an invisible force.

Seher could hear the wind howling outside and in that moment, she wanted to be just like that. She wanted to scream and howl and let out all of the frustration and rage that was pent up inside her. Her mind raced with thoughts of what it would feel like to just stand on top of a hill and scream; scream until her throat went dry and her lungs gave out, until she felt nothing except raw soreness along her insides.

Their words still rang in her ears like the lyrics of songs that stay with us forever, except in this case, she did not want them to. She wanted to forget she had ever heard those words.

"We really are doing it for your own good."

"He will change afterwards. Marriage changes people."

"He has money."

That last one really made her want to roll her eyes. Of course if she did roll her eyes, she would be the disrespectful daughter who had no idea what was good for her. So she had refrained from the unholy gesture and had resorted to her old habit of cursing everyone in her head. Her thoughts seemed to be the only thing that belonged to her now. They could not control them even if they tried. They could not tell what was going on inside her mind. She was free there.

Seher could not stop the wave of disgust that rolled over her as soon as she started thinking about what had happened mere hours ago. The memory of her father coming home, and announcing her fate as if she had no say in it whatsoever was still engraved in her mind, and then her mother, beaming with happiness when she heard that the groom's side had offered to pay for the entire wedding if they had it within four weeks, was enough to make her want to throw her guts up. She remembered how she had cringed when her mother had started talking about the clothes she needed to get stitched and about how much money she needed for them, and when her father had told her he would get her the money for all of that by tomorrow, Seher had almost laughed out loud.

It was almost funny how nobody seemed to want to know what she thought about the whole ordeal. Almost.

She had been engaged to Arshad for three months now, and needless to say, it was not a happy engagement; not on her end at least. But then again, why would that matter? According to her mother, she should feel lucky to have gotten engaged right after she had completed her education, and her definition of a complete education for her was different from her definition of a complete education for her brother. After completing tenth grade, she was eligible for marriage, and if she had found a man from a respectable family who was willing to marry her, she would be stupid not to take the opportunity. Of course if it had not been for her father, she would not have even studied past eighth grade, she let a small smile grace her lips as she remembered the argument her father had won for her two years earlier. But now, with ten years of education behind her and a man willing to take her, it was time for her to be married. What was love again? She had thought incredulously, but had of course kept her mouth shut because that was what she had done her whole life.

Maybe she should have spoken up; she realized, and cursed herself for not having the courage to do what she believed was right for her. If she had spoken up, perhaps she would not be in the predicament she was in now. She shuddered at the thought of living in a completely different house and sharing a bed with a man she barely even knew. She could almost hear her mother's response to the latter statement and rolled her eyes. She would tell her that of course she knew Arshad. They had been living a few doors down from each other for years, and had he not been bringing them milk for the past five years? Her father knew his father and that was a perfectly good reason for her to marry him. Seher could also imagine what her reaction would be had she told her mother that just because her father knew his father, it did not mean they were a good match for each other.

"That is not the way decent girls are supposed to behave, Seher. Your parents know what's best for you."

What defined a decent girl really? She found herself wondering, and realized that she did not have an answer. According to her entire village, you were decent if you did whatever the society demanded of you, and indecent if you dared step out of the parameters laid down by it. She scoffed, thinking of the various other criteria of decency she could come up with, and about just how many people would fulfill that.

As the first drops of rain hit the roof above her head, she sighed. There was no way in Hell she would be able to stomach spending the rest of her life with Arshad. The man did not know how to read or write for God's sake. She had pointed this out to her mother of course, only to see her laugh in her face and tell her that she had ridiculously high standards which she really needed to change if she wanted to have a decent life. So what if he was illiterate? He was the son of her father's friend and she was just being petty.

Maybe she was being petty and shallow, she thought and let another sigh escape her lips. Not liking someone just because they were not exactly how you wanted them to be sounded exactly like the kind of thing she would hate anyone else in her village for. Maybe she was just like them after all.

Turning on to her other side, she tried to remember the last conversation she had had with Arshad, but could not think of anything. That was the main problem, she thought. If she could just convince herself that she knew him well enough to know that he was a good man, maybe then she would be able to agree to spend her life with him.

After another thirty minutes of just lying in bed and listening to the pitter-patter of the rain outside, Seher gave up on sleep and quietly clambered out of bed, silently praying that she did not wake up anyone else. She rolled her eyes yet again as she thought about what they would say if they saw her getting up in the middle of the night and going out, even if it was just for some air. She could almost imagine the assumptions they would make, and the questions they would put forth.

As she was about to shut the door behind her, she almost jumped when she saw her mother stir in her sleep, but breathed a sigh of relief as she went still again. Outside, the cool air felt like a gentle caress as it washed over her face and blew her hair around her face. She almost sighed as she felt it touch her face; it felt as if it were a salve meant to sooth her scorched and clammy skin. Scorched. That was how she felt on most days. She felt as if she was burning from the inside and there was nothing she could do about it. Each day was a struggle, and she was going to completely burn out one day.

It had started a couple of years ago, she recalled. She had started thinking differently; about herself, her parents and the world in general. She attributed it all to age of course. When she had been a little girl, she had believed everything she had been told without a shadow of a doubt. She had believed, for example, that if children stayed out past five in the evening, they were carried off by evil witches. She had believed everything that they had told her about the world, and had never questioned it, for good children were not supposed to question their elders.

But then she had begun to "think." She had really started to get curious about the logic behind everything she had ever been told. Why was she told to do something a certain way, and why was it so wrong if she did it a little differently? Why did her parents think a certain way and were unwilling to listen to anyone with a different opinion? She had tried on numerous occasions, to ask them, to get them to understand how she imagined the world should be, and about how she believed that as long as you were not doing anything morally wrong, you did not have to worry about anything. But of course their definition of being morally wrong differed from hers, and their only answer was; "What will people say?"

People, she had come to realise, were the main problem. It was either them, or the assumption that what they thought and said about you mattered. It made her blood simmer in her veins whenever she heard those words, and she always felt like screaming when they were uttered. She could not understand why her parents would care about what people thought as long as they knew the truth. She began to remember the conversation she had had with her mother only hours ago and could not help the white hot wave of anger that washed over her. She had asked her mother why she could not just wait till she found someone else, and what if she said no to Arshad?

"I've already told everyone. Do you know what they will think if I say it isn't happening now? They'll think you went and got yourself pregnant by another man!" She had stood there for two minutes; her feet had been stuck to the ground, and she had not been able to breathe past the lump in her throat. She remembered how she had felt the wetness behind her eyelids, and had watched as her mother had continued explaining just how much damage she would cause if she said no. She did not want to ruin her father's reputation, did she? He had a name in this village and she was his pride and joy.

She had not been able to say anything at that time, but now she could practically hear the words that she should have said at that time. She had felt at that moment- and it was a feeling she had started getting quite used to- as if she was not her own person anymore. Her body was not hers, and the only thing she did have was her mind, because that was what allowed her to think things nobody else knew about. Everything she did, or said, was for someone else. She needed to be careful about what she said just so her father's precious reputation was not tarnished, or so she would not be thought of as the disrespectful daughter. Her heart felt so heavy that it felt as if it was weighed down by stones because of all the things she had to refrain from saying out loud.

The wedding was in four weeks, and she felt another wave of anger towards her mother and father when she imagined herself sitting there as the *Nikkah* ceremony was performed. She imagined looking at Arshad and seeing his dark brown eyes fixed on hers and a victorious smile stretched across his mouth, and then she imagined what would happen if she said 'No'. Nobody would bother asking why, all they would care about was that she had ruined what would have been a really happy marriage. They would say she was being improper and that no other man would want to marry her, just because she had exercised her birth right.

It was sick, she decided. The way everyone's mind worked here was utterly disgusting. But there was also nothing she could do about it. She could complain about it all she wanted in her mind, but the truth was that she was weak and she despised herself for that. She hated how she was powerless against everyone who had claimed complete control of her life, and she wished she was like those strong, independent girls she saw on television sometimes. But she was not, and that was the harsh reality she had to live with.

She stood there and watched an old tree that had stood in the courtyard ever since she could remember. Its leaves rustled as the wind swept by them, and the whole tree was leaning so far forward that it had to be a miracle that it was still standing there. She remembered all the times she had thought that it would fall; after all, this village had seen its fair share of thunderstorms. But it had not. It had stood there in all its glory and held against every single one. It had bent forward at some point, and sometimes, a branch or two would snap, but when the storm cleared, the tree would still be there, tall and proud, and she would be reminded that no matter what happened you could always survive.

She hated herself for thinking that way though, of simply surviving and not living her life the way she wanted to, but she knew that was also something she had to live with, she realized as she once again, began thinking about what awaited her at the end of four weeks.

"What are you doing out here in the rain?"

She almost jumped out of her skin when she heard the voice, her hand reaching for the wall to steady her, but relaxed when she saw that it was her sister, Zara. Having Zara see her out here was a lot better than having her mother or father catch her instead.

"I couldn't sleep," she said quietly. Zara moved closer to her to hear above the roar of the wind. Her sister looked pale in the dull light, her once prominent cheekbones and bright eyes were barely recognizable, Seher realized with another pang of sadness. The village had been cruel to them both in different ways. While she had taken to despising everyone around her including her own self, her sister had resorted to accepting the cards that fate dealt her with little resistance, choosing to believe the worst of her own self.

"You should really try to get enough sleep these days," Zara told her, looking out at the courtyard. Their house was not exactly spacious; you only had to walk five steps to get to the door that led outside into the street, and apart from the old elm tree, there was nothing standing between them and that door. Seher had often dreamed about getting out of the house, to a better place that hopefully did not make her feel as if she were suffocating, but she had given up on that option now, because getting out of here meant moving into a house that may be larger, but would only be another kind of prison.

Zara took her hand. "I know what you're thinking," she whispered, her voice soft and comforting as it had always been. "It might not be that bad, Seher." She knew she was referring to her upcoming wedding and shook her head. It amazed her to think how her sister could be so calm and optimistic about her marriage after seeing what had happened to her own.

"I don't love him," she answered. "How can they expect me to be okay with this?" She said, and felt Zara squeezing her hand gently.

"Because you're their daughter." Her tone had changed, and was almost bitter as she continued, and Seher's heart broke for her sister when she noticed that she had her other hand pressed protectively over her stomach before she seemed to realize something, and the hand dropped limply to her side while her eyes brimmed with unshed tears. "They expect you to do what they think is right for you. This village and the people here… they won't consider your feelings or think of what you have lost…" her voice shook as she blinked, and Seher realized that she wasn't just referring to her. "They will put people's opinions before your feelings."

She realized that Zara was not optimistic at all. She knew what was coming would be hell, she knew that they had been dealt harsh blows, and that they had little power to control their future. But she had convinced herself that the only way to survive was to do absolutely nothing about it. The idea that the village had managed to completely rip her sister's soul apart drove Seher further towards that endless pit of hatred and despair,

Chapter 3

Ahmed

The girl had died. Ahmed heard about it on the news the next day as he was getting ready for a meeting; a meeting he had been forced to attend by his father. It was a meeting that would once again "ignore trivial matters and focus on the real problems faced by the country." He had sat there for hours as a bunch of people, including his father and grandfather, had sat around a table and discussed exactly how they could bring the economy back up and decrease the poverty gap. To him, it just sounded like they were coming up with ways to convince people that they were doing their best and would continue to do their best if they elected his father. The meeting had really been a way to sniff out potential allies and beneficiaries who would not be afraid to get their hands dirty for his father as the election drew nearer.

He tried not to think about the look in her eyes as the girl had stared at him; the steely determination that had taken his breath away for a moment. Her raven hair and olive skin was etched in his mind, and he was trying his best to think of something, anything that would get his mind off the guilt that he was feeling. But then again, he thought to himself as he drove through the city towards his grandfather's house; maybe he deserved this. Maybe he deserved to feel as though he were being stabbed with razor sharp knives over and over, and as if the girl was still looking at him with that gaze of steel. He knew that her gaze would haunt him forever, and that he would always recall that night and imagine what might have happened if he had not driven away from hcr like the coward that he knew he was.

The city whizzed by in a blur of grey and black as he struggled to keep his eyes on the road and his mind blank. He could not afford to be distracted right now, as his father had reminded him countless times that day. The people that they would be meeting today would prove to be valuable allies if they played their cards right. He scoffed unconsciously when he thought about all the lies that would easily roll off his tongue tonight.

The sun had begun its slow dissent over the horizon, and everything was bathed in a soft orange glow as he neared the outskirts of Lahore. Traffic here was different as compared to the rest of the city, and he struggled to keep up as people rushed by him, not looking back at the lone SUV driven by the son of an aristocrat. His father had told him on countless occasions to make use of the driver that he had been assigned, and he had always waved him off, however now as he was forced to meander between angry drivers who honked at him from all sides, he was beginning to reconsider. Bedian road stretched before him, a never-ending sea of grey, dotted with trucks, buses and cars alike.

His phone buzzed in his lap and his gaze drifted down for a moment to see a familiar name flash across the screen. This time, instead of the resentment or hurt that usually passed over him when he saw his phone, he only felt a tinge of longing that was gone almost instantly. Irene had been a welcome distraction during his time at Oxford, and he could not help but smile at the memories as they washed over him. But that was all they were; memories. He knew he could never get that time back. No matter how much he hated this life he had been forced into, going back to England was not an option anymore and getting back in touch with Irene would be like fooling himself into thinking that he could run way from all of this.

He still remembered his first day there as a bitter nineteen year old who had had his future decided for him even before he had turned five years old. Oxford was where his father had studied and his grandfather before him, so it was only fitting that he graduate from there as well. It was 'expected' and his father had reminded him of that fact every time he had gotten in trouble at school. *"You have a legacy to uphold," he would always say.*

That legacy could go to Hell, he thought as he swerved right, narrowly avoiding being struck by a cargo truck that continued to push ahead through the other vehicles. He remembered his last day in Pakistan, when his mother had told him not to do anything that would bring shame upon their family name in any way. His father had sneered at him from behind her, already expecting the worst. Perhaps it had been that look that had steered him towards Irene and all the drama that had come with her. His mouth curved into a smile yet again as he remembered his first night out with her and the rest of the crew. They had gotten high out of their bloody minds that night, and had narrowly escaped getting arrested. The memory still sent a thrill of pleasure down his spine.

He wondered why she would call six months after he had left; a whole year since they had stopped seeing each other. She's probably wasted and wants to whine about her miserable life, he thought with a small smile, and turned onto the narrow winding road that led to one of his grandfather's many mansions. This road was a welcome reprieve after the noise and bustle he had just witnessed, and he let his gaze wander over every small detail as he drove. The tall evergreen trees that bordered it were still there, towering over everything, and the barriers that sealed off the end of the road that led up to the house were still in place as well, yet another reminder to the common man of the class that he served but would never be part of.

He carefully drove around them and towards the charcoal black gate that marked the end of the road. Rolling his eyes at the unnecessary display of guards, he waited to be let into the massive compound. They had been there ever since he could remember, and he had always hated seeing them whenever he had come to visit. As the gates slid open, he saw that numerous cars were already lined along the long driveway and his heart sank, knowing he would have to play by his father's rules tonight. A feeling of deep revulsion washed over him when he realized that not a single person here would actually be willing to do anything they were currently promising the general public. "Just enough to keep them at bay," were words that always hung in the air, unspoken, but true nonetheless.

He spotted his father as soon as he handed over his car keys to the valet. Dressed in an immaculate grey suit, and with his salt and pepper hair carefully combed back, he looked as imposing as ever. This was how he was used to seeing his father, dressed in suits, with a cigar dangling from his lips, or a glass of scotch in his hand. He could not remember the last time he had had a conversation with him that had not involved politics.

"You're late," were the first words that dropped from his father's lips.

"There was traffic on the roads, dad." People had started to turn, eager to see who the newcomer was. They saw Ahmed and within seconds, the whispering started. Raza Ali Khan's son was here, and he really had decided to step into politics. He had been at Oxford, hadn't he? There were rumours about the way he had spent his time there, but surely they weren't true?

"That would not have been a problem if you had left with me when I told you to," his father told him referring to that afternoon when they had just gotten back from the meeting, and his father in his usual workaholic fashion, had asked him to ride with him so they could both go over talking points in the car. Ahmed had declined because he had needed a break from politics after three hours of being stuck in a room full of people like his father, making plans that would only involve more palm-greasing and shrewd tactics to get people to do what they wanted. "Just try to go with the flow for once. Your grandfather and I know these people well."

Ahmed did not miss the jab at his inexperience, but he nodded his head as his father waved at someone across the lawn. "He was asking about you earlier so make sure you talk to him. I don't care if it's about the damn weather, but you need to show him you're truly invested." He wanted to ask why it was so necessary for him to talk to him when his father and grandfather were doing such a fine job fooling people on their own but something pulled at his gut and stopped him.

"I will."

#

"His wife just left for London…"

"That's how they pay for the house in Paris."

"You know you will always have my full support."

Snippets of conversation reached his ears as he sat alone, sipping his water while all around him, people attempted to mingle and make small talk. Ahmed had just managed to get away from a group of men that his father had steered him towards nearly thirty minutes ago, and his ears were still ringing with their questions and the lies that had spewed from his mouth on behalf of his parents. He hated himself for it, but had done his best to get him in their good graces. It had worked too, he realized, as he noticed the same men clamoring around his father; all eager to hear what he had to say.

Of course they had agreed to help him, he thought with a scoff. People were very quick to side with anyone they thought would be of use to them in the future. A favor or two now would mean they would have his father's support once he was elected, and that possibly meant a free pass on anything that might have been frowned upon otherwise. His father knew people, and they would take full advantage of that. But Ahmed knew that his father would have plans for when that time came as well.

His mind drifted back to the previous night again, and he found himself wondering what that girl's family would be doing right now while the people responsible for the conditions that had led to her being brutally raped were feasting on expensive food and laughing; laughing as another group of people mourned the loss of a girl, too ashamed to come forward and demand the justice that they were owed. He knew she had not been the only one. Countless women were raped in this country on a daily basis, and either lived the rest of their lives in shame or never lived again at all.

"Ahmed!" He looked up from his glass and locked gazes with his grandfather at last. He had not run into him ever since he had arrived, and had been hoping it would stay that way till the end of the night, but clearly that was not happening now. After he placed the nearly empty glass of water on the table next to him, he only had a second to spare before he was pulled into a tight embrace. "You look well," his grandfather commented as he drew away. "Oxford did you good, son."

He bit back a retort that was nearly at the tip of his tongue before nodding, and remarking that the old man looked very healthy himself. It was not a complete lie, he realized as he took in the rosy cheeks and lean figure of the man standing before him. Jaffar Ali Khan had managed to keep himself healthy despite his age. He remembered the last time he had seen him; a month before he had left. He had not been doing too well back then, but clearly the diet and early morning walks as well as the weight loss treatment he had been paying an oversees doctor for, had changed him.

"I must say I was expecting to see you sooner," he was saying as they gazed out across the lawn. "I heard you arrived six months ago."

"I would have come earlier," he found himself saying. "But then things started piling up, the trip to Switzerland for example." His grandfather shot him a glare that was sharp enough to cut through glass.

"Why don't you just grab a microphone and tell everyone about it?" There he was, he realized. The cold, calculating man who had groomed his father into who he was today, was standing before him and had not been able to stay down for five minutes. Ahmed bowed his head apologetically while every fibre of his being told him to demand why they did things that had to be covered up later I the first place.

"You've had the fountain replaced," he noted in an attempt to divert his grandfather away from any talk of politics and the election. He knew that was what it would eventually come to anyway. Their party was all they had left, him and his father, and this election was crucial for them. His grandfather was bound to bring up the election in their conversation eventually.

"Yes," his grandfather responded with a cool smile. "I had it done last year." Ahmed remembered all the times he had chased his cousins in this very lawn. They had run around the old fountain, just children not knowing where they would all be in fifteen years. Now they had all either left the country, or had removed all ties with them after the last election. Nobody talked about it but he knew that was a huge reason behind the vigorous campaign this year. His father wanted to prove a point and his grandfather would do anything to relive the old days when his own father was alive and the party had actually been in power.

"Talk to him." Ahmed had been expecting those words. They wanted him to mingle with the supposedly influential people at the gathering and he had been sitting down for a while now, away from the crowd at a table that provided an excellent view of the entire lawn, further strengthening his belief that these people did not deserve half the things that they had. Women drifted from group to group, pausing only to ask tactfully constructed questions that may or may not guarantee someone's support for them or for a close relative, and exchange those mandatory kisses on cheeks that seemed to be a clever way of avoiding an actual embrace.

He nodded and started making his way across the lawn, taking in the men seated around the tables; their plates piled high with food, half of which they would no doubt leave lying around. They talked in loud booming voices that masked any hidden grudges that they might bear for one another, and he knew for a fact that nobody who was there that night genuinely trusted another, or was willing to grant favors unless they benefited from the exchange.

All around him, men clapped each other on the back, laughing at jokes that were probably not even remotely amusing, and he swallowed the bile that rose up in his throat when his gaze fell on a man his father considered quite close following a woman across the garden with his eyes, his mouth curving up at the sides when she bent to place her glass on a table, the neckline of her dress slipping down to expose a significant amount of cleavage. He could practically see the man's gaze roving over her body as she straightened herself and walked away, casting a soft smile over her shoulder.

The smell of tobacco mixed with barbecue was thick in the air and he let it wash over his senses, calming him as nothing else was likely to. His eyes soon found his father who was sitting at a table not far off with a group of men smoking cigars that were courtesy of his grandfather. When he noticed him in the vicinity, a look of apprehension passed over his features, and Ahmed knew he was trying to determine if it had been a good idea asking him to come, trying to figure out if his son would keep his reputation intact tonight. It was not like the man had any other choice but to trust him, Ahmed thought, and smiled to himself. They needed him. So he looked his father in the eye and winked at him, grinning from ear to ear, before turning towards the man his grandfather had mentioned.

The rest of the night went by in a blur, marred with more superficial conversations than he could have imagined possible in one night, lies that made his blood boil as he uttered them, and promises that may never be fulfilled. He spent the few rare moments when he was alone deep in his own thoughts, knowing he was helping a cause that he had no sympathy for. He also knew that there was nothing he could do about it, nothing he could do to change the course his life had taken. Everything had been decided, and deep down he knew he would never have the nerve to stand up for what was right. He could spend years hating himself for everything he was doing but none of it would matter in the end.

As the night drew to a close, he found himself alone by the fountain he had talked about with his grandfather. It looked different now without all the people milling around it. The lawns were silent; caters having cleared them out an hour ago, and the guests having left in their luxurious cars, for their extravagant homes in Gulberg or wherever else Lahore's elite chose to live. His father and grandfather had retreated into the house a while ago, but he had chosen to stay outside a little longer.

The water in front of him was still, and he could see his own face reflected in the clear surface. What he saw did not shock him; he had gotten used to it after all these years. Hollow cheekbones and eyes that had long ago lost the light they once held greeted him, eyes that would soon be bloodshot and swollen. His reflection shivered as a cold breeze blew over the water and he shivered too, feeling the cool air caress his skin and ruffle his hair. He reached into the pocket of his jeans, and his fingers found his lighter, he thought he could already feel his nerves steadying in anticipation as he slowly began to let go of the bottled up anger and hate he felt inside.

It would just be a few hours, he knew. But at least, in those few hours he could be someone who was not held back by his demons, who was not responsible for any form of injustice, cared for and valued. He could be anyone he wanted to be.

Chapter 4
Seher

The rain had stopped by the time she woke up the next day, and the sky was back to its usual deep blue. This was usual, she thought as she slowly dressed, already knowing that she had overslept and that her mother would remind her of that fact when she greeted her. The weather in this part of Punjab was something she both liked and hated; it could be raining heavily one day, and then a few hours later, the village would be plunged into scorching heat, and it would be as if it had never rained in the first place. Right now, the courtyard was bathed in golden sunlight and the puddles that had formed the night before were already starting to dry up. The tall elm tree that stood a few meters away was as upright as ever, its branches reaching up towards the sky in silent prayer.

"The milk has already been put away," her mother said by way of greeting when she walked out. "Zara had to do it alone since you wouldn't budge." She resisted the urge to ask why her sister had had to do it alone since she had a brother to help as well. It was obvious that they had decided that pouring the fresh milk into containers was somehow beneath him, but fit for a woman. Seher rolled her eyes and wordlessly took the cup of tea her mother had set aside for her.

Talking felt more like a physical effort with each passing day, she realized as she sipped slowly while watching her older brother, Hamid bent over his phone. It was a small rectangular device that he had only gotten a week ago, and would now never be seen without. He claimed he had gotten it with the money that he had been getting for working at the cement factory that was located an hour away from the village, but Seher doubted that; the job had never paid him enough to even pay for his daily fare.

Yet nobody had raised an eyebrow at him when he had strolled into the house one day with the new phone, boasting about its touch screen and camera. She had seen him hastily close applications upon noticing when someone else was nearby, but had never spoken about it, knowing it was useless to point out flaws in her parents' only son and source of comfort in their old age.

"It was not a problem." She was saved from answering her mother as her sister walked out of the other room, having heard her remark. Her mother turned and sighed, looking over at her daughter with such despair and anger that Seher had to resist the urge to scoff. She knew that Zara had seen the way her mother's gaze lingered on her stomach and sighed. Her sister had always had low self-esteem. Did their mother have to make it worse?

She sighed and made her way to the old elm tree, a slight breeze lightly ruffling her hair as she walked. Resting her back against the thick trunk, she turned her face up to the sky and inhaled. It would be a long day and she knew it, another pointless mix of meaningless conversations and awkward silences. She allowed herself to think about a time when life had been simpler, or had seemed simpler anyway. The earlier years of her life had been full of endless games with the kids in the street outside or the fields where her father tended to the crops. She had been her father's princess back then.

"It could rain again today." She knew it was Zara before she even turned to look at her. Her sister was the only person who attempted to start a conversation with her that did not involve her wedding.

"Yes," she answered, trying, and yet again failing to come up with a way to carry the conversation forward.

"Come on," Zara bumped her shoulder gently. "Smile. Sometimes it looks like you're the one who lost her whole future and not me."

She knew the remark had been intended to lighten the mood but she found herself biting her lip in anger. "You haven't lost your future," she said, knowing Zara would not believe her. Sure enough, her sister just sighed, and brought her hand to her stomach before murmuring.

"I couldn't give him what he wanted." The pain in her voice was indescribable, and Seher could practically feel the sadness and frustration rolling of her sister in waves as she clutched the place where her baby bump had been. She still remembered the day Zara had come back home, crying and alone. Her eyes had been swollen and red, and she had been repeating the same words over and over. "My fault."

Her mother had taken her daughter in her arms and had stroked her hair, not saying a word. Later she had heard her talking to her father about how their daughter's life was ruined. Zara's husband had sent her away after hearing about the miscarriage, claiming she needed to be with her family for a while. They had then found out that he had married his second cousin the very next month, leaving Zara to choose whether she wanted to come back to a house where she would now be looked down upon because of something that had been out of her control, or to stay with her own family to whom she was now a burden. She had chosen to stay, and their mother had not been successful in hiding the fact that she was not particularly wanted at home either.

"It was not your fault," Seher told her sister for what seemed like the thousandth time.

"You don't understand these things, Seher," Zara sighed before turning away. "You should be happy. You're getting married." She debated arguing, but stopped herself. After all, what was the point really? It was not as if her sister would agree with her. Zara had been conditioned to think a certain way, she decided, as had everyone else she knew in the village. Nobody was willing to entertain the idea that a woman was more than what she was expected to give.

"You need to take care of yourself too," she said instead, turning to look at Zara. She had lost the baby weight, and with it, the glow that had always seemed to surround her ever since they had been little girls. Seher remembered a time when her sister had always worn her long, naturally wavy, brown hair down, and it had fallen in soft curls around her shoulders, much to their mother's disapproval; she had always insisted on her daughters' tying their hair, or tucking it away.

Zara had also once had beautiful, bright eyes with long lashes that lightly brushed her cheeks, a full mouth that would always be curved up in a smile, and a voice that seemed to breathe life into a room. But Seher did not see any of that in her sister now. All she saw were sallow cheeks, listless hair that was now permanently tied back and an ever present vacant expression on her face.

Her mother chose that moment to call out to them from where she was sitting. "Someone needs to clean the courtyard." Her gaze was fixed on Seher as she finished the last of her tea. "Samina is coming for lunch, and I don't want her to see the leaves from last night's storm." She was talking about Arshad's mother, and Seher could not help the wave of annoyance that washed over her. The woman had obviously decided to come to check on the bride before her son married her.

"As if a clean courtyard is a valid judge of character," she muttered, and Zara nudged her side before gently pushing her away.

"Who knows?" she commented. "Maybe it will get you in her good books even before the wedding." She rolled her eyes before walking over to where the broom was. Hamid had left for work now after assuring them that he would be back in time for lunch, and their mother had retreated into the room to get ready for the day ahead. Seher could hear her mumbling to herself inside about how she was stuck with taking care of everything herself, and about how her daughters had not made anything easier on her.

She tried to think of a time when her mother had not been like this, when she had been considerate and compassionate, but come up with nothing. For as long as she could remember, Fauzia Bibi had been the same shrewd and bitter woman that she was today. She could not even remember a time when she had seen her mother genuinely laugh or smile.

Her mother had married young, she knew that much. It had been right after her own father had died, and she had been coerced into marriage by everyone around her at the age of thirteen so her own mother would be free of the financial burden. She had not loved her father in the beginning and she doubted that she did now. Most marriages in the area were never about love anyway.

You grew to love your husband later if you were lucky, but she doubted that her mother had ever allowed herself to feel that emotion for her father. They never exchanged the sweet greetings that she had seen couples exchange sometimes on television, nor did they address each other with endearing names. Short phrases, careless accusations and occasional requests and inquiries about food or money were what made up her parents conversations.

Fauzia Bibi had quickly molded herself into the role of a mother and wife after she had been married, choosing to let go of the little girl who had just lost her father and instead, adopting the persona of a housewife who waited on her husband and tended to her children. There was no life beyond those two things, she had decided. Sometimes Seher wondered if that was why she was so adamant on marrying her daughters off early as well.

The village they lived in certainly had not helped. A forced marriage at thirteen had set the tone for how the rest of her life was going to be, limited and controlled by the shackles that society had constructed for her. Soon, she had become part of that very society without even realizing it and had spent her life within its confines, choosing the same for her children.

Seher's movements were mechanical, taking the broom, moving it over the floor slowly so the leaves would all be swept to one side, and then moving it back so the process could be repeated. She was ashamed to admit it to herself, but this was the only thing she did not mind doing here. It somehow allowed her to be at peace with her surroundings, and to think at the same time. She could tune out the rest of the world and be alone with her thoughts, dark as they may be.

She knew there was no way she would ever be happy with Arshad, and yet again, she felt that white hot anger burning inside her, anger at herself and the rest of the world. There was no way they would let her say no to the wedding, and no way that she would try to get out of it either. She might criticize her sister for not changing her fate, but the truth was that she did not have the courage to change her own either. She pictured herself in four weeks and swallowed past the lump in her throat.

Seher would sit next to him, in the red dress that she was expected to wear, a soft smile pasted on her face, her eyes done up in black, and lips painted an outrageous shade of red. She would sign the papers that would seal her fate, knowing it was not what she really wanted, but that there was nothing else to be done about it. Her mother would be smiling from ear to ear because she now had one less burden to carry. Her father and brother would be happy because it meant they're honor was perfectly intact seeing as she had in fact, married the man they had given their word to.

That was not how it had to go down, she found herself thinking. She could in fact get away from all this. A half- forgotten image began to form in her mind, and she tried to push it away, yet it stayed, solidifying into actual memories and ideas that she had had two years ago.

She felt the warm wetness behind her eyes before she could blink, and soon she was a little girl in a field filled with mustard flowers, her hair undone and blowing in the wind as she walked arm in arm with a boy with dark hair that curled at the nape and brown eyes that seemed to understand her for who she was and not who she was supposed to be.

She had been clutching a sketchbook in her hand and he had been holding a pack of colour pencils. The book had not been cheap, but she had been saving for it for six months and he had gotten it for her two weeks ago. She could draw, and he would colour all that she drew. He had convinced her to let him be a part of her art because he claimed they were better together, a force to be reckoned with. They had made beautiful art together and she smiled as she remembered their first picture, a cotton field topped by a grey sky.

They had planned on going to the city and making something of themselves, perhaps selling their art. It had been her dream to go there, and he had agreed, telling her every day that he would do everything to take her away from this village that was too small for them both, from its people and their opinions. They would be happy together there, he had promised.

She had longed for the day when she would finally be free to live her own life, to earn her place in the world. She would not be like the rest of the girls in the village, because unlike them, she had a man who would help her do what she wanted. They had planned to get out right after he finished school, and there was nothing keeping her in the village because her sister had just gotten married, leaving the house dull and unwelcome.

Seher had always been the outcast in her family given her disregard for social norms and expectations, and Zara had been the only person who even bothered to sympathize with her when she was subjected to yet another of their mother's disapproving lectures after she had supposedly found a way to taint their family's name.

Saad had promised her everything when they got to the city; love, support and a home. He would find work there and find them a place to live, and she could continue sketching. They would find a way to sell her work and make more money and then move into a larger house. He would do everything in his power to make sure that she lived her dream.

Her first mistake, she realized later, had been to rely completely on a man. After all, no other man in her life had ever even entertained the idea of her controlling her own life; her father and brother were proof of that.

Her own father, a man who had regarded her as his world had slowly started to let the opinions and assumptions of the people around him get to him. Why would Saad have been any different? She had told no one about him because she knew her parents would immediately jump to conclusions. Her morals and virtue would be questioned, thus ruining any respect anyone had for her family, which would lead to them giving her hell, seeing as she was the sole entity that preserved their precious honor.

He had, however made the mistake of telling his mother about her in the hopes of having her blessing to start a life in the city, and she had responded by accusing him of letting a harlot trick him into leaving his family behind. She had told him outrageous stories of girls who were out of control and became the reason their husbands were laughed at in public, and the reason they drove away their parents.

In the end, she had asked him to choose between his own mother and a girl who wanted him to stand and watch while she tore his honor to shreds. He had married his aunt's daughter a week later and now had two children. They had not spoken since.

Sometimes she wondered what would have happened if she had actually gone alone; if she had left the village behind and taken her fate in her own hands, but she had always come to the same conclusion. She would never have made it, and she despised herself for putting so much faith in Saad that just the mere thought of leaving alone chilled her bones.

The sketchbook had long since been buried at the bottom of an old tree near the outskirts of the village, along with any hopes and dreams she had had about the future. But she still remembered that day as if it had been yesterday. It had been raining hard, and she had laughed bitterly at the coincidence. She had heard about Saad's wedding from her mother who had come home beaming with happiness at the prospect of having an excuse to dress up. Seher had fled to the confines of the room she shared with her sister, and had vomited all over the floor before rushing out, the sketchbook held close to her chest.

She had ran for what seemed like forever, until she had reached the tree, and had then sunk to her knees and wept like the pathetic girl she knew she had been. Her tears had mingled with the rain as she dug the shallow hole that would hold her drawings and her dreams.

That had been the day she had decided never to expect anyone to put her first, or care enough about what she wanted. She had been a little girl and she had to grow up now; let go of the expectations she had of the world and its people. People, she had come to realise, were always going to believe what they wanted to believe, and they would do everything they could to make sure their version of the truth actually happened. It had also been the day she had begun losing her faith in men in general.

So she had wiped her tears, pushed the naïve idea of escaping reality out of her head, accepted the fact that her life was in fact, meant to be in this very village surrounded by the same people, and had then headed home, her hair pulled away from her face and eyes hard as steel without a trace of the child-like hope and optimism they had held mere days earlier.

She hated herself for letting that day change her, for letting someone else decide that she needed to change. She despised herself for letting Saad take her dream away from her, and for forcing her to stay in the village. But she also knew she could have been happy, away from all of this had they both gone away. He had filled her head with visions of a life she could never have had, and she had chosen to believe every promise he had made.

Seher also knew that in the end, she alone was responsible for her happiness. After all, she had had such high hopes and had allowed herself to think that a man from her village would actually stand by her.

The broom was getting heavier in her hands as she reached the end of the courtyard, and she sighed before straightening and looking back at her work. The leaves had all been swept into the corner, and by now, the scorching hot rays of the sun had almost dried the remaining patches of water on the ground as well. Their mother was exclaiming in joy as she saw the large dead chicken that her father had just brought in in hopes of impressing Arshad's mother who would be arriving in an hour.

"Where's my daughter?" Her father was asking for her now, and she could hear her mother mutter a reply, telling him that she had not managed to finish cleaning the courtyard for the past hour.

Sighing, she tossed the broom aside and began walking towards her parents, bracing herself for the torturous meal ahead.

Chapter 5

Ahmed

Warm sunlight was trickling into the expansive living room as he walked in, the evidence of last night evident in his eyes. He had gotten home at around four in the morning to see that his father had returned some while before him and had gone straight to bed. He knew that he would be expected in his study shortly to talk about everything that had happened yesterday; how many people seemed to be buying the lies that had dropped from all of their lips. After all, Raza Ali Khan expected his son to support him completely in the upcoming elections, at least that was what everyone at the event had seemed to think the previous night.

"The seat will be yours after him," his grandfather had said to him on countless occasions. "You need to be ready for that day and helping in your father's campaign right now will only help you, Ahmed."

And conveniently ensure it does not go out of your family, he had thought to himself at the time.

Mrs. Raza Khan looked up from her tablet as he walked in, her face already primped for the day ahead. A set of silver diamonds rested around her neck and he nearly winced as his eyes fell on them, the harsh sunlight that was reflected on their surface seemed to intensify the pounding in his head.

"Hey, you," his mother called as he sat down at the opposite end of the couch. A copy of *Vogue* lay open between them. She had dyed her hair yet again, he noted with a grimace. It had been a light ash brown the previous month, but now it was back to the auburn shade she had been using earlier. Ahmed considered asking her when she was planning on settling on one colour but decided against it, knowing he would never be able to understand his mother's reasons for anything she did.

"Hi," he replied, trying and failing to mimic her chirpy tone instead. Ahmed had no idea how she managed to be so cheerful this early. Then again, he also could not figure out how she could stand by and watch as their family fed on the poor, how she watched and helped as her husband and others like him took from the country, not caring who they hurt in the process.

His mother had not always been this way, he thought as he watched her continue to tap away on her tablet; probably making sure all the wives of the important political workers were coming to the brunch she had organized for the next day. Ahmed knew that there had been a time when she had been all about the people, finding out what they wanted, and then doing whatever she could to make it happen. She would write about it, and then try to convince her husband about what needed to be done. The inquisitive journalist within her had made sure the people's voices were heard.

But she had given all of that up now. As soon as she had realized that if she wanted to live the kind of life she secretly dreamed about, with glamorous parties and an extravagant house, she had realized that dirty politics was the only way, the more convenient way anyway. Writing the truth did not guarantee that Sabyasachi saree or those expensive vacations after all.

The fact that her husband's family was already into it certainly made things easier, and so she had changed from an ordinary journalist to the woman who would be the reason his father's lies were believed by everyone around him. She would find ways to convince the wives of people who mattered and sometimes even the men. He guessed the journalist inside her had never left, she had only found a better way to make use of her abilities.

"Your father says yesterday was a success." She looked up at him and he did not see any trace of his mother in the woman sitting before him, only a willowy woman in her fifties who looked to be in her mid-thirties, the skin on her face stretched to such an extent that he was surprised that she could even manage to smile. She had not been at the dinner the previous night, something he attributed to another one of his grandfather's political strategies. The men at that dinner had been greedy, hungry for favors and so her persuasive voice and quick wit had not been required to sway them.

"If by 'a success' he means that everyone was stupid enough to believe the lies we told them, then yes," Ahmed replied, taking a sip from the cup of green tea that had just been brought in, the manservant quickly disappearing after having placed the cup on the coffee table in front of them. God knew he needed this, he thought, as the warm liquid trickled down his sore throat. His mother shook her head at him. He could see her typing quick replies to emails, and he considered asking her just how much she was willing to do for someone who was so in love with the idea of possessing power that he was willing to do anything for it, but bit his tongue, knowing that his mother was equally in love with the comforts that power brought her.

"You know he has no other choice," she told him and he scoffed, the headache that had slowly started to recede returning tenfold now.

"Do you realise who you're defending right now?" he asked her. The sunlight streaming in through the large French windows was piercing into his eyes and he could barely see straight as he stood up, his head spinning due to the sudden movement. He knew it was pointless to ask her that, and yet he could not help the words as they left his mouth.

They had never had much of a relationship, the two of them, and on some level he had always blamed her for it. After all, a normal relationship with your parents was impossible when they spent all of their time trying to climb to the top of the social ladder and trying to impress people whom they knew would be of use to them.

His mother stood up. "Ahmed," she reached out for his arm, her dark brown eyes going wide as he carried on, his anger fueled by the fact that she did not even have a logical answer herself.

"Lying is never the only choice," he said and started to make his way outside. Arguing with her had never yielded any results. But she followed him to the door, her six-inch heals clicking on the hardwood floor.

"He wants you to go with him today. You can talk to the people..." Her words got caught in her throat as the door of the entryway slammed shut.

Warm sunlight greeted him as he emerged outside, and he grimaced as he was temporarily blinded by the sudden light. There was no trace of a breeze and he could hear no birds chirping in the trees as he made his way towards his motorcycle which was parked at the back of the large mansion that his parents called a home. He rolled his eyes. He knew that they could not have it parked outside with all the other cars, would not want to ruin the image of sophistication and class they had worked so hard to build after all.

He gazed around at the perfectly manicured lawn and the fountain that stood proudly in the middle. The scene might have been considered tranquil by some people, he realized as he looked over at the towering trees that bordered the whole garden. The lawn with its lush green grass and trees would be enough to make a person stop and wonder about the social standing of its owners. He supposed that was what it all came down to in the end; where you were at in the social hierarchy. Politics was just an excuse to get there for people like his parents.

Social security was what everyone craved, he supposed as he revved the engine before backing out of the paved driveway. His parents had not loved each other for a long time, he realized as images of them arguing and storming away from one another began to enter his mind. The three of them had not even shared a meal together in ages, and the only time that they were together was when they had to show a united front in front of people. He knew that his mother had no feelings for his father, but ever since she had gotten a taste of what being a part of the aristocracy could get her, she was not willing to let go. Add that to her need for stability and you had an explanation for why she put up with her husband.

This house and his grandfather's houses were the only things the family had now after the successive defeats that they had suffered in the two previous elections. The houses, and the large amount of money they had stored in offshore accounts. Nobody would ever know about the latter, he realized as he caught a glance of their house behind him as he rounded a corner. The money would remain safe and sound, never to be investigated because the right bribes had been offered to the right people. He was filled with a sudden feeling of disgust towards his grandfather and father as his attention was caught by yet another little boy begging for money at the corner of the street.

He really did not blame the rest of the family for cutting off all ties with them. Nobody wanted to be associated with a family of corrupt politicians, and he envied his cousins for the life of freedom they enjoyed far away from the mess that he was in.

He knew his father had wanted him to accompany him on a trip to one of his constituencies that day. Raza Ali Khan had been talking about it last week as well; how they would go to one of the villages outside of Lahore and talk to the people there. They would do anything from offering monetary bribes, to promising irrigation systems in order to win the people over. If those villagers had a single intelligent bone in their body, they would know it was all just words. But then again, they really did not know how to choose who to vote for.

These people voted on the basis of historical trends and whoever paid them enough, and most of them were not even educated enough to know if they were being made fools out of. He knew that his father would take advantage of that, and Ahmed did not want to be a part of it. He also knew in his heart that he would have to be sooner or later. The fact that he had gotten away today did not mean that he had gotten away for good.

Beads of sweat were starting to form on his forehead, but it did not bother him as he drove on through the city, passing through traffic without paying attention to where he was going. It was still early in the afternoon so the roads were fairly less crowded, and he was able to navigate without too much difficulty. Soon he was driving down a familiar route towards a park that he had grown quite used to visiting lately.

The park had allowed him to observe people of all kinds as they came to get some cardio done, or to simply watch their children, not to mention the maids and drivers who brought children from well-off families, whose parents were probably too busy planning their society events to bring them themselves. So he had grown used to sitting alone and just pondering over the world, and how it worked. Nobody here seemed to want to know anything about the strange rich boy who always sat alone in his designer clothes, and that was just what he wanted. He did not want people associating him with his father but that seemed to be impossible in most places, except here at the park.

As soon as thoughts of his father started to pour into his head, his phone buzzed with a text and he sighed.

Your mother says you told her you can't make it today.

He scoffed, his father would not let it go until he had texted him, letting him know that he knew. With a small smirk playing on his lips as he imagined his father's expression, he typed,

Yes, something came up. I'm sorry.

He put his phone away and found himself imagining his father's reaction. Of course he would be angry. After all, how could his only son just decide to abandon him in his hour of need? How was he going to tell the others that his son would not be with them? He knew they needed him. Everyone was talking about young blood these days, and how important it was that the young generation be given a chance to change their country.

His face was a weapon according to his mother. The youth of the country would be able to connect to them better if someone younger was seen in a prominent position. Besides, after his father, the seat was going to be his so the long-term benefits were there to look forward to as well. Leave it to her to want to use me for publicity, he thought bitterly as he watched an elderly man take the bench next to his and pull out a newspaper.

The park was empty apart from them but he knew that soon, children and adults would start trickling in and the air would be filled with the sound of them talking and mingling. Somehow, that was when he felt most at peace with himself. He could get lost in the noise and forget about his own problem, or he could retire into his own mind and focus on nothing but himself. It depended on the time really.

The old man next to him turned a page, and he instinctively looked over at the sound to catch a glimpse of his father's face. It was a group shot, probably taken last week, of him and his fellow party members at a conference. He had grown up seeing his father on the news and in newspapers but had somehow still not gotten used to it.

The photographer had caught him clapping another man on the back with a broad smile on his face. It was a good picture, he admitted. It showed exactly what they wanted the people to see. They were willing to work with everyone for a better future, and old rivalries were definitely just that. Ahmed also knew who the other man in the picture was, and he could not help but roll his eyes as he recalled a conversation he had overheard between his father and grandfather. They had talked about just how "willing" they were to work with him.

"They are talking about educational reforms." His head snapped up and he realized the man had caught him looking. Smiling at his expression, the old man continued. "I'm not into politics myself, but that's what my daughter told me." He tapped the picture of his father with his index finger.

Realizing it was too late to turn back now, Ahmed turned so he was directly facing the man. Not wanting to tell him that the educational reforms were probably not going to happen, he decided to go for a different topic. "Why aren't you into politics?" He supposed it was a personal question but did not know how else to respond.

"Because, son," and the man now looked older than he had only a minute ago. "I know the truth about all these thieves." Ahmed felt a small smile starting to form on his lips as he heard those words, and guilt in his heart at the prospect of agreeing with a man who was quite clearly not a fan of his father. He pushed it away.

"All of them?" He asked, mild curiosity edging into his voice.

"Every last one of them," the man replied with a cold sneer, putting the newspaper down on his lap and turning to gaze directly at him. "Their pockets are filled with our money, and what do they do with it? Send their kids abroad to study while our children rot in the despicable public schools here. They spend thousands on their houses and food, while we are left with people begging on the street for scraps."

"You know, they send their kids abroad so they can come back here and help," he was repeating his father's words, and hated himself for it. This was what his father said whenever someone asked him about why he had chosen to send his son abroad instead of getting him to complete his education in his own country. He knew that what he had said was wrong. After all, what had his father done for the country after coming from Oxford himself?

"I know people who don't send their children to school because they are too expensive for them," the man answered. "I know children who get beaten brutally in public schools if they don't write what is expected from them. Tell me, what this man or his children have done for them?" The man had a gleam in his eyes, and Ahmed wished that there was something he could say to him to placate him, but there really was nothing. "The educational reforms that he talks about," the old man continued. "They are what people like him have been promising for years now."

"You might be right."

"I heard he sent his own son to Oxford," the man remarked, and it was then that Ahmed found himself wishing he had not come to the park today. It was one thing to hear people talk cruelly of his father, and he was okay with that because he knew the man deserved it. But hearing this man talk about him as if he was partly responsible for something he had no control over was enough to make his heart clench.

The man kept talking about how he had seen various forms of social injustice in this city alone, and Ahmed kept listening, knowing that every word he uttered was true, that he might not be like his father, but would always be linked with him. The park eventually started to fill up as children began to walk in, and soon laughter could be heard all around them. He supposed it was a good thing that nobody else could hear them as they talked about how completely corrupt the present government was, and how the upcoming elections would not change anything if the people continued to eat up the lies fed to them by every political party.

"These reforms will probably come long after the children of my children are dead," the old man concluded and Ahmed nodded in agreement.

"Probably."

"My daughter practically idolizes this man," the old man sighed and he laughed.

"He has that effect on people," he replied. Ahmed was really not surprised. His father had managed to draw a substantial amount of people to him, simply by talking passionately about subjects that people wanted to be talked about, such as social justice and education. He had managed to convince them that he was the only person who could achieve these things for them and they believed him simply because he sounded sincere to them.

He sounded like a man who would do things for them, and women and teenagers looked up to him. He supposed if he was successful this year, it would be because of them. Their party had been suffering considerably in the past, but judging by the polls on social media, this election year would be different and his grandfather was counting on that. The new angles and strategies that they had been using seemed to be working, and nobody had come up with any allegation against them yet either, not one that was accompanied with proof anyway. So it really felt like they were in a good place.

"You make a good point," the old man said finally. "It's the way he talks." He added as an afterthought, and Ahmed nodded. "My daughter says he is bringing his son forward now too."

"What do you think of that?" He genuinely wanted to know his opinion because it was clear to him that the old man knew what he was talking about.

"I think the kid would be better off in Oxford." Ahmed smiled as he continued. "Politics is not for children, and if you have parents like this guy," he pointed at the newspaper. "I doubt you would know the first thing about the people of this country." They fell silent for a while and Ahmed was almost considering asking the man if he had a personal vendetta against his father when he added. "I bet the poor kid didn't have a choice. That's how it is with these high class aristocrat types."

"You sure you aren't secretly one of them?" Ahmed found himself teasing the strange old man that he had just met. It was a nice feeling, he realized, having someone sympathizing with him. This old man barely knew anything about him and yet he seemed to understand him more than his own mother.

"Like hell I am," the man replied with a laugh.

They sat in silence yet again for a while until the air around them grew colder, and the sun started to set. The smog was back, clinging to the air and forcing the children to leave. He felt it brush over his face, and noticed the old man shiver a little before finally deciding that it was time for him to go. Ahmed watched him go, not knowing whether he should ask for a name, or if he even wanted to. They had had a nice conversation, he thought to himself as the man disappeared from his view at last, swallowed up by the ever-present clouds of smog that blanketed the city that he loved to hate so much.

Chapter 6

Seher

"So they're all coming over then? His mother too?"

"His mother, two sisters and his father as well."

"Of course."

She had not been out with her friend in months, it seemed. Rabia had been one of the few people in the school who had actually bothered to talk to her despite her outrageous qualities, and the two of them had been friends since the fifth grade. Seher had gotten in trouble for standing up to one of their teachers after she had hit a girl on the palm too hard with a ruler for a mistake that she had not made, and Rabia had come up to her after class that day and told her, more like demanded that they be best friends. That memory still managed to bring a small smile to her face. Although Rabia had gotten married right after the eighth grade, the two of them had stayed friends, despite the fact that her husband obviously hated her guts.

"Maybe he will be better than you think," her friend said as she unwrapped yet another candy, and popped it into her mouth. The two of them had been coming to this shop on the outskirts of their village for years now, buying treats and then eating them together on their way back. It was a tradition both of their families had despised since the day it started. That had not stopped them from going.

"You don't need to try to get me to be happy about this," Seher bumped her shoulder gently. "I know it doesn't matter how I feel, so why bother?" Yet, even as the words left her lips she knew that despite her cynical tone, the closest she would ever get to being truly happy was when she was with Rabia. The two of them shared a bond stronger than blood, and she knew that in the few moments that she got with her, Seher could truly be herself without fear of being judged.

"You deserve to be happy though," Rabia said. "Everyone does." They continued to walk down the narrow, winding road that led back into the village, past men who were lounging around outside their houses and sneered as they walked by. Seher's hair blew around her shoulders because of the breeze that had started up and she quickly tucked it behind her ears, knowing that it was only a few minutes before she would be back inside that house where smiling had become a thing of the past, and staying in the present nearly impossible.

The sun cast its yellow light upon the path in front of them, but she was shivering slightly, knowing that it would not be long before the sun set, and the mysterious clouds of fog settled down upon the village, enveloping it in their cool embrace.

Soon, they were walking down the familiar street that had Rabia's house at the end of it. Her two year old son was waiting for them outside the door and Seher smiled as her friend bent to pick him up. He often stayed home when Rabia went out to work in the large *haveli* owned by the *Chaudhry Sahib* that was not far off, or to run errands, and her mother would watch over him in the meantime.

Seher knew in her heart that she would never be able to even think of having a child with Arshad, but she was glad that her friend had been able to get something good out of her own marriage. The boy stared back at her through confused brown eyes as she reached forward to hand him one of the sweets they had gotten.

"Those things make him sick," Rabia sighed as her son took the candy with curious hands and a smile.

"They make him happy," Seher answered. "Someone here should know what that feels like." Thoughts of the impending supper ahead had started to enter her mind now, clouding her senses. She had known, all this time that she was going to marry the strange boy down the street whom she knew nothing about, but somehow, now it felt more real. She was feeling the walls slowly closing around her, and hating the fact that she was helpless against them. Rabia had started moving about the house now, getting water for her mother who was about to leave, and then putting a pot of tea on the stove for her husband who was due to arrive at any moment. That was her cue to leave she realized.

"Take care of yourself," her friend squeezed her hand at the door and she nodded, her mind already a mile away. "And tell me everything tomorrow."

#

The sky had darkened quite rapidly that day, and Seher was starting to wonder if winter really had come with the rain they had had a couple of days ago. She could certainly feel the chill in the air now as she sat by the stove, her hands held out in front of her over the fire in an attempt to warm them. She could hear an owl hooting in the distance and then a cuckoo, and she closed her eyes as the warmth from the stove slowly seeped into her skin. She knew this would not last long though. Soon, her father and brother would come home from the fields where they had been working and she would be expected to help make supper for them. So she decided to make the most of the time that she had to herself before she would have to open the door.

The day had been hectic, she recalled; more hectic than usual anyway. She had come home only to find out that Rabia's husband had been looking for them while they had been outside. He had gone by the house for lunch, and upon not finding his wife waiting for him by the stove, he had gone back outside in a fit of anger. Zara told her that he had come by twice.

Seher supposed her friend's husband had started to despise her the day they had taken that first trip to the shop together after her marriage. He had been away then, and a friend of his had informed him that his wife had been seen out in the streets with "that girl Seher" and with her head uncovered no less which was absolutely scandalous.

Rabia's husband had a habit of deciding what would displease God on his own. She thought this was ironic considering that fact that he had probably never read a word of the Holy Book himself. He made her sick, she thought, as memories of him sitting on the side of the street before he had gotten married began to surface in her mind. He would sit there and stare at every woman that walked by, and his gaze had felt like a razor sharp blade cutting her open and leaving her exposed for everyone else to see. He liked to pretend that he was different now, but she had caught him countless times outside the girls' school, supposedly just selling crushed ice in the middle of the blistering hot summers, but he still managed to run his eyes over the bodies of his customers in spite of them having their heads and bodies covered.

There was a sharp knock at the door, and then she could hear the raucous laughter of her father and brother. Wincing slightly, she stood up as her mother started yelling at her to open the door from where she sat knitting something a few paces away. Seher's movements felt slow and she also felt as if she had opened the door in a daze. It had been like that for a while. Her head felt light as she walked, and she slowly detaching herself yet again from the present.

She remembered a time when it had not been this way, a time when she had rushed to the door every time she heard her father's voice outside. She would open it and throw her arms around him, and squeal as he picked her up. She would smile as he pressed his lips to her forehead while her brother and sister bounded up to them, chattering away, and then they would all walk back to the fire together where her mother had a pot of tea ready.

Those days were gone now, she told herself as the door opened to reveal her father, his back bent, and a small sack of rice over his shoulder. She supposed that was a good sign, they had been running low on food items for a week now. Her mother moved forward to help him bring it inside and he visibly relaxed. His joints had been getting worse over the past few months, Seher realized. They had stated hurting him over the past year and he had been taking pills prescribed by the village doctor, but they did not seem to be working long-term. He would have to go to the city soon.

Her brother entered a few seconds later, deep in conversation with another man who was standing in the shadow cast by the low wall of their house. They paid no attention to her as they walked in, and her father had a wide smile plastered across his face now as he brushed his hand on top of her head in a practiced manner, and then his voice as he spoke his first words to her sent a shiver down her spine.

"Look who came for supper!" And it was then that she realized who the other man was. His shawl was wrapped tightly around his shoulders and covered his head as well but there was no mistaking that face, those dark brown eyes that looked as if they were staring right through her, and that hard mouth that curled into a smile when his eyes had roamed every inch of her. Her mother gave a squeal of utter joy and moved forward to greet him as they walked further into the house, the sack of rice now lying forgotten against the wall. After polite greetings had been exchanged, Arshad regarded her with a cool, steady gaze, and she realized that she had not moved from her spot by the door. Pure revulsion was coursing through her and she could not bring herself to feel otherwise as his lips parted again to reveal a slightly softer smile that was supposedly meant to make her toes curl.

It was not as if she was not trying to feel some form of affection for her soon to be husband, she truly had tried. But something in her heart had always clenched when he was around, ever since he had been bringing them milk for all those years. It was as if her body was trying to warn her and now, as he stood before her once more and gazed at every inch of her, she felt that familiar feeling again.

"You look good," he commented, and she involuntarily ran a hand through her hair which was hanging in lose curls around her shoulders. She had just bathed a while ago and let it hang lose for a while before tying it.

"Thank you." The words felt like drops of poison as they left her mouth, and for a moment they hung there in the air between them as he continued to look at her, and she tried to look anywhere but at him.

"Did you go to the shop today?" The question was simple enough, and she knew she might be reading too much into it, but she could not help the wave of defensiveness that crept over her as she looked back at him. Rabia's husband's face flashed before her eyes as she realized that Arshad would quite possibly be just like him. She did not know if she had imagined the slight edge in his tone so she nodded.

"What did you need?" He definitely sounded different now, and Seher could see that he wanted to say more but she simply shrugged.

"Rabia and I went to get something for Zara, and we wanted to get some sweets for ourselves." He nodded and she closed the door behind them.

"Next time just tell me to get whatever you need," He smiled at her, and she realized that in his mind, he was doing her a favor. She simply nodded and tried to block away the disgust she felt for him in that instant. He was trying hard, she realized. Had they been married, he would have said more; the hardness of his mouth and the way his shoulders were shaking were proof enough. A shiver ran down her spine.

"I thought Amina and your mother were coming too," Seher said in an attempt to change the topic. Amina was his little sister and the two of them had often talked outside. She quite liked her too, and up until that moment had thought they would both be coming. Her mother had been worrying about the courtyard for nothing then.

"They were busy," he said dismissively and then smiled. "Besides, I wanted to talk to your father about the expenses of our wedding, so I expected this sort of thing would go over their heads anyway. Yours too."

The jab at her gender was enough to form a lump in her throat, and a wave of fury to wash over her but she bit her tongue. He, thinking it was because of the fact that he had not come to see her sooner, smiled and tipped her chin up. She flinched inwardly.

"Don't worry," he whispered. 'You'll be with me soon." He started walking towards the fire where the others were waiting but looked over his shoulder. "The sooner your mother finishes the dowry arrangements, the better it will be."

She knew she had to follow him, of course she had to. The others were now looking over expectantly, and her mother was signaling for her to serve them tea. Her fists clenched at her sides and she could practically feel her veins turn to ice as she walked back. His words were ringing in her ears, and she knew that there was a chance that she was being unfair to him, but her mind was racing a mile a minute. She remembered when Zara was getting married and her mother had been frantic about the dowry, mending old clothes for her and buying crockery with what little money she had saved up. She had even asked the *Chaudhry Sahib* that their family worked for to help, and his wife had given some jewelry, and money they had used to buy a small television set that was still being used by the man who had abandoned their daughter, and his new wife. But Seher had never understood why a dowry was necessary and had gotten in an argument with her mother which had ended in her being sent to her room and a firm "you will not understand."

But she did understand. She understood that a dowry basically meant that the girl's parents were paying the groom's family to take their daughter, as if she were a goat that had been taken off their hands. She hated what the dowry represented. Arshad's family would think less of her parents if they did not give enough because the dowry was another way to preserve family honor. Her mouth went dry at the very thought, and she tried to swallow past the lump that had now formed in her throat.

Supper seemed to take forever, and she yearned to be away from the heat of the fire that had felt like a gentle balm upon her freezing fingers mere minutes ago, but now felt like it was going to burn her very skin off. She was reminded yet again of the sensation of being slowly burned from the inside and her thoughts drifted once more to that place where she knew she was safe and yet in danger. It was dangerous because she knew quite well exactly where her thoughts would lead her, and how powerless she would feel. The feeling of being powerless would then be followed by anger at her own self for not being stronger. She hated it and yet she loved it.

She knew that the moment was near now. She would soon be leaving this house, and it would be like leaving one form of prison for another. When was a girl like her supposed to grow then? When was she supposed to find her true self? The answer rang clear in her head and she knew she had sighed out loud. A woman found her purpose as soon as she became a mother. She could almost hear her mother saying that and she knew she disagreed as she watched her sister take slow mournful bites of the food, her eyes cast downward as though she were afraid Arshad might look at her and start a conversation that would most likely lead to him asking about her husband, or him looking at her as if she were a lost cause, a burden for her parents.

She longed to somehow show her sister that she was more than what she thought she was, that a miscarriage did not have to mean the end for her. But she also knew that it would be impossible to do that while they lived in this village. Nobody ever let you forget anything here.

Seher knew that she did not want to bring a child into this world only for it to drown under the social norms and obligations of their village. She felt like it was a sin to be the cause of someone completely innocent being broken like that. And yet, she realized. That was what was expected from her after she married Arshad. His mother would start pestering her right after they got married, and God forbid they have a daughter!

She could feel the bile rising in her throat, and struggled to keep it down as she realized that he was watching her. Her mother and Zara had always said that she would grow to love this man, but now she was almost sure that that would never happen. He would be the reason she finally went under, and she knew that once she was there, there was no way out.

"Why don't you girls start washing these, and we can talk about the wedding?" She was jolted out of her reverie by the sound of her brother's voice and her blood boiled. He was a whole two years younger than her and yet he went around acting as if her were five years older. He had never even touched a dirty plate in his life, because it had been decreed that women be tasked with washing up, and a man surely did not need to bother himself with such chores. Her father was nodding his head, probably preoccupied with thoughts of exactly how much he would be asked to pay. Although Arshad's family had agreed to pay, they had only found out yesterday that this deal was basically a loan that they expected to be repaid by the end of the year. As if it was not their son's wedding too, she thought bitterly as she prepared to leave.

As they began washing up a few meters away, Seher caught snatches of conversation from the other side of the courtyard, and could not help the momentary smile that curved her lips upwards. They were struggling with adding up numbers and she knew that she would have been able to do that in just two minutes. Even though her parents had invested more in their son's education, he was now straining to do something she had taught herself when she was barely seven. She almost laughed. Almost.

"That could take a while," Zara laughed nervously beside her, and when she turned to look at her, it was to see her looking back at her with concern written all over her face. Her sister placed a clean steel plate on top of the pile they had made and sat back.

"It could," she agreed and realized that this was probably the first time she had spoken that night ever since her conversation with Arshad by the door. Her throat felt parched, and her own voice sounded as if it was coming from far away. It was strange, she thought. She knew this was not normal, that whatever was happening to her had a name for it. It had to. But she also knew that nobody in her village would even bother to think that this feeling of detachment was anything more than a girl gone astray from the Right Path, who needed to be brought back on it. It could be the devil himself, they would say. The fact that he was sending evil spirits after her was a perfectly logical explanation.

"I'm worried about you," she heard her sister say and she turned to look at her, not having it in her to ask her why. She was worried about herself too, but would that change anything? "What was he saying to you when he came in?"

Sehr considered not answering. After all, that would be the best way to avoid a pointless conversation that was most likely to involve her sister telling her about the compromises a woman had to make, but she shrugged.

"He wanted to know why I was at the shop today." Zara visibly paled, and the silvery moonlight highlighted the numerous dark circles under her sister's eyes. She was now looking back at her with her lips slightly parted and a look of utter fear in her eyes. Seher tried hard not to smile at the absurdity of the situation, because the sight might have suggested that Zara was the one being questioned by her husband and not her.

"I told you not to go," Zara said. "And you did not even cover your head!"

"And what a crime that was," she replied bitterly only to hear her sister gasp.

"Seher, I've told you a million times. There are men…"

"If those men had a shred of decency in them, they would mind their own damn business," she snapped and her sister sighed.

"God, Seher."

Silence reigned after that, and she was left again to ponder upon the irony of things. She knew that she could not change things but she also knew that simply covering her head would not make sure that men stopped treating her body like an object to be ogled at. It would just mean they would have more room to their imagination. If the problem really had to be solved, it was the men who had to be educated. She knew girls, some of them from her own school, who had been dragged into alleys and raped by the men of their village while they had been covered from their heads to their toes. But they would not come forward either.

Hours seemed to go by as they sat there after the plates had been washed and dried, while their father and brother talked things over with Arshad. Their mother had gone inside and had probably fallen asleep, already thinking about how soon her loud and shameful daughter would be off her hands. She then realized how there was a chance that that was not the case, but quickly dismissed it. Arshad was getting up and she realized that was her cue to start moving towards the door because she was expected to see him out. She got up and it was as if she was making her way to the door in a daze, her feet moving of their own accord.

She was trying her best not to make eye contact because his words from earlier were still ringing in her head, and she longed to be in bed and away from him. The door had almost closed when he stuck his foot out, stopping her from closing it all the way.

"It will be soon now." She felt herself nodding without meaning to. His dark brown eyes seemed to be boring into her then, and she noticed that his jaw was tense as his lips started to form words. "Just a few more days and we will be sleeping in the same bed."

His words sent chills down her back as she imagined herself lying next to him and shivered. But her lips had started to move on their own now.

"Yes."

"You should stop going out so much though."

A small flame, barely an ember started to burn inside her and she felt as if it would fuel the fire that would burn her, but she found herself talking and then there was no going back. Besides, it was also quite likely that he would listen to her after all, she hoped. A part of her knew he would not and had already given up.

"I was with Rabia." He had moved closer and had somehow griped her thin arm, his expression unreadable.

"I don't like her husband." His fingers were moving softly over her, and yet they felt like razor blades digging into her skin. When she looked up into his eyes, it was to realize that they were narrowed and she could see anger in them that she had never seen before. She hated to admit it, but in that moment she was scared. She knew for a fact that he did not hate Rabia's husband; they were close acquaintances to be precise.

"Rabia is not like him…" The words were barely out of her mouth before he had started squeezing her arm, and she was biting her lip to keep herself from crying out.

"You will be my wife and I do not want you seen outside, especially with people like them." His nails were digging into her skin, and she knew there would be a bruise the next day.

And then, she could feel herself drifting away, away from him and the village. This was exactly what she had been afraid of when her parents had told her about the proposal. This was what happened to most of the girls who got married here, and her fate had been sealed the same way. Slowly, she felt herself becoming numb. His hand was still clenched around her arm, but she had stopped feeling it. She could only see his dark eyes running over her and the sneer that stretched across his mouth as he realized that he had at last managed to shut her up.

"Okay."

Chapter 7

Ahmed

Raza Khan did not like to be kept waiting in the morning. But then again, he was always most likely to lose his temper whenever he was sure he was not being watched by the public, something that was guaranteed in his own house. Here, he sat at the head of the table, impatiently taping his knuckles on the hardwood that his wife had picked during those few prior months of marriage that tend to present an illusion of eternal happiness.

He was waiting for that morning's newspapers, and in doing so making sure that his breakfast went cold which the kitchen staff would then be blamed for. His wife sat on his right, clad in a black and gold saree, an exquisite set of rubies around her neck. Her hair was piled atop her head, and she would reach up now and then to sweep a stray strand back behind her ear, a sure sign that she was nervous. Ahmed supposed the looming election was the cause, after all, the next few days were crucial if they wanted to win.

His father wanted to know what the papers had to say about his election campaign, because even though most of his rivals considered the news channels on television to be a reliable source of information about their chances of winning, he considered them to be 'fickle' and 'unreliable.' This was true because Ahmed knew that they tended to decide which party they wanted to win, and then sway the public away from the others using the tools at their disposal. But Ahmed knew that the newspapers were no different. His father just liked to believe he was in control and in some way, looking at the papers, having them in his hands at the breakfast table seemed to fulfill that particular desire.

"We are doing quite well in the Sahiwal district." He had at last gotten a copy of the *Express Tribune*, and the slight smile on his face indicated that he was not entirely disappointed with what he had read. "They seem to have liked our food drive there last week. Shahid actually has a chance, so that's one base covered." He leaned over to show the article to his wife who smiled in the practiced manner of the wife who was used to appearing to be proud of all of her husband's accomplishments.

When the newspaper had been cast aside, Ahmed had to try hard not to roll his eyes as they fell on the picture that had been attached with the article. It showed a man from his father's party.

Shahid Khan, the same one that they had just been talking about, with a huge smile plastered on his face as he handed a food package to a young boy of about seven. The boy looked like he had just been handed the keys to the universe.

Ahmed supposed that was true in a way, seeing as the boy was probably thinking of the money he had been bribed with to smile for the camera. He knew his father was more likely to jump into a river than help ordinary people, especially since they had not even won yet.

"We need to focus more on districts closer to Lahore now," his mother observed, and his father nodded in agreement, putting down a copy of *The News*. The front page had a picture of him from the dinner that they had hosted at his grandfather's farm, and it showed them talking to another political worker while the other guests mingled in the background. "These dinners can only get us so far unless we combine them with interactions with the actual voters."

He knew the blow was coming before the words even left his mother's mouth. "Maybe you should take Ahmed with you to one of the villages today." They had not spoken since their previous argument when Ahmed had walked out of the house and left her staring after him, but that argument, like all their other heated conversations had been forgotten now, swept under the rug, never to be brought up again. That was how his parents coped, by casting problems aside and pretending they did not exist.

There was silence in the room as the idea was processed by his father, and Ahmed stared ahead, waiting for his reply, not bothering to say anything because he knew it would not make a difference. "The boy doesn't have a political bone in his body." He then resisted the urge to point out that he had obviously thought differently yesterday when he had wanted him to accompany him, but kept his mouth shut, knowing that they, despite their snide remarks did in fact need him. His father was just too proud to actually say it. "But I suppose it would be helpful just to have the people there see a younger face."

He knew he had made the right decision when it came to politics. He wanted no part of it, the lying and manipulating came easy to his father, but he hated it with every fiber of his being. They knew that as well, he supposed, and it was probably why they had not pushed him to compete in the elections this year. It was either that or they were afraid that he would openly challenge everything they stood for.

So he had wordlessly agreed to be in the background, helping with PR and at dinners, and wherever else they wanted him to. He also knew that they were all expecting him to have learnt the 'way the world worked' by the time it was his turn to take his father's place, but he doubted he ever would.

"You don't have other plans, do you?" His father asked him.

"Even if I did, I would have to go, wouldn't I?" Mrs. Raza Khan sighed, and her husband looked up, his eyes blazing.

"Keep that attitude in check, Ahmed. We don't need you crying about how you're above all of this right now. We need to stick together." Raza Khan stared at him over the rim of his glass of orange juice and Ahmed's heart clenched, silently urging him to speak up, but just like all those times in school, when his father had assumed the fights he got in were purely because of his son's attitude problem, he stayed silent.

#

An hour later, they were speeding along the Grand Trunk Road while truck drivers honked and yelled at each other on all sides. The day was slightly warm and when Ahmed rolled the window down, he felt the crisp air wash over his face, right before being advised, quite politely, by one of the guards seated beside him to roll it back up.

"Your father hates the smell." He glanced over and sure enough, Raza Ali Khan had scrunched his nose up and was glaring at him from the seat in front of him. He might have found the sight slightly funny had he not let himself think about what this implied about his father. The man was a hypocrite and there was no doubt about it. He was going to see a bunch of people who had probably never even been in an air conditioned room, and he would tell them he understood what they had to go through when in reality, he could not even stand to breathe the same air as them.

"Of course he does." The guard smiled politely back at him again and turned away. He was then reminded about the simple undeniable fact that these guards were stuck in the same position that he was, forced into a life they never wanted. He knew all of them had families to feed and his father made sure they were kept happy, but in truth, nobody really wanted to spend their life protecting a man who had hurt countless others to get where he was now. It was ironic how he and people like him even felt the need to be protected from the very people they deceived every single day.

"We're almost there," the same guard said after a while and Ahmed nodded, bracing himself for the swarm of people that would surely be waiting when they disembarked. Of course the camera crew would come first, the people who had been paid quite handsomely to make sure that their visit was recorded from every angle, and that it was enough to make people fall in love with his father. He also knew that he was a pawn in that process, but he tried not to think about it as the dark tarmac turned to light dirt, and the trucks behind them receded into the background. Now it was just them followed by the line of black SUV's that appeared to follow them everywhere. They followed at a respectful pace behind them, and he imagined that if someone were to see them from above, the line of cars behind them would look like a dark silent ribbon, bound in the same direction, surrounded by an expanse of green sprinkled with shades of brown.

Soon, they could see crops on both sides, and he marveled at the towering stalks of wheat as they swayed in the light breeze that had started up. The wheat soon gave way to cotton fields that spread out in both directions. The white balls shivered as the cars sped past, and he wondered if it would be a good idea to take a picture as the sun's rays turned them golden.

"It's picking season right now." The guard next to him was staring wistfully at the endless acres of fields, and Ahmed realized that he was probably from a village just like this one.

"It looks like hard work," he commented and the guard nodded wordlessly. He was about to answer when his father cleared his throat. He knew that he was going to instruct him the way he usually did before a public appearance. He rolled his eyes.

"Talk to them," he told him, and Ahmed stopped himself from asking if he would talk to the people as well, or if it would just be his son and the other political workers. Normally his father just made sure they got a couple of pictures of him shaking hands with someone who looked reasonably poor ,and then let the rest of them talk to them while he stood off to one side 'observing' and recording a short video that showed him talking to a gathered crowd.

Ahmed nodded. "Yes, sir."

As they slowed down, he noticed the slowly gathering crowd, and tried to keep his face expressionless as he realized that half of these people had gathered because they had been promised free cold drinks after they had gotten a few minutes of footage. The media was likely to be in on it as well. The rest of them were here simply because the long string of cars coming from outside were likely to be the most entertainment they would have for a while.

They stopped when a sufficient amount of people had gathered, and he watched as the camera crew disembarked from the car in front of them first and then set up their equipment, before they were asked to walk out slowly. Ahmed noticed his father's expression change in a matter of seconds as he put his phone down and flashed a dazzling smile at the crowd before looking over his shoulder at him. Ahmed loathed himself for knowing exactly what that look meant, and for the fact that he would do everything to make sure he acted on it as well. He could criticize all he wanted but he knew he would never go against the man who paid for everything he had.

So he looked out at the crowd, a smile already formed on his lips. He could feel himself drifting away, to that place where he knew he would not hear or see what was going on. He would be safe and away from his father, and everything that he stood for. It was ironic how sometimes he did not even need to be buzzed to get to that place nowadays.

Ahmed sighed as he heard the faint sound of people cheering as some juice boxes were distributed among the children. Then, he only felt a vague sense of revulsion as he smelled the cow dung and dirt on the air, and scrunched his nose up when the cameras were not focusing on him.

"Thank you." A little girl of about ten had just come up to him, food package in hand and a smile on her face. Ahmed was just debating how to answer when the girl's mother started calling for her. She was standing at the edge of the crowd and she clearly did not want her daughter near the cameras. "I'll vote for you when I grow up because we haven't had a meal in two days."

Ahmed considered telling her that he was not running, but his chest ached at the thought of the girl having been hungry for two whole days and him not being able to do anything about it.

"Thank you," were the only words that he could muster before she was called away.

"Talk to someone else so they can get a shot of that." His father had walked by him and was now quickly making his way over to another group of villagers, his face perfectly at ease, and his lips curved upward in the smile that was guaranteed to win their hearts.

#

The day had been grueling to say the least, he noted; not that he had noticed the time go by. But judging by the fact that the sky had started to darken and the sunlight was starting to fade, he figured it was about to end, the torture and misery his body had endured while walking around, smiling at people and enquiring about their lives was finally about to end. As the people from the media began to pack their things, and the guards went to collect his father from the house of one of the landlords of the village, Ahmed found himself drifting back to the present and walking away from the cars and the crowd of people gathered to see them off.

He only remembered vague details about the village and how the day had gone by, but they were enough to make him want to look around on his own for a while, even if the smell that lingered in the air now clung to his nostrils. He remembered how they had walked along the dirt streets, passing out food packages, smiling at the children who had greeted them with hungry smiles plastered on their faces. They had terrified him. The little boys and girls had been shivering when evening had drawn closer, and two of them had lips that had gone blue in the cold. Yet, they had stayed outside, desperately awaiting the food that had been promised to them. Their parents had been no different.

He still wondered whether the people here even believed that his father could bring a change for them, because any sane person would question a man who was asking for votes in exchange for food and drinks. But they had not, and he supposed it could be attributed to the fact that his father had promised them another well to water their crops, and to fund their school. But they did not know that he had promised another village the same thing the last time he had run for elections. It had not happened.

The street that he was walking along was narrow, with mud houses on each side. The stench was stronger here and he resented himself for turning his nose up. The cold dug into his skin, and he could feel his toes going numb in his boots, but he walked on, determined to erase the day from his mind before he got back in the car. The sunlight was dying fast, and he could see his shadow elongating before him as he walked.

Soon, he began hearing sounds from the houses, of people talking, preparing supper or fighting. The latter drew him to a house at the end of the street, and he was then unable to move as the sounds got louder. He knew what they were in seconds, and then despised himself for having come there after all. The feeling that washed over him then was just like what he had felt when had seen that girl on the street. That night seemed so long ago now.

Someone was being shoved against a wall, and a man was yelling, his voice carrying across the silent winter air. "You bitch! Don't you know we are running out of money!?"

"We were out of flour. I had to ask them…"

"You looked like a whore!"

Ahmed stood there, transfixed as he heard the blows, followed by the sound of a woman whimpering and then collapsing on to the ground.

The blows did not stop as she fell, and he could hear her begging him to stop, to go inside. He felt sick when he heard her scream that he would kill the baby. The harsh sounds stopped then, and he heard the man's footsteps as he neared the door and then stormed out into the night, leaving the woman quite possibly still sprawled on the ground.

He did not know how long he stood there, only that he now had a sick taste in his mouth and wanted to throw his guts up at the mere injustice that was going on right under his very nose, injustice that he had the power to stop, but would not dare to. Just as he had heard it that night, he heard his father's voice ring in his ears again.

We cannot afford to get mixed up in a petty scandal. He walked away, while his blood ran ice cold in his veins.

Soon, he came out onto a wider road that probably led out of the village. The air was cleaner here somehow, fresher, and it burned him as it rushed over his skin. The sun had nearly set, and yet he could see the dying rays casting everything in a warm orange glow. Here, it almost felt magical, the cool air, the dying sun, and the sounds of night birds that were just waking up. He could see fields stretching out on both sides and as he got closer, he realized they were the same cotton fields he had seen when they had come.

He heard her before he saw her.

The girl was sitting hunched over under a tall tree at the edge of the field. Her hair was lightly brushing the ground behind her as it trailed under the *dupatta* that covered her head, but she did not seem to mind. She was bent over a piece of paper with a pencil in her hand, and he had heard the sound of her pencil scraping against it on the ground. She looked up when he drew closer, and then he was forced to stop. It was not due to the fact that she was beautiful, or that she had no form of warm clothing on but looked to be doing fine. They had locked eyes for a second, and he knew he would not forget that moment for a long time.

If he had known what a gaze of steel was before, this girl's had to be of iron. That was the only way to explain it, he realized as she continued to stare, her grey eyes boring into his as he struggled to think of what to say. He could sense sadness in them, but there was no proof of that in the way she was looking at him and he realized that he admired her for that. She turned away first.

"Hi," he said immediately, before realizing that perhaps he should have gone for the traditional term for greeting people here. When she did not answer, he began looking over her shoulder at what she had been drawing. It was a picture of the cotton field that they were in now, only during the day, and it was filled with people, women, he realized, picking the balls off the stems.

The picture was perfectly done too. From the way she had drawn it, it was obvious she had had some practice as well. The girl obviously had talent, talent that would be wasted here without a doubt. Ahmed was now thinking about everything his father and people like him had the power to do, but chose not to, and a strange feeling settled in his stomach.

He knew there was a lot this girl and others like her could do, if given the chance. She probably had not even heard of an Arts school, he realized, and something stirred in his stomach. Ahmed allowed himself to imagine her going to one just for a second. He knew she would make the most of it, more than the children of most of the wealthy elite of Lahore did anyway. She could have a shot at something.

We can't get involved in petty scandals.

Stick together.

They need to see you are just like me and your grandfather.

His father's voice began to ring in his ears as his hand reached into his pocket for a pen and an old receipt. The girl had turned around again, and was looking at him as he scribbled his number on it, and then dropped it on top of the sketch she had made. She had still not said a word.

As he stood over her thin yet stiff frame, images began to resurface in his mind, memories that he had tried very hard to bury. The girl at the edge of the road had been bleeding, he recalled, and there had been blood pooling around her as well. But she had stared right at him, perhaps daring him to do something, to help. He had failed her. He had failed her as well as countless others.

The girl's *dupatta* rustled in the slight breeze then, and he blinked, slowly coming back to the present. His mouth was dry, and he spoke quickly, his words tumbling out.

"You can do a lot more," he said, and waited for her to say something. She still had that intense look in her eyes as she took in the small slip of paper and then his expression, as he stood there. She had not moved a muscle since he had come there, only her eyes, and as the last rays of the sun began to fade away, he realized why those eyes had had that effect on him.

It had been as if he was looking at himself.

Chapter 8
Seher

"He did that to you?" Rabia asked, brushing her fingers over Seher's wrist where the marks of Arshad's nails were still visible. The two girls were sitting inside the room that Seher shared with her sister, a plate of sliced apples between them. Neither of them had touched the apples, and the makeshift curtain that separated them from the world outside was slowly moving from side to side. It was early in the afternoon, and her mother had gone to clean at the *Chaudhry Sahib's* house for a dinner they were hosting that night, and her father and brother had left for work a while ago. Zara was sitting outside in the courtyard next to the stove absentmindedly stirring a pot, she had been there for the past thirty minutes.

"He did." Her voice sounded alien to her own ears. She knew that had something to do with the fact that she had not expected things to start going worse for her so soon. They had not even gotten married yet and he had already bruised her,

Seher could not bring herself to imagine how the days after the wedding would be like.

"Tahir told me someone saw us coming back that day," her friend told her in a resigned tone. "'That must be how he found out too." She knew Rabia's husband had probably yelled at her about going outside with her as well, seeing as being seen with someone like her was something these people deigned to be outrageous, but she could not bring herself to ask about it. Any kind of words felt foreign on her tongue, and the last two days had simply gone by with her being closed off from the world, not saying a word to anyone because the effort seemed useless. Zara had tried talking to her that night, but had stopped after it was clear that Seher would not agree with her notions about marriage, and after a full day of silence, Rabia had finally decided to check on her at her house while her husband was at work.

"I can't think about him without wanting to vomit," she whispered, and her fiend squeezed her hand.

"It will be okay, Seher," she said. "Things will make more sense after you get married."

"I can't marry a man who thinks it is okay to do… these things." She answered, knowing that Rabia, like the rest of the village would not understand.

"It's what they all do here."

Despite being her best friend, Rabia would not be able to see that they did not have to live the kind of lives they were living, that they could all be a lot more than what the confines of the village allowed them to be. Her hand was resting on top of her pillow as she watched her friend finally reach for an apple slice, and as these thoughts warred in her head, images from the previous day began to flood it as well.

A thin line of black cars passing through the village, filled with people who lived far away behind fancy brick walls, and hid behind their guards. A tall young man in black shalwar kameez. A slip of paper. A few whispered words. Seher shook her head, refusing to think about that encounter.

#

Two weeks. Seher knew she only had two weeks until she was to be married, and yet she had not come out of that dark place that was in the very depth of her soul. Her thoughts had completely engulfed her in their cool embrace, and coming out of there had never felt more daunting, not that staying there was a pleasant experience either. But then again, it was a lot better than staying in the present moment and pretending to be happy when her mother talked about her upcoming wedding, the jewelry she had managed to find for her, and how her daughter was finally going to 'her house.'

She had not met Rabia since that day either and she hated to admit it, but it had been fear of her fiancé that had stopped her. Her skin had almost healed, and the bruises were barely noticeable now but the scars were there, reminding her of what would happen if something like that happened again. She had instead, kept to the house, choosing to stay inside while her mother and sister went about their daily routine. Her mother was working extra late at the *haveli* now, hoping to earn some more money and Zara, it seemed, had given up on trying to make her smile. Seher did not blame her for it. After all, her sister had her own problems to think about too.

"Do you want some tea?" Her sister's voice pulled her out of her thoughts for a moment and she nodded, knowing that trying to start a conversation would be futile at that point. She heard Zara leaving the room, and then the clatter of steel and porcelain as she poured the tea from the pot and into the cup. Her gaze drifted over to a lone phone placed on the highest shelf in the room. It was a small grey device, not nearly as sleek or wide as the one Hamid had but it performed its functions all the same. It was Rabia's, she had forgotten it here the last time she was there, but Seher had not found a way to give it back yet.

She had gotten the phone the previous year, and she could not help but smile as she remembered the days when her friend had worked at the *haveli*, cleaning and cooking for the *Chaudhry* and his family. They had joked about how the day she got paid would be the day the world ended, because that had been what it had felt like. "We live on their property," her mother had told her when she had asked her why they always paid late. "They can pay whenever they feel like it."

The money would go to Rabia's parents and not her, even though she had worked at the house ever since they had been ten. So when Rabia had at last gotten the money that she was expected to take home to her parents, Seher had suggested she take a small sum for herself and not say a word about it. She had, and they had gotten Hamid to get them a phone, one of the cheap ones but a phone nonetheless. That memory was one of the few happy ones that Seher had of the previous years. Most of them were marred with despair. She was just considering seeing if she could call Rabia's sister, letting her know that she had it when Zara walked back into the room.

"We're out of sugar and flour," her sister sighed, before sitting down next to her, a tray laden with two cups of tea on her lap. Seher wordlessly took the cup meant for her and took a sip, the scalding hot beverage burning her throat.

They seemed to be running out of a lot of things lately, and she knew they had not restocked because that meant spending money, money that her parents were saving to pay for her wedding later. Seher did not answer her sister, and so they sat in silence, sipping their tea.

Zara soon got up to go clean up and then get started on lunch. Their father would be home soon, she had told Seher, and she had nodded absentmindedly, thinking about how after a few days, she would not be seeing her father at any meal. The two did not have the relationship they had once shared, but sometimes she liked to imagine that things were fine between her and her father, that she was still his little princess and he would do anything for her happiness, even if it meant going against what the village wanted him to be. She almost laughed at the absurdity of the thought.

When he came staggering in through the door, Zara greeted him with a smile, reaching to take the small sack of rice from his hands. Seher moved to help her sister and her father brushed a hand over her head.

"My daughter," he said, smiling. "Get me a glass of water, won't you?" She nodded, leaning into his touch without realizing it, before walking towards the steel jug a few paces away. Her heart ached at the thought of leaving him at that moment, but she could not think of any words to say. Despite her lack of faith in the male gender, her father was the only one who still held a place in her heart. Yet, she knew things would never be the same between them, and her eyes burned at that thought.

"God bless you, *beta*," he said as she handed him the glass. "May God always keep you happy."

I will not be happy with Arshad, her heart was screaming but her mouth refused to move. She stood there, waiting, as her father drained the glass in one gulp. He was clearly tired from the day's work. When he motioned for her to sit down next to him, she did so without a word, quietly retreating back into that familiar cool dark place at the back of her mind, and his arm slowly wrapped around her shoulders, drawing her closer to him.

#

One week

It was now just one week before she would leave this house forever, only to come back occasionally, and then be expected to leave after a certain period of time, because it would not be her home anymore. What was home anyway? She often pondered over that question, but had not come up with an answer yet. But she simply could not believe that a place Arshad called his home could ever be hers as well.

"Eat something." Zara's voice was a beacon, momentarily guiding her out of the place that she had grown so accustomed to retreating to now that it almost felt like it was real, that the reprieve she had created for herself in her mind was more real than the actual world around her. "You haven't eaten at all today."

She had stopped eating since two days, only forcing herself to eat when her father was around, because he had suddenly taken an interest in whether she ate or not. Perhaps it was the fear of finally watching her leave that had caused the change within him, and there might have been a time when Seher would have welcomed it, but not now when her whole world had shattered around her, and going back sounded impossible. There were times when she felt like a foreigner in her own body, like she was a visitor in the house with no idea how she got there. Those days were the worst.

She felt herself getting up from her cot in her room and making her way outside. There was a slight breeze blowing, but she did not feel anything on her skin as she walked to the fireplace where her mother was sitting. It was just the three of them for lunch that day, she noted. Talking had started feeling more taxing than it ever had before so she had resorted to staying silent. Her mother now started to say something about how she had lost weight, and that she looked like a frame of bones now. Seher did not bother saying that she had been adamant that she ate too much, and needed to lose weight just a few weeks ago.

She reached out to take the plate that Zara was offering and flinched inwardly as she saw yet again, the dark circles under her sister's eyes. She obviously had not been sleeping either, Seher noted, and then smiled bitterly to herself. She could give Zara all the lectures she wanted; she could tell her to think for herself and not care about what people said. She could also remind her over and over not to value a man's opinion of her over her own opinion about herself or to not let him dictate the choices she made, but who was she trying to fool really?

Zara had slowly dragged herself to an endless black pit because of the simple undeniable truth that what people thought of her mattered, and then fallen into it headfirst which had resulted in the dark circles and worry lines in addition to her life being snatched from her. But she was worse and she knew it. Seher knew what was right and just, and what was not, and she had let herself believe that she was different; that she would not make choices that countless girls like Zara made, and yet she was the same now. She was going to marry a man whom she knew would snatch her very existence from her. She had not even dared leave her house since that night because the slight stab of pain in her arm was a fierce reminder of what would happen if she did and someone decided she looked like a bad woman.

"I made it, you know. You could tell me if it's any good." Zara was still sitting next to her, and she realized that her mother had already left the house on one of her daily cleaning errands. It was just them now. She nodded, grateful for her sister's attempt at teasing her, to get her to talk. The food had tasted bland on her tongue though, and she had found it hard to swallow. The plate was lying abandoned next to her feet.

"Seher, it's not as bad as it seems." She looked up to see her sister gazing at her from beneath long lashes that had once been dark, her lips pale in the golden light of the sun. She could not even think of what to say to her, seeing as these were the exact words she had said to her the day she had come back to their house a year ago, and Zara had just shaken her head. She also could not bring herself to tell her sister how grateful she was to her for still trying with her.

"You're going to look beautiful," Zara continued, and she scoffed, which was perhaps the first sound she had made in days and rolled her eyes. What was beauty anyway? Seven days from now she would be decked out in layers of cheap powders, and her eyes made up to look larger than they were while her lips would be pained a sick shade of red that only reminded her of blood. She had seen the new lipstick Arshad's mother had sent over, and the first thought that had entered her mind had been of the lines of dried scarlet blood she had seen that night on her arm a few nights ago after he had left her house.

Nodding her head slowly, she got up and started to walk back towards her room. She could hear Zara's sigh behind her as she swept the makeshift curtain between them. It was even cooler here, and yet she hardly felt it as she climbed into her cot.

She was then reminded again of the short amount of time that she had in this house. It was borrowed time, she realized. She would be trading this miserable life for another one in just one week. Her arm felt like it was throbbing at her side now, silently mocking her. There would be a lot worse to come, she knew that. She knew she would have to change if it meant a guarantee of safety and security. Her life flashed by behind her eyelids, and she saw herself running carefree in the cotton fields, her hair blowing behind her, her going to the shop with Rabia, the sound of their laughter echoing in the streets, and she saw herself smiling with a sketchbook in her arms.

Her pillow was damp, she realized a while later, and there was a dull ache in her chest. All of that was no longer possible now, she told herself as she struggled to swallow past the dryness in her throat. Her lips were dry as well when she ran her tongue over them, and she suddenly began thinking about the last piece of memory that she had just recalled. The girl who used to draw and smile while doing it sounded like a completely different person to her. She knew those days were gone.

And yet, some part of her, some small nerve in her body slowly tugged at that memory, and then she was reaching under her pillow until her fingers closed around the small slip of paper that had been lying there for days, carelessly shoved away but never completely forgotten. The paper felt foreign to her trembling fingers as she closed her eyes. It was a constant testament to the fact that someone out there thought that she actually had a chance, that her drawings might just be something precious. She only remembered snippets from that day but they clung to her memory like bees cling to honey on a hot summer day.

She had somehow ended up going outside a few days ago when the sun was about to go down, and her feet had dragged her to the open cotton fields at the edge of the small village. Arshad had gone out of the village that day with a friend to sell some of the milk their cow provided, to the next village, and the news had felt like a balm on her aching heart. She had not gone by Rabia's house that day for fear of being seen. But she doubted anyone had seen her at all that day because she had taken the long route to the fields, past the graveyard, and clad in a thick shawl that had hidden her well enough. It had been a temporary relief of course, and she imagined that it had been the last day that she could truly call her own. She knew that after that, everything she did would be linked to Arshad.

    Seher did not remember the walk there or the events of that day, just that she had felt an overwhelming sense of being suffocated between the four walls of her house. But now she was starting to remember sitting at the edge of the cotton field, and taking out an old frayed piece of paper and a pencil that she had found on her father's cot. She did not even remember exactly what she had drawn that day, just that even though it had not been as good as the ones she had been used to drawing before her life spiraled downward, some small part of her had felt content in that moment.

    The little girl inside her had felt at peace sitting there with the air caressing her face, and the sounds of the birds making their journey back home as the day drew to an end. She had still been in that place that she had created for herself then, the safe haven in the depth of her mind, but a small part of her had felt at peace with the outside world in that moment as well.

The boy who had given her the piece of paper had not changed that, he had not even managed to get her to utter a word, and she supposed that had been because she had never fully registered the fact that he was there. That could be attributed to the fact that she had not really been fully there in the present moment ever since the day Arshad and his father had come to visit. The little girl who had smiled at the fact that she had drawn again had not considered the moment important enough to register either.

The elections were coming up, she knew that. So far about four different groups of people had come to the village, and had made promises so absurd that she was shocked the people actually believed them. But then again these people believed anything, so it had probably not been hard to fool them. She knew that because last year they had voted for someone who had promised them bottles of mineral water.

But in the end it was actually pointless to come here and talk to these people anyway. The people of the village did not care about who came and made false promises that would not be kept. No, they voted for whoever the people in charge of them living here wanted them to. The landlords who let them stay on their land in exchange for hard labour were the ones who dictated their choices, not sound reason, never.

Yet, they had wasted a day talking and mingling with the people while they were filmed as if they were some form of entertainment. The children of the village had been filmed as they had gazed in awe at the small parcels of food that had been passed out among them. Seher knew exactly what that had meant too. They were trying to make money off the naivety of the common man while they hid behind their wealth in the big cities. She knew they were enjoying five meals a day, while they could barely afford two here in the villages. She also knew that they, the people in the villages, were the ones providing them with those meals. Most of the rice and wheat that they grew here was shipped away to the cities.

But that boy had sounded sincere, she thought. She had no idea who he had been since he had looked too young to be in government, and too wealthy to be part of the camera team. She still remembered the way his shoulders had been bunched against the cold village air. The moment when he had dropped the slip of paper with his number in front of her had felt real. He had sounded like he actually believed that she could do a lot better. She did not know what exactly he had meant when he had said those words considering the fact that he did not even know her or what she was being made to do, but she did know that she could do a lot more than what this village allowed her to do. She did not have to be with Arshad and she knew she did not deserve that either.

Her sketchbook flashed behind her closed eyelids again, and she could not help a fresh wave of tears as it crashed on to her, and it was then that she remembered Saad again and all the promises that he had made her. She shook her head slowly. No, she could not think about that strange boy now, or about what he had implied. Arshad's face flashed before her eyes as he had pinned her against the wall, and she thought of her father and brother, so willing to let her go.

This boy could not be trusted either. He was probably miles away now, asleep in a comfortable bed while he was waited upon by people like her, forced to serve him and his family. She imagined him behind towering brick walls, oblivious to the struggles of the outside world, and scoffed. He was likely to have forgotten about her and her village anyway. At that moment, she despised herself for even imagining him to be different from all the men she had come across in her life. Sighing, she turned onto her side, silently vowing never to trust any of them again.

Chapter 9

Ahmed

The drive back was longer than he had expected, and he marveled at the other villages as they crossed them, blanketed in soft velvety darkness and emanating waves of tranquility out into the world. The road was bordered by trees on either side, their leaves rustled in the slight breeze that was blowing. The windows were rolled up but he imagined it to be eerily quiet outside. Clouds of fog were clustered around them, engulfing everything else in grey, and the only signs of life on the narrow dirt road were the line of cars that was making its way to the main city, their headlights casting the road in front of them in an eerie glow.

"It's sad the way these people have to live." His father's voice broke through the spell of silence that had been cast over the car and its passengers, and the guards sitting on either side of him snapped to attention. Ahmed's mind flashed back to the house he had been standing outside mere hours before and he then wanted to ask his father why he did not do something about it then. If he wanted everyone, even just the people in this car, to think that he was a kind and considerate person, why not actually do something to prove it? But then again, his father had always been a man of just words. Raza Ali Khan had never felt like he needed to prove anything as long as it was said in the right manner. The guards surrounding him dutifully nodded in agreement.

He could however, still hear the woman screaming at her husband to stop and think about the baby, and it was almost impossible to get the sounds of the blows out of his mind. He imagined her going through it on a daily basis, and his heart broke for her. Before he knew it, he was thinking about the girl whose body they had found a few days ago after she had been raped and left to die in that street. He still felt partly responsible for it, and when that familiar self-loathing washed over him, he let it engulf him completely.

He knew he could do something about the atrocities in his country too, but going against his father was something he could never even fathom. So he let the hatred consume him, followed by guilt and then grief, grief for all those people who lost their loved ones every single day just because people like his father ran the country.

They were back on the main road now and he could see lights glimmering all around them.

The trucks were back, their drivers honking and waving impatiently in an attempt to make the traffic move faster. Silvery moonlight was streaming in through the windows and he imagined that the people back in the village could see the stars as they glittered down at them. In the city, it was a miracle if one spotted just one or two. That was the first time he allowed himself to think about his encounter with the girl again, he had shoved the memory away in his mind as soon as he had gotten back to where the cars were parked.

He wondered if she had ever tried to draw a picture of a clear night with the stars shining over the fields and if she had, had it been difficult? He had always imagined drawing the night would be harder than drawing a sunset or sunrise. That was why he preferred taking pictures, it meant he could capture moments like these without putting pen to paper himself. Yet, he recalled, she had looked so at peace while she drew. Her pencil had moved across the paper as if it were second nature to her, as if she was in a different place altogether. He still got chills when he remembered the way her gaze had fixed on him for a second, and then the moment started to replay in his mind as they drove on.

Those eyes had looked so familiar to him that it had almost been haunting. The grief mixed with anger and disgust that had been buried in them had instantly reminded him of the way he looked at his own self in the mirror. Was she really that angry at the world or at herself? After spending one day there, he could think of plenty of reasons why she might be angry, but the look of self-loathing he had seen still confused him. Had it really been self-loathing?

"We might have to come here again," his father was saying. "The *Chaudhry* invited us to dinner next week."

"I might be busy," he said automatically. There was no way he was going back there knowing what people like that woman had to go through, and whatever it was that had driven that girl to look the way that she had.

"Busy?" Raza Ali Khan scoffed. "When was the last time you were busy with something of substance anyway? We need this. I imagine he will gather the other landlords, and they will want to talk about whatever they need me to fix in that miserable village. We need to make them believe that we can do those things for them."

Ahmed looked around and sure enough, the guards were all quiet, their full attention turned towards the two of them, his father had worked hard to maintain his image even among them. What further drove his anger forward was the fact that he knew he could not say anything else about not being able to go during the car ride. He was again reminded of the fact that even though his father had little concern about the way he projected his son in that moment in front of the guards, he would not dare say anything to him when he was surrounded by other people from his party.

"I just had plans with friends." That was not entirely untrue seeing as he had been thinking about getting together with the old crew for quite some time now. They had not met ever since he had gotten back from Oxford, and Fahad had been texting and calling for weeks now.

"Cancel them."

He forced himself to stay silent, choosing to ignore the words for now, and drifting back into the past instead, the constant sound of the air conditioner acting as a beacon between two worlds.

They had always had a strained relationship, ever since he had been a boy, he had done whatever he had been instructed to do by his father and grandfather. 'What you do reflects on us and this party.' They had always said, and the words had been etched in his memory. His early teenage years had been filled with pleasant family dinners and parties where he was considered the model son. His academic accomplishments were proudly displayed on the walls; for people to see of course. Everyone knew Raza Ali Khan had the perfect son, bound for great things, except Raza Ali Khan himself.

More had been a word that his father had used endlessly throughout Ahmed's childhood, or at least the parts he was there for anyway. He needed to be more if he wanted his father to pat him on the back with a smile on his face. More was necessary to survive in the dark world that they lived in, and if he could not give more, he may as well be someone else's son. Politics demanded more as well, his father had always said, and until his late teens, Ahmed had been passionate about it. Becoming the co-chairman and then eventually the chairman of the party formed by his grandfather had always been the plan, and his educational path had been carved accordingly. Until he was about fifteen and all hell had broken lose.

He had cracked somewhere in the beginning of ninth grade, he recalled. It had been hard enough to make friends seeing as he was the son of an aristocrat, and one of the lessons his father had imparted to him was that nobody was his friend, not really. But when an opportunity presents itself, friendship is bound to come out of it. He had found that you only needed to have something in common and that would be it. Being in a school meant for the children of the elite, it had been easy enough to get in with a crowd with similar problems. It still shocked him how his father had been responsible for one of the longest lasting friendships in his life.

He and Fahad had been thrown together because of their mutual need to please their fathers, the thirst to accomplish more, and then eventually the need to escape when it became clear that the latter could never be achieved. So when it had been established that 'more' would never be possible, they had drowned together. Unexplained nights in Lahore's more questionable areas, and hours under the influence of even more questionable substances had been the product of their friendship and the lack of a bond with their respective fathers.

The next few years of their lives had gone by in a blur. Ahmed's parents had attributed his declining grades to Fahad's presence, whereas his parents had held Ahmed responsible for their son's lack of interest in family values. But by that point the both of them had gone past the point where they wanted to fix the bond with their families.

As he spent more time out in the underbelly of the city, Ahmed had begun to realize the bitter reality of life outside of the high walls and fences that sheltered the country's rich and powerful. His fundamental beliefs had come crumbling down, and there was no going back. He was consumed with a hatred for the world he lived in, the dinner parties were not dinner parties anymore. To him, they were now events held by the wealthy to feast on meals that had been stolen from the countless people out on the streets. His private guard was a man forced to serve a class that he despised while he struggled to feed a family back home, and his father was a man constantly trying to convince people of an image of himself that could shatter any moment.

His friendship with Fahad was what had consumed him for the rest of his teenage years, and the two of them had been inseparable. The parties they had thrown and been to were still embedded in his memory, and he could often feel the thrum of familiar energy as he drove through the city, and nights spent with his friend flashed before his eyes, ones where they had floated through reality, joked about it even, and then woken up with pounding headaches.

Lahore thrummed with energy all around him, the music was so loud that the beat was echoed by his heartbeat, and the lights seemed to be ten times brighter at this time of the night, in this house, far away from his own. He felt light as a feather as he floated through the air, stopping now and then to mumble a greeting or two. The pill he had swallowed twenty minutes ago had finally kicked in and he was in heaven, treading on soft clouds of grass, and watching the shapes blur on all sides, creating beautiful patterns in the air. He sucked in a breath as he felt a touch of the cool air upon his skin. It was electrifying.

The rest of the crew would be here soon, and he smiled as he imagined them being stuck in traffic. It was a good thing he and Fahad had taken a shortcut after the brief stop at Heera Mandi. The girl had been mesmerizing that night, a petite brunette in a gold dress, her hips moving sensually to the beat of the music being played by the old man behind her.

Ahmed had gone to see her specifically after being told about her by Fahad. She had not disappointed in the slightest, and his eyes glazed over now as he thought of her coming closer to him in the middle of the song and placing a porcelain white hand on his shoulder, teasing him before swaying her way back to the center of the gathered group, her mouth curving into a wide smile at the sight of the pile of money at her feet.

"You look like an angel," Someone was talking to him, but all he saw was a bright golden light in front of him surrounding another slender girl, a model perhaps. The light was too bright to tell for sure.

"I'm anything but." His words were slurred, jumbled together as he smiled, a half-drunken smile that masked nothing but anger and pain. They stood together on the side of the lawn for a few seconds, or minutes it seemed before a hand patted him roughly on the shoulder and the girl started to giggle and retreat towards the sound of

the party, promising to be waiting for her angel. He slowly shook his head as his friend, Amaar's face materialized in front him.

"We got slowed down but we made it." There was liquor on his friend's breath, and Ahmed pictured him being pulled over by the police before driving away, a few thousand rupees lighter and grinned. At least their parents were good for something.

They were now entering the city and he smiled again as the images rolled behind his eyelids. The result of that friendship had eventually been a decline in academic performance, and then the eventual decision that Ahmed was not suited for politics just yet, that he needed to be kept out of the public eye because he could ruin everything that his father and grandfather had worked so hard on over the years. The next few years were crucial for his father, and a troubled son was not what he needed to worry about at that time. So assumptions had been made and tears had been shed, by his mother of course, as he had entered his nineteenth year, and Oxford had been given as the only option to pursue a higher education.

College had really done a number on them both, Ahmed realized. Somewhere along the line they had lost touch, and he had gotten in with a new crowd, one that had only driven him farther from the person he had been in the past. It had gotten easier to completely lose himself, to forget, and just live in the moment until it ended. The four years had been some of the best and worst of his life. He had been conscious of the way things were back home, but it had been easier to pretend that he was not a part of that world when he was at Oxford, drifting through classes and smoking his way to graduation. The friends he had made had made it easier to forget the world he was a part of and he had been more than happy to burry himself in the booze and the drugs, until he was stripped completely of his former self and what remained was a man without a tether to this world, a drifting soul with enough bitterness to consume its very existence.

It had torn him apart, and he could barely recognize the person in the mirror nowadays. The face of the girl he had seen before she had died was one of the many reminders of the result of his utter incapability to go against his father and do the right thing. And yet, the previous day had stirred something inside him, he still could not put his finger on it, but it was definitely there. He did not know whether it had been the whimpering of the woman inside that house, or the sight of the girl that had caused it, but something had been tugging at his heart ever since they had left the village.

#

The next day found him sitting at the breakfast table while soft golden sunlight poured in through the high French windows and his father was, as per usual, scanning the newspapers. Their visit to the small village would be broadcasted around noon today and Raza Ali Khan was ecstatic about it. It appeared as if whatever he saw in the newspaper had pleased him as a smile was starting to form at the corner of his mouth, and soon it stretched across his face, making the stretch marks around his eyes all the more visible. Politics certainly had taken a toll on his health, but he refused to acknowledge that fact.

"They said your visit might make the front page tomorrow," his mother was saying as she buttered some toast for herself. When he looked at her, Ahmed was again reminded of the fact that she had gone from being a journalist who had been considered to be quite reliable, to simply being a pawn in political power play, and that she had embraced the role willingly. But then again, the woman had always craved wealth and stability so it was no surprise. If she could have them both, then to her, losing her own voice was a small price to pay. It was not right in the slightest but there was nothing he could do about it, and he had accepted that a long time ago.

"It better," his father answered, reaching for his coffee. "We spent good money on them."

"Ahmed's face probably did the trick," his mother said, smiling. "Did they get enough shots of you?" He nodded, and her smile widened. This was followed by a short discussion on whether he should be at the next dinner that they were planning for the other political workers and diplomats; he tuned out of the conversation when his father started talking about how he knew exactly where he would rather be.

"I will not have you off gallivanting with your friends when people are just looking for an excuse to badmouth me." His father was looking at him from the end of the table with his lips pressed in a thin line, and Ahmed could see the vein pulsing in his temple, but something in him prompted him to plough on. Something about the way his father had completely dismissed him the previous night, and how he had decided to go along with it had been eating away at him since then, and he realized that he wanted to stand his ground this time.

"Maybe if you actually gave them something they actually wanted, they would not be so keen to find flaws."

The room was silent. His mother had put down her knife and he could see the sunlight reflecting off its surface, and off the jewels in the necklace that adorned her neck. She must be headed to another one of those charity events later, he thought; the ones that were held in the name of charity but were really just an excuse for the wealthy to show off their money, and the gossipmongers to exchange news. His father was still gazing at him from across the table, and his expression had hardened into a sneer. That was not surprising, he noted. He was probably trying to understand how his son had even managed to contradict him. But Ahmed gazed steadily back at him, unblinking while his mother looked like she had forgotten to exhale. The scene might have been comical in an old movie. Raza Khan raised an eyebrow.

"Are you suggesting you know more about politics than me?" His tone was icy and his eyes had narrowed considerably. Ahmed could see the shock written all over his parents' faces, and a part of him was already drifting away, telling him to back off and go along with his father because there was no point in arguing, but another, much larger part of him wanted this, wanted to feel like he could stand up and say what he believed in.

"No," he began, his voice steady. "I'm only suggesting that if we give them a small incentive, people might be keener to vote for us." Us. The word reverberated through his head as it left his lips. He could not think of another moment where he had acknowledged himself and the party in the same sentence. It had left a bitter taste on his tongue.

"And just what would you suggest this incentive be?" The vein was now pulsing furiously.

"I don't know yet." He had not thought that far ahead, but he suddenly imagined the girl from the village siting in a classroom, studying Art with an actual smile on her face, her expression curious and not filled with the intense self-loathing that he had seen the previous night.

His father sneered, and he could already feel his resolve faltering. But he held on as he answered. "How convenient." Raza Khan's voice was dripping with sarcasm, and Ahmed clenched his fists at his sides. The conversation was beginning to feel like the ones they would have had before he had gone to university; he wanted to prove something, but did not know how. Time had frozen still, and he could feel himself trembling with the effort of restraining himself. He had no idea what he was refraining himself from doing, just that he needed to do something, anything. The moment stretched on for an eternity, with them gazing at each other, neither backing away, until his father's phone started to buzz.

The eye contact was broken. Ahmed unclenched his fists, and sat back as a sigh escaped his mother's lips. Raza Ali Khan got up and wordlessly made his way out of the room, his face scrunched in confusion and contempt.

They sat in silence for about two minutes, the only sound being the ones made by his knife and fork as Ahmed started to eat his pancakes, and the clinking sound that his mother's glass of orange juice made as it was taken and then replaced on the table. Through the huge windows, he could see the leaves of the evergreen trees in the lawn slowly swaying in the cool breeze, while the fountain bubbled merrily in the distance. He could see the gardener tending to the new flowerbeds opposite the dining room window. But he forced himself to look at his mother across the table.

She was gazing at him from beneath hooded eyes, and he could see that she wanted to say something. At that moment he felt sorry for the woman sitting before him, she tried to appear in control and content all the time, but in reality she was scared to say one word against the man who made sure she was near the top of the social ladder among the wives of other aristocrats and diplomats.

"Where is the brunch today?" He asked her in an attempt to fill the void of silence between them.

She stared back at him, and he knew that look only too well. Disappointment and regret was written clearly across her face, and he had a feeling he knew exactly what she was going to say before the words left her mouth. But he did not get a chance to find out as the door to the dining room was opened so forcibly that the sound of the hinges reverberated through the room.

Raza Ali Khan strode into the dining room, and Ahmed sucked in a breath without realizing it. His mother's eyes shot towards her husband within seconds and her lips parted as if to ask a question, but she stopped herself when the door slammed shut. He had seen his father going through various emotions. Anger, grief and regret had always been frequently observed by him and his mother, and they had been dealt with however his mother saw fit. They would all either pass, or be fixed with a few bribes here and there. But this was different, and Ahmed knew it as soon as his father had entered.

His face had gone ash white and his eyes were bulging. With his lips parted in a half gasp and his hair ruffled, a clear indication of him having run his fingers through it multiple times, Raza Ali Khan looked as if he had seen a ghost. His hand was trembling as he sat down, and placed his phone on the table with enough force to rattle the plates and cutlery. Ahmed could only watch as his father reached for his glass of water and took a sip, before placing it back. When he spoke, his voice, to their surprise was steady. But his words were enough to send chills up his spine.

"They have something on me," he paused, as if waiting for the words to sink in. Then, seeing his wife's confused expression, he continued. Words tumbled from his lips in a jumble, and it seemed as if any control he might have managed to gain over his tone a moment ago had slipped. "Corruption. Fraud. Money laundering. They have evidence and they're talking about putting my name in the bloody Exit Control List." He exhaled, and Ahmed realized that his own blood had run cold in his veins. When his mother did not utter a word, he carried on, fixing his gaze on Ahmed. "We need to push the dinner today. And you're going to be there."

He nodded. He would be there.

Chapter 10

Seher

Two days.

Seher only had two days until the day finally came. She had seen the small trunk that her mother had prepared for her, and had resisted the urge to roll her eyes when it had been placed in front of her. She knew it held some cutlery and crockery tucked under layers of cheap clothes that her mother had managed to mend for her to take with her. The crockery had come from the wife of the landlord they served. Although the very concept of a dowry still repelled her, along with the whole idea of marrying Arshad, she realized then that she resented her parents for not being able to provide more.

Seher had always wanted more, she realized. She had wanted more than what the village provided her, and that had never boded well with her parents. Her father had, in the beginning tried to give her everything, and with a smile that was barely there, she let herself think of the days they had spent together out in the fields where he used to help in the harvest of the wheat crop. He would let her go with him and help him pile the stalks before they were carried away. He would tell her how she was his princess and could do anything she set her mind to. Those days had ended the day the villagers had started to gossip, and defending her had started to seem like a chore. So their outings had slowly decreased, and then stopped altogether. She resented him and the entire village for that. They had been poor then too, she recalled; had barely managed three meals a day. But times had been different then. Life had been different.

The day was a warm one, with birds singing in the trees all around them, and the tall stalks of wheat slowly moving in the breeze. The smell of dirt mixed in with dung was thick in the air, but she did not mind that at all as she sat on the edge of the field and drew, while her father worked a few yards away. It felt as if time had slowed down for the two of them alone.

"That looks beautiful, my princess." She looked up after what felt like ages as her father leaned over her shoulder to look at what she had been drawing, a sketch of an old tree that stood a few meters away, its branches tipped towards the sky. Seher smiled as her father took the sketchbook from her, peering at the picture more closely.

"I started it yesterday," she told him, getting to her feet. Her father had piled a few stalks of wheat at the edge of the field while the other men and women continued to work, oblivious to the pair.

"Your sketchbook is almost finished," her father observed, running his thumb over the edges of the few pages that remained. *"I'll try to get a new one for you when I go to the city."* He had been saying that for the past two weeks now, promising to get it for her the next time he went. But every time he had made a trip to the city, something else had come up. The last time it had been her brother's new schoolbooks and his uniform the time before. Seher had not complained then, believing her father was doing all he could.

"Thank you," she grinned, as her father held out a hand for her. She took it, and he spun her around, a smile lighting up his face as he saw his daughter's eyes shining under the golden sun. Her laughter echoed around them and she could feel other pairs of eyes on them as her father continued to swing her in his arms.

"Someday," he whispered. *"You will have everything you have wanted, my child. I'll make sure."*

She did not know exactly when she had started resenting her parents for being poor, or whether it was actually them whom she resented after all. All she knew was that had she been born into one of those families in the city, where their only worry was deciding where to get the best clothes from, things would have been different for her. Here she had to worry about whether she would even have a roof over her head after it rained since the houses were made of mud and tended to collapse quite often. She had to worry about what lay in the future for her, and that alone was enough to make her hate the place she had grown up in.

"Your dress just came." Zara was peering at her from behind the curtain that separated the room they slept in from the courtyard. "Hamid brought it from their house." Their mother had gone over to the *Chaudhry Sahib's* house to help with dinner, promising to bring back some supper for them seeing as they were out of rice again and had still not gotten more flour. Their father and Hamid had at last gone to the city to get a doctor to prescribe something for his joints. They would be back later that night.

She simply stared ahead, refusing to acknowledge the fact that in less than seventy-two hours she would be wearing an atrocious red dress that had belonged to Arshad's mother, next to a man she had come to loathe with a passion. The mere thought of wearing something that his mother had worn at her wedding made her sick to her stomach. She would never admit it out loud, but she had been hurt after finding out that her own mother had sold the dress she had worn in exchange for some extra money, and that she could not wear that instead.

"Rabia just came too," her sister told her. "She's practically drooling over it."

But even the thought of seeing her friend was not enough to lift her spirits anymore. She had given up trying to find solace in anyone. Who knew if she would even be able to see Rabia after the wedding?

Seher heard her sister sigh before the curtain was swept back in place, and her footsteps started to fade away. She had, no doubt gone to retrieve the dress from outside seeing as Seher had not made any move to get up herself. She could not bring herself to move. It was as if the blood in her veins was running slower than usual, and she could feel a kind of hollowness spreading through her entire being, consuming her. This was worse than the fire that had been in her not even three weeks ago. Seher knew that the fire still existed within her, smothered for the time being by the sheer state of helplessness that she had dragged herself into.

She had found peace in the hours she had spent alone recently. Her heart felt like a hollow vessel that was only meant to pump blood lazily to every part of her body, and she could feel herself being drowned by her own thoughts; it felt like she was wrapped in a blanket of soft darkness that cocooned her in its embrace, and when someone spoke to her, that blanket was lifted slightly, letting in cold gusts of air that bit into her very skin. She knew the fire inside her was compelling her to give in to that air, to welcome it and do something about it, but it was as if Arshad's face from that night had been imprinted at the back of her eyelids, refusing to go away. So she stayed there, engulfed in the darkness of her own mind.

Zara had walked back into the room, and was laying the dress on her cot for her to see. "Look at the gold neckline!" her sister gushed, and she squeezed her eyelids shut, feeling the warmth behind them. Her sister had moved away from the cot and she could feel her behind her now, gently brushing away the hair that had fallen out of the bun on top of her head. "You will look beautiful in it." She heard Rabia walk in at that moment and stand next to her sister. She took her hand and squeezed but Seher barely felt it.

"It goes with the jewelry too!"

Seher just stood there, her feet rooted to the spot. Seeing the dress she would be wearing soon would somehow make everything real, she thought. It would mean that her wedding was a confirmed fact and there was nothing in the way. Her heart sank even further than it already had as she opened her eyes at last.

The dress was mocking her, its bright red and gold hues symbolizing happiness and love, while all she could think about was the hatred that ran through her, and the grief and resentment that was buried deep within her. Her fingers brushed over the red fabric, and then she was clenching her hand around it, imagining the dress burnt to ashes beneath her palm. But the gold lace dug into her skin instead, and she felt as if a knife was digging into her skin. Her eyes ran over the shirt and took in the neckline that her sister had mentioned. She grimaced, imagining herself in the dress sitting next to Arshad as their families celebrated around them. She pictured him looking at her from beneath those long lashes and those brown eyes that seemed warm enough, but could be filled with a monumental amount of anger and hate. Her throat tightened.

His face loomed at the edge of her mind, and she pictured him reaching for her hand as they sat there, his fingers stretching to curve around hers, and she shuddered. She winced, remembering his fingers digging into her arm and pictured him pining her to the wall, she would not even be able to scream if that happened. Nausea swept through her at that image and her hand shot to her mouth, trying to hold back the bile before she realized that there was nothing that would come out because she had not been eating. She felt sick.

"Seher," her sister was saying but Seher was quickly drifting away.

She was in a room with Arshad after they had been declared married, and her *dupatta* covered her face as she waited for him to enter. The dread that had settled in her stomach was enough to make her want to throw her guts up, but she was trying to keep the bile at bay. Nothing had prepared her for this and she resented her mother again for straying away from this talk. She had no idea what to expect, and that scared her, especially because she had seen a part of her husband's temper. Her skin crawled just thinking about the next few hours.

And then he was here, lifting her *dupatta,* and looking into her face as if he were looking at a prize that he had won. Her breath caught in her throat as his fingers came up to cup her face, his other hand reaching for her hand. She gasped.

Her heartbeat quickened as his mouth stretched into a wide grin, and as his hand moved up her arm, caressing her skin at first but then squeezing. Her blood chilled as his fingers pressed into her, his eyes daring her to utter a word. This was his house after all.

The room was spinning, she realized. Zara was asking her something, but her voice had abandoned her. She wanted to scream and she could not. She wanted to breathe, but the walls of the tiny room were closing in around her, and she felt herself incapable of breathing or of swallowing the bile that had risen to her throat by then. Her vision was starting to blur and she knew that if she closed her eyes, she would be gone forever, knew that she would never be able to escape if she let herself be dragged under. She staggered towards the door, Zara's voice echoing behind her. Rabia was calling after her as well, but she barely heard them as she rounded the corner, a faint "I'm going to get food," dropping from her lips.

The cold December air bit into her skin as she walked, the narrow dirt road barely visible in front of her because of the thick clouds of fog. It was deserted outside, she realized. Everyone was probably inside because of the cold, and she supposed she could have waited for her mother to come back from the *Chaudhry's* house as well since she would have brought some leftover food with her after all. But she needed this, she told herself. She had not left that house in weeks.

She could breathe easier now, and she marveled at how wonderful the air felt going into her lungs here, away from that room with its four walls that always felt like they were closing in on her, and that dammed dress that had pushed her over the edge. The street was stretching on in front of her, the houses on either side as silent as ever. She would hear voices every now and then, people sitting down to supper or tea, she guessed. The idea made her stomach grumble as well. She was not hungry, not really. Seher had stopped feeling hungry for a long time now. But she knew that she needed to get some food in her before she started dry heaving again.

She soon reached the school building, a sign that she was close to the house. Seher had taken a shortcut unknowingly, but was glad now because it meant she would be in and out of the house quicker than she would have been before. She had not seen any of Arshad or Tahir's friends either, which was a good sign. Her breathing had slowed down, and the blood in her veins had stopped rushing as well, she felt calmer here. Her thoughts had yet again managed to reel themselves back into that quiet dark place where they could be free and undisturbed.

Seher swallowed, not allowing herself to dwell on the images that had flashed behind her eyelids. She kept walking, past the grey fence that ran around the building, and then sighed in relief as she saw the familiar turn up ahead. The banyan tree that had always stood by the school was shrouded in grey because of the fog, and her breaths came in slow, grey puffs.

"Where are you going?" Seher stopped. The streets were deserted, she had guessed because of the thick layer of fog that had blanketed the village. She had gathered that Tahir and his friends had gone to their houses hours ago as well because of the cold. So she looked around her, not entirely sure whether she had imagined the voice. Her shawl blew around her in the cold, and she struggled to hold it in place against the cold.

"I thought I would not see you until the wedding." It was a different voice now, and her blood ran cold in her veins when she recognized it as Arshad's. Every part of her screamed at her to run and yet her feet refused to move. Seher stood there, her heart racing a mile a minute.

A man's face loomed in front of her out of the clouds of grey fog, and her breath caught in her throat as she realized it was one of the men Rabia's husband hung around. "I'm going to the *Chaudhry's* house," she said, her voice coming out in rasps, and she realized, with another wave of self-hatred that she was scared. She was scared of becoming one of the many nameless women who got raped in the streets of the village, their only sin being that they were out too late.

"Of course you are," the man said, his words slurred together. "At this time." Her fists clenched at her sides as she cast her gaze around her. The fog had shrouded them all, she realized. They had been sitting under the tree and she could still see a heap of empty glass bottles there. The fact that her soon-to-be husband was drunk outside the girl's school while it was pitch dark made her want to throw something, anything. Yet, she stood there, her body refusing to cooperate as his friend came forward.

"I need to go." She tried to step past him and to her horror, realized that there were three other men with them, standing by the wall, their hands clenched around stained, dark bottles.

"But your husband is here too." Seher's pulse quickened at the words. "Where else would you rather be?" Arshad was staring at her now, she realized. The bottle in his hand was shaking as he came forward slowly, his dark eyes narrowed. Anger was burning through her at the man's words, at what him and men like him represented. She yearned to reach forward and snatch the bottle out of Arshad's hand and to scream until someone heard her.

"My…" But she was cut off as she was slammed against the tree. It had happened within seconds, and her mind had not even fully registered the contact with the hard trunk behind her. Arshad's face was inches from hers, his eyes bloodshot and swollen. Sehr felt as if her insides were on fire.

The others were standing a few paces behind him, watching. Seher tasted bile in her mouth as he brought his face closer, his liquor-coated breath fanning her face.

"I told you to stay inside the house, you whore." The words hit her like a ton of bricks as he pushed himself onto her, his weight crushing her against the trunk of the banyan tree that had stood there for years. She could feel her back ache in pain as he dragged his nails down her arm. This was a thousand times worse than what had occurred that day at her house, and she could feel the fear creeping up on her. It was pitch dark and anything could happen. The cool blanket that had been a barrier between her and the rest of the world for the past few days was slipping. She could feel warm blood on her arm.

"I needed to get food from the *Chaudhry Sahib's* house." She struggled to speak as the men around her sneered and whistled, their drunken laughter echoing around them. There was a mad gleam in Arshad's eyes as he slapped her across the face before his hand reached into her hair, yanking it from its roots, and then slamming her against the tree again. She could taste blood in her mouth now. But she would not cry.

Arshad's hands were all over her, touching and squeezing, and she writhed beneath him, struggling to breathe. Each touch, each prod, felt like a knife slicing her open, and she felt herself being dragged under, towards that familiar abyss of darkness. But something inside her cracked as the men around them laughed louder, applauding Arshad for teaching his disobedient wife a lesson.

A scream began to form on her lips, and before she could marvel at how long ago it had been since she had actually felt this way, trapped and struggling, and yet wanting someone to hear her, his hand clamped down on her mouth. She swallowed again, tasting the bitter bile on her tongue.

The cold seeped into her exposed skin and she tried to speak again.

"Like hell you did," Arshad growled, his teeth glimmering in the dim light. The bottle he held in the other hand shattered as he dropped it, and she shivered, the sound reverberating through her. Images of her parents and brother flashed behind her eyelids, and she bit back a sob as she realized what they would say when they found out. They would blame it on her. His hands were at her sides, holding her in place while he fixed her with a cold stare.

"You will do what I say while you are married to me, you understand?" Arshad's voice came from a million miles away, and Seher struggled to stay conscious as he stumbled in his drunken state towards his friends. Blood dripped from her forehead and arm, and she could feel the pain coursing feverishly through her veins.

Her heart was thudding against her ribcage, and it felt as if the world had started to spin around her. The men had stated to walk away, their arms slung around each other's shoulders, and their voices fading in the distance. They retreated into the fog, and she sat there panting as she watched the thick drops of blood pool in the dirt around her. She had no idea how long she sat there for, alone in the freezing cold, her hair sticking to her face with her own sweat and blood, but eventually she stood up. Her legs shook and her arms throbbed as she walked slowly back, all thoughts of food completely gone from her mind.

She also did not know how long it took her to get back to her house, did not hear when her sister and best friend shrieked in shock as they saw her, or when they started to ask what had happened. Zara had continued to yell frantically as she had bathed, the freezing water feeling like a balm on her sore skin.

She put clean clothes on with trembling hands, Arshad's hands still roving her body in her mind. She did not even feel remotely clean. She knew it would be a long time before she was able to look at herself again, but for now, she needed to get away. The ground was siding quickly beneath her feet, and she reached out her hand to grip something, anything to tether her to that moment and to reality. Trembling fingers closed around a battered slip of paper on the cot, and her arm throbbed as she felt Arshad's touch on her yet again.

Their mother still had not returned, and Hamid and her father had not come back from the city either. When she came outside, a battered bag clutched in her hand, she realized that Rabia had gone back home. A faint sense of regret filler her as she realized that her friend was not there to see her, but it was quickly overpowered by anger. The anger and hatred was coursing through her, lighting her insides on fire, and filling her with adrenaline that she had not even know she had buried within her. She was not Seher anymore.

Zara was calling out to her frantically and she might have even run after her for a while, but Seher doubted she would want people to see her. Losing a baby had brought enough humiliation after all. Her mind was still spinning, and the ground felt like what she imagined ice to feel like in the north, slippery, as if she would lose her footing any minute and collapse. But she kept going, her heart beating rapidly inside her chest.

The frigid wind bit into her face as she ran, but she did not stop. Arshad's face from moments before was still carved into her memory, and she realized then that she was ready to do anything to get rid of it, to somehow get out, to be more. It seemed as if her whole world was crumbling and she was the one who was responsible for it. But this time, she did not hate herself for it. Pride blossomed in her chest as she felt blood oozing from under her foot because something sharp had cut through the thin sole of her shoe and pressed into the heel of her foot. Blood roared in her ears, and she welcomed it.

She did not know how long she ran for, or how many people had seen her, just that she was almost at the edge of the cramped village. The streets she ran through widened just for her, and she could see her breath in front of her before it was carried away on a phantom wind. The smell of the village snaked up her nostrils, and she wished that she were outside already, on the other side. Midnight was approaching and she realized that her mother would be home by then.

Upon discovering that she had fled out of the house, her first thought would be if any of the villagers had seen her daughter running through the streets. She also knew that her father would find out when he arrived, and the fear of being known as the man who could not keep his daughter under control would overcome his paternal instincts. So he would allow anger to consume him until he could no longer see reason. Hamid would tell Arshad and together they would start combing every inch of the village for her, because their most precious possession had been taken right from under their very noses.

So it was futile to run now, she realized as she neared the cotton fields that lay almost near the edge of the village. Hamid had friends on this side who helped with the harvesting of the crop. Surely, they would have been asked to keep an eye out for her, so she decided to wait for a while, just to be safe. The cotton fields looked as tranquil as ever as she gazed at them. Tomorrow, the numerous people who had no choice but to work here or the nearby factories to feed their families, would come and start the arduous process of picking the small balls off before they were taken away to be processed. Seher stopped and allowed herself to breathe in huge gulps of air that felt like they would burn her lungs. Her hair was a tangled mess around her shoulders, and she could feel her feet throbbing after running so fast. But she did not care.

The fire that had been thrumming inside of her for so long was back to the surface now, only now it felt different. The fire was not anger at herself at that moment. It was something more. Her blood was boiling in anticipation for what lay ahead. She sank to the ground under the cover of an old tree, hoping she would not be seen. Her arm still hurt, and she could still imagine the way it had felt to have Arshad's hand over it, to have him look at her with that predatory glare that seemed to say that he would as he pleased with her body. She leaned to the side and finally threw up the contents of her stomach,

"I will leave." She said into the silent evening, and waited for the fear to set in. It did not come, and she did not know if that was a good thing, only that she could not turn back now. Going back now would be suicide, she thought, as another image of herself in that red wedding dress flashed in her mind. She had to do this. A small part of her yearned to see Rabia before she left, but she ignored it, telling herself that it could cost her too much, and she had come too far to look back now.

The silver moon shone down on the cotton field, bathing it in a soft pearlescent glow, and she wondered when she would ever see a night like this again, if she even wanted to. The owls were starting to wake up, and she could hear cuckoos in the distance; she knew cities did not have them. She allowed herself to stare at the fog for a while as it hovered over the village, thickening as the night wore on. Her palms were cold, and she tucked them into herself in attempt to get some warmth to seep in, thinking about where she would go.

In her heart, she knew where she wanted to go, knew that some part of her had always been prepared for this moment. The reassuring weight of the folded banknote against her bosom was enough indication of that. She would go to Lahore, she told herself, and then let herself look at the piece of paper that almost felt like a lifeline now. It had remained in her hand as she ran, clenched between her fingers. She did not know if believing what that boy had said made her a fool or not, just that she was desperate.

He had seemed sincere enough, she recalled his face, and felt a smile begin to form on her lips. His tone had been gentle, sweet even. If he, a stranger, thought she could do more with herself away from this village, then maybe she could. She would never allow herself to feel the way she had today again, she told herself firmly. Seher also knew that she would do anything necessary to make sure it never happened again, anything. Her heart beat faster at the thought of what she was about to do, at the ridiculousness of the very idea of seeking help from the people she despised, but she smiled. She would show them all.

She could see headlights on the main road in the distance, hear the honking of trucks on the road beyond, and then knew that she had to leave. Thankfully, nobody had spotted her sitting under the tree waiting for night to settle in. Then again, who would expect to find a girl outside under a tree at the edge of the village anyway? Hamid had probably told his friends to keep an eye out on the streets as they went home, and she had seen them a while ago, laughing and talking amongst themselves on their way back to their houses. None of them had noticed her. There was also the possibility of her parents not noticing and Zara keeping her mouth shut, she mused, but then quickly shoved the thought away. She needed a clear head for the next few minutes.

    Getting to her feet, she let herself gaze at the field, and her tree before taking a deep breath. She exhaled, and caught a puff of white air in her palm before letting it go. Anticipation thrummed in her veins as she made her way to the main road. The dirt road beneath her feet felt steadier, and she finally felt like she could breathe again. A small part of her hesitated as she rounded the corner and she paused, letting the memories wash over her one last time.

Chapter 11

Ahmed

News really did travel fast in the world of politics, he thought as the night wore on. He had noticed the furtive glances people had been throwing at each other through the evening, clearly not wanting to be remotely associated with someone who had been accused of corruption, but still not wanting to lose that person's support just in case the claims were proved false in the end, because he certainly was a good ally to have.

His face ached with the effort he had been putting in his smiles that night, and he yearned to sit down in a corner and let the news of his father's possible future sink in, of what was expected of him now. They had had a short informal meeting earlier with his grandfather and a few other prominent party members, and had come to the conclusion that it was imperative that Raza Ali Khan's son make his debut in politics this year. His father had obviously found the suggestion outrageous at first, but had then realized that it was perhaps the only way to gain the people's favor. If they could make sure the people loved him, it would surely mean their party had an actual chance. It was just a rough patch, his grandfather had said. And they just needed Ahmed to make sure the people were still on their side after the charges were cleared. An older man could never hope to achieve that. They needed Ahmed to start taking charge so that when the time came, they could use him as a back-up plan just in case things had not settled down until the elections.

So the dinner had been hurriedly organized, with frantic last minutes invitations to people in a desperate bid to have them see the face of the youth of the country, to have them talk to him in a closed setting, and to make sure that he managed to woe them with his words just as his father was known to do. In other words, Ahmed thought to himself as he slowly sipped from a cup of green tea. They wanted to use him as a distraction while they got his father out of trouble. That would not be a problem considering the fact that a bribe here and a bribe there could basically do anything in this country.

"Yale was always a strong possibility for me." Ahmed turned his attention back to the people surrounding him, only to notice that the group of four he had been standing amid had now grown to include two new people, one of whom was slightly younger and looked to be near his age.

He wondered whether he was leeching off his father's money, or was in the same boat as him.

His question was answered moments later as the man continued. "But Princeton won me over in the end. I think I made the right choice as well. This country could learn a lot from the way they teach there." The last sentence was added as an afterthought, cautiously, as if he was not sure of the reaction it would receive. When the other men surrounding him, including his father, nodded in agreement, he continued. "The way they talk about World Systems and views there is truly fascinating really." As other people started contributing to the conversation, his grandfather drew him aside for a moment.

"That's Ghulam *Sahib's* son talking," he said in an undertone. "You want him as an ally because chances are his father might be the new CM."

"He sounds like a snob." He had no idea why he had pointed it out, seeing as he had once again agreed to do something to help his father, regardless of his own moral code.

"He's an ally," his grandfather repeated. "We have worked hard to gain his father's favor and you calling him out or appearing aloof will not help that purpose, Ahmed." The old man looked tired, he noticed. His father did too, and both men were on edge, though they were trying to appear as nonchalant as possible. It was as if they both knew that there was a huge chance of everything they had been working towards going to hell soon.

Begrudgingly, he bowed his head and joined the group again, this time making sure he heard every word the Princeton graduate uttered, and even going as far as to jovially patting him on the back when he mentioned reforming the current export market of the country. By the end of the conversation, they had set up a date to play tennis at his farmhouse, and Ahmed had caught a triumphant gleam in his father's eye then. He did not know what kind of person it made him but he felt a small sense of relief wash over him. This meant they were going in the right direction and that people had not entirely given up on their party.

His father had been engaged in conversation with numerous people throughout the night, trying to subtly convince them that they had nothing to worry about, that the allegations meant nothing, and that soon it would be over. He was trying to win their unwavering support in exchange of more promises and assurances. Ahmed was almost impressed by how fast the man had managed to slip on a mask of utter calmness and control as the night went by, as if he had not been considering fleeing the country a day ago. Ahmed still remembered the hurried conversation his father had had with his own father minutes after they had gotten the news. In the end it had been decided to wait out the blast by the media, and to play the cooperation card. The public always ended up having a soft spot for someone who was willing to be investigated and then proven not guilty.

He was just making his way over to another group of men, the independent runners, when his phone buzzed. Trying not to let his emotions play out on his face, he pulled it out and saw the notification flash once on the screen before it went black. But his stomach had knotted at the mere sight of the name. Irene. Sighing deeply, he slid the phone back in his pocket. He had been meaning to check on her for a while, but had never gotten around to it. To him, Irene would always represent another life that was miles away now, one he still yearned for sometimes, but knew he could never have. That life involved going far, far away from this country and all of his father's problems, living his life the way he had lived it while he was at Oxford, not caring about how anything played out, because he only had that day, that moment, to live.

She represented the part of him that would always prefer to smoke and get stoned until the pain was a dull throb in the back of his mind. The numbness that would take over would be welcomed with open arms. It was easier to blame her for all the bad choices and decisions that he had made, not that he would ever admit they were bad.

"Ahmed!" Wincing slightly at the pitch of the voice and at being jolted out of his thoughts, he looked up to find another familiar face. It was one of the older men from another party who would be an ally in the upcoming years if everything went well, and he realized that he had probably come to size him up. He vaguely remembered the man being on very good terms with his father ever since he had been a boy, and could almost hear his father's voice telling him that the man was an asset, and therefore needed to be impressed. "It's so good to see you, *beta*. How was Oxford?"

So he tried to ignore the fact that the man had basically asked about Oxford as one would enquire about a short vacation and offered his hand forward with a smile. "Likewise," he greeted. "Oxford was a great experience really. But it's even better to be back." His grandfather was smiling at him from a few yards away.

"I bet it was," the man winked at him, and Ahmed was grinning back at him. "You really should have told us when you got back though. I bet Sana will be glad to hear it." Sana, he nearly choked on air as the name was mentioned. The girl had been the very definition of obnoxiousness ever since they had been kids, and he had hated her with every fiber of his being, which had always made their dinners interesting affairs. But he tried his best to keep the smile in place.

"I would have," he apologized. "But they wanted to keep it low-key. You know how everyone's busy with the elections and everything."

"Yes, of course," he answered before adding. "I should have known you would have wanted to arrange something for your friends. A huge party!"

Something snapped inside him as he heard those words, at the implication behind them, but Ahmed kept his expression neutral when he answered. "Oh," he waved a hand dismissively through the air. "I'm past all that now." He added a small chuckle at the end for good effect and when the man joined in, the hollow feeling in his stomach returned.

He knew exactly what he was doing, and why he was doing it and resented himself for it. All his morals and personal beliefs had seemed to melt away as soon as his father had mentioned that he was being investigated and that they needed to take certain measures. He had not objected when this plan had been laid out in front of him, had merely nodded his head and agreed to do his part. So he had laughed and talked to the very people that he detested with everything in him all night, and had made sure that they saw him in a good light, just so his father could have a decent chance at deceiving more people.

The air was filed with the sounds of loud laughter and chatter as the guests milled about the lawn, huddled in small groups on couches with low tables placed in front of them. Almost everyone was sitting now, clutching small cups of steaming pink tea. For the first time that night, his eyes sought out his mother. She was sitting in the midst of a group of women nearly in the middle of the lawn, her face showing no signs of worry or stress at the fact that her husband might be in trouble, because if anyone asked, he was not.

Her neck was adorned with a diamond necklace that sparkled as the light fell on it, and glittering jewels dangled on her ears, and moved as she talked. Her smile never wavered as she chatted with the wives of the political workers, trying to make sure that they heard exactly what they wanted to, and that her husband and son were regarded well by them.

He supposed that was what it meant to be part of a family that was so involved in politics. But at that particular moment that was not why he felt sorry for her. Despite not having a real relationship with her, it was times like these that made him want to try. He felt ashamed at the thought of her having to be there for the night's special entertainment, to see what her husband got up to when he was completely trashed.

Ahmed was now sitting squeezed in between the Princeton man and another political worker who was close to his father, he could not for the life of him remember their names. But he supposed that would not matter for the rest of the night at least. They would all soon be too preoccupied for long conversations anyway.

A stage had been set up at the front of the lawn with twinkling fairy lights around it, and the other lights were now starting to dim, signaling everyone to cast their gazes away from each other. The women gave each other knowing smiles, probably waiting to use the next few minutes to blackmail their husbands later. The men were already gazing at the stage, clutching half empty glasses and smirking at each other as the music turned to a slow sensual beat.

The girl that emerged was skinny, dressed in a silver *saree,* with a short white blouse that looked as if it was on the verge of tearing open due to her enlarged breasts that she took care to highlight when she leaned forward to offer her hand to a man sitting on the left side to kiss. She started to sway on the spot, and he realized that the men did not even care whether she was dancing. Their eyes followed the thrusts of her hips and pelvis, probably savoring the only few minutes of excitement they would have before they went back to their bedrooms and the drains on their bank accounts. He knew the women did not even mind because being married to a politician meant a bottomless tab.

As the minutes ticked by, his gaze drifted to his father. Raza Ali Khan was grinning at the girl who was now being passed from man to man as they groped her front and back while she batted her eyelashes at them. His stomach twisted as he caught his mother looking in their direction just as his father's hand found the girl's left breast. She put her hands on both sides of his face and planted a kiss on his cheek before moving on to the next one.

He knew these things happened when you were in politics, and it was not as if he had been a model citizen all of his life so it was not for him to judge the actions of the people around him. His father needed to make sure these people had a good time today, he tried to reassure himself as his mother looked away, her mouth curved downwards for just a second before that poised smile was back in place.

He realized that his throat was parched dry, and he was just about to ask a passing waiter for a drink when his phone buzzed in his pocket again. Some part of his mind hoped it would be Irene but as he took in the number that hope was easily cast away and he found himself wondering who was calling at the late hour. It was nearing three in the morning.

"Hello?" There was a long pause at the other end, the silence on the line was a sharp contrast to the music and chatter around him. The number had been unfamiliar, a landline in Lahore from the looks of it, and he had picked up out of sheer curiosity, seeing as most people did not even use landlines unless it was an official call; which he doubted was the case here. "Hello?" He was just thinking of ignoring the call, considering the fact that nobody had spoken on the other end when he heard it. Someone was clearing their throat on the other end, a woman from the sound of it. Now more intrigued than ever, he struggled to get to his feet before making his way to the back of the lawn.

The air was cool as he stepped away from the comfort of the heaters that had been placed around the area where the guests sat, and it bit into his skin as he held the phone to his ear. "Irene?" He did not know why he had asked that, knew that there was no way it could be her, but she had been the only woman he could think of who would be calling him at that time, especially since he did not remember being with a girl in the last few days who would have his number.

The woman cleared her throat again, as if struggling to find the right words to say, and he waited, partly feeling stupid for thinking it had been Irene, and partly hoping that the voice that he heard next would be hers. He hated to admit it, but it was then that he realized how truly lonely he really was. Irene had been one of the few people who had understood his need to let go, to forget who he was and where he came from. That was the only thing he missed about her.

"Hello?" The voice was so faint that he thought he had imagined it at first, before it came again, louder this time. "Hello."

It definitely was not Irene, he realized and mentally kicked himself. The voice did not seem to belong to anyone he knew either, and had an accent that vaguely reminded him of the way his father's chauffer greeted him.

"Hi, who am I speaking to?" Ahmed's teeth were nearly chattering due to the cold and he wished he was closer to the warmth of the marquee.

"I'm Seher." He tried to place the accent, and then nearly gasped when it finally dawned on him. The girl continued. "From Zaleemabad." That had been the village they had visited a few days ago. He could still picture it; the rolling cotton fields, and the girl who had sat under that tree. Her drawing of the field was still imprinted at the back of his mind.

"Seher." Her name sounded strange on his tongue, and he started wondering what had prompted her parents to name her that, seeing as it sounded like a name for someone in the city. He immediately hated himself for thinking the way his father would.

"Yes," she replied, breathless as if she had been running for a while, or because she was having trouble forming words, he could not tell which. "I got out of there."

He stood there and let the words sink in, let them form meaning in his mind, and when they finally did, he was terrified and elated at the same time. "You got out?" He could hear the tremor in his own voice. "Where are you right now?" This was not how he had planned for things to go for her, and he could again, hear his parents' voices rising to a crescendo inside his head. This was not what his father needed right now. A girl from a village that he had convinced to run away was not what would help him make sure that his father won. But then she spoke again, and something cracked inside him. Her voice was small, and she sounded as if she was terrified but was doing her best to hide it.

"I came to Lahore. I got off the bus and started walking. This was the only phone I could find. I have nowhere to go. I want to be someone here, but I don't know how."

Chapter 12

Seher

She had seen dawn breaking out over the city, and it had taken her breath away. Seated on an ordinary park bench with her shawl wrapped tightly around her, she had watched the sky change to a pale orange flecked with pink as the sun had slowly risen over the horizon. The air had been cold and it had rushed over her skin, but she barely noticed it. Her thoughts had been elsewhere, they had been ever since she had found the park.

Would he actually come? She hated the thought of waiting in an abandoned park for a man she had only talked to twice, one of the conversations only being one sided. Everything inside her was screaming at her to leave, to not put herself in a position where her actions were directed by someone else, but, she reminded herself. She was prepared for this. She would not let herself be taken advantage of by anyone here.

He would help her, she had told herself over and over as she had waited, alone in the park. He had asked her to describe the place she had been, and then calmly explained the way to a park where he said they could meet. There had been music playing in the background when he had picked up, she recalled, and wondered where he could be at that hour. He had certainly sounded awake and surrounded by people. Then again, he had come with the politician so she supposed it was considered normal for people like them to mingle at odd hours of the night. Nevertheless, she had been glad when he had answered.

Her heart had been hammering inside her chest as she had gotten off the bus and looked around at the sprawl of pale yellow lights and lingering fog, and she had had no idea where to go, just that she was not going back. She had felt like a fool then as the full weight of what she had done hit her. She had come all this way just because a man she had only met once had told her that she could do a lot better than her village. The money that she had would only last her a couple of days here, and she shuddered to think about how she would survive in these streets. Women who stayed out late were more likely to be taken advantage of, her mother had always said. She had found that out just hours earlier herself.

Then, every shadow had felt like a man lurking behind her as she walked, and every brush of the wind upon her skin had been phantom touches of men like Arshad who prowled the streets at night. His nails had left marks on her skin, and she could still feel the weight of him pushing her up against the tree. Her sides still throbbed with pain. She had been shivering with fear, and had then resented herself for it as she reached a lone shop that had a phone. With trembling fingers, Seher had made the call, her breath coming in steamy white puffs as the old man running the shop had watched her curiously. She doubted he had many girls from villages showing up to use his phone in the middle of the night very often.

 She had silently prayed for him to answer as it had rung, hoping he would hear the phone if he was sleeping, and pick up instead of dismissing it as merely a wrong number. When he had picked up, she had been unable to form words at first. Her voice had caught in her throat at the thought of what she was doing, of how terribly wrong this could go. But she had managed to get a few words out before he had recognized her. She would not admit it but she had been relieved then, because she had also told herself what to say in case he had forgotten who she was.

 He would help her, he had said, and sweet relief had flooded into her at the words He would be there within an hour, he had told her, and she had not told him that there was no way she would even be able to tell when an hour had gone by.

Instead, she had started walking, keeping close to the streetlights and praying she would not run into anyone at this hour. Arshad's iron grip on her arm was not easy to forget. Luckily, the park had not been too far from where she was. But she had decided long ago not to expect too much from this encounter. If things went downhill, she would find work somewhere, maybe in the house of a wealthy family who needed work done. But she would not go back to that miserable little village.

She had watched the pale morning sun rise into the sky and cast the city in its warm golden glow. Its rays had softly touched the grass, and she had seen them glinting off the freezing dew that had fallen the night before, and shine on the hovering clouds of fog that lay suspended in the air. She had watched it with awe coating her features, and marveled at how peaceful the city looked in these minutes.

A dull roar sounded in the distance and she glanced towards the entrance of the park where a motorcycle had pulled up. She could feel dread sinking into her as the rider started to take off his helmet. After all, this was a park and anyone could come here. Nobody would even know she had been here. Seher started to get up from the bench, picturing Arshad pinning her to the wall at her house, and then to the banyan tree outside the school. The men here would be far more dangerous, she thought to herself. But then, just as she was drawing her shawl tighter around herself and preparing to leave, her mind already starting to register the fact that the man she had called had not come, he turned around.

It was him, she realized as he tucked the helmet under one arm and signaled her to come outside. He looked different than she had imagined him to, or from the way he had looked that day when he had talked to her at the edge of the cotton field. His hair looked golden in the light of the sun, and he ran a hand through it to smooth it down as she made her way towards him. The leather jacket and jeans that he wore was a sharp contrast to the way she had seen him only a few days ago, and she could not help but roll her eyes when he smiled. God knew she was not going to fall for that again. Arshad had looked decent when he had smiled too. Then she silently reprimanded herself for even thinking that way, seeing as there was nothing between her and this strange boy except the fact that he had agreed to help her.

"Hi," he greeted when she was near enough, his voice oozing with wealth if that was even possible. She was quick to pick up the slight accent that it held, declaring that he had spent years abroad on his parents' wealth, while people like her had been forced to skip meals or miss out on a chance at a decent education. But she forced herself not to think that way.

"Hi," she said back, unconsciously wondering whether she had managed to make her voice sound less like the village girl that she was, and more like the people he was used to associating with. She hated herself for even wanting to sound like them, but there it was.

"Well, that's an improvement already," he was saying. 'You refused to talk when I last saw you." She realized he was talking about the time when he had talked to her at the edge of the cotton fields and dropped his number on her sketch. That encounter seemed so long ago.

"I was not okay at that time," she started saying. He made no move to walk further into the park.

"Clearly." He looked her over. "You look better now." She narrowed her eyes, and he continued. 'I'm Ahmed by the way. I don't think I introduced myself when we met earlier."

"You didn't."

His mouth turned up slightly at the corners as he patted the seat of his motorcycle. "Yeah, you could say I was not okay then either."

"Do you really want me to get on that?" She raised an eyebrow and he smirked.

"If you want to get something to eat then yeah," he answered, and she realized that she could not remember the last time that she had eaten. She also found herself admitting that she actually wanted to eat now; the growls her stomach had been emitting proved that. So she tentatively took the hand he offered and slid one leg, and then the other over the side before taking the helmet he offered her. Most girls from her village would have balked at the thought of getting on one of these things, but she was ready for it. She felt a wave of anticipation pass through her as Ahmed revved the engine.

"Where are we going?" she asked once they were both settled and she had slowly placed her arms around his waist. He looked over his shoulder, and this close she could almost make out each individual strand of his hair, and see the exact colour of his eyes. They were a dark brown that grew lighter in the middle.

However, it was not their color that made her breath catch in her throat. It was the hint of something she only knew too well, something she had tried to hide ever since reaching Lahore, and she was quite sure he was now trying to do the same thing for her sake. But it was there, the disgust shone clear for a second along with resentment and pain. If she guessed correctly, it was likely to be aimed less at the outside world and more towards his own self. But it was gone within a second, and he flashed her a small smile.

"We're getting tea and some breakfast,' he said, before slowly backing out towards the road. Seher's stomach turned slightly as she imagined what her mother might say if she was there to see her, but she quickly dismissed the thought, choosing instead to look around as the city slowly stirred to life.

Lahore whizzed by them as they drove and she marveled at the billboards that rose up into the sky, advertising new products and companies, and at the few cars that were already out, their drivers making their way to huge corporate buildings for work. The fog had started to thin by now, and she could make everything out clearly, the roads with tarmac that was grey with age, the few trees that bordered them, and the slight stench of smoke that lingered in the air. The roads were wide and the few cars that drove alongside them were sleek while their drivers maintained an expression of cool disregard as they drove past.

"Why don't you drive one of those?" she asked as yet another one of those cars sped past them.

"That's certainly the method of transport my father would have me use," he commented. "But I prefer this. It lets me feel the wind on my face." He paused for a second and then said. "You feel more alive on a motorcycle." She agreed with him.

"Is your father one of those rich men who sit behind a desk then?" She had wondered why he had shown up to their village with that politician since he seemed like he already had enough money of his own. Even though a voice inside her had told her not to judge. She had ignored it.

"In a manner of speaking," Ahmed answered before turning a sharp corner. The cars on the roads had increased by then, and everywhere she looked, she saw people blaring their horns or looking impatiently out of their windows at the cars in front of them. She remembered a time when she had come to the city before with her parents, and winced at the memory. That day felt like a day from another person's life now. She then began to wonder what her parents were doing at that hour, if they had decided to look for her or told Arshad. Would they simply call off the wedding, or would they ask for more time? She shook her head and focused on the road in front of them. She would have to call them eventually, but now was not the time to think about it.

They rode in silence for a while after that, Ahmed expertly cutting between the lines of cars, and she was soon glad that they were not in any of them because they seemed to be moving at a snail's pace compared to them. She was glad to feel the wind brush through her hair and on her face. It was still cold and she felt it seeping into her bones and breathed a sigh. It had been days since she had felt anything it seemed.

Soon, the roads narrowed and the number of fancy cars that she had been seeing ever since they had started driving decreased. The billboards and corporate buildings receded in the distance, and they were now surrounded by rickshaws and the stench of smoke mixed with something else that she could not quite place. The people here were louder, more expressive, and everywhere she looked, she saw colours. There were vendors selling spices and clothes, and it looked as if Ahmed knew his way perfectly between them as he weaved through the crowd of people and rickshaws alike. Even though she had always told herself not to judge, she found herself wondering exactly why someone like Ahmed would ever come to a place like this with its tight roads and loud noise.

They stopped after about five minutes and Seher looked around in awe. This looked to be the heart of the *bazaar*, vendors selling spices called out as they passed, and the smell of exhaust fumes hung heavy in the air. "This place has the best *halwa puri*," Ahmed said as they reached a small shop at the end of the street. It was at the corner, and a few tables had been set outside. She could smell fresh *halwa* being made.

"Why here?" She blurted out.

"Why not?" Ahmed replied as they sat down.

"I didn't think you would want to come to a place like this," she answered and watched his eyes narrow slightly. "I mean don't people like you go to fancier places? Where they serve other things?" She had always looked at the upper class with distaste, and had assumed everyone that belonged to it had some kind of completely different lifestyle that included eating habits as well. She supposed that was going to have to change if this boy was going to help her. Ahmed's mouth turned up at the corners as he waved over a young boy carrying a tray.

"They have good tea," he said simply and then added. "And I'm not one of those people." She noticed how his expression had hardened at the words, and decided not to press further. When the boy came over, he greeted him with a smile and Seher hid her shock as he addressed him with his first name.

"You come here often." She tried to hide her surprise, but Ahmed had noticed because he turned to her and smiled slightly.

"I come here a lot," he said. "It's the perfect place to get away when it feels like the whole world is watching you."

"Does your father mind?" She was curious and she knew she was asking too many questions for someone he had just met, but she had not been able to help herself. He appeared to be debating something with himself, and she was almost sure he would not answer but then he nodded.

"He would if he knew I was here." His mouth quirked up at the sides. "You're full of questions for someone who just escaped being suffocated to death." His eyes shone with warmth, she noted, warmth along with something else that she could not quite understand. But she was starting to feel comfortable in his presence. She had felt like she could trust him the minute she had called him, but had still been weary. Yet now, as he sat there peering curiously at her from across the small table, she realized she wanted to tell him something, as if to prove that she could be trusted too.

"I was almost married," she confessed. It had not been what she had planned on saying, but the words had simply tumbled out of her mouth. He did not gasp as she had expected him to.

"Wow, I didn't realize it was that bad." He laughed softly and she smiled. "And I thought me being forced to watch my father feel up a woman with my mother in the same room was bad."

She could not help but laugh then, at the sheer absurdity of their situations, the fact that they were sitting and talking about them, at the fact that she was sharing a meal with one of the people she had grown up resenting, and at the fact that she liked this stranger more than she would ever like the man she was supposed to marry.

The tea arrived first, followed by *the halwa puri,* and she had to admit that it really was good. While everything she had been eating lately had tasted bland on her tongue, the *halwa puri* was divine, and she ate more than she had in months.

Chapter 13

Ahmed

He could tell that she resented people like him from the minute he saw her. Her eyes had narrowed in contempt as they had first landed on him, and her expression had hardened when he had greeted her, no doubt picking up on his accent and judging that he was indeed one of the wealthy policy makers responsible for the conditions she had lived under for years. He did not blame her in the slightest. But as the minutes had passed by, they eventually settled into a comfortable rhythm.

They had ridden through the city, her arms slung around his waist and her hair blowing around her face. He had expected her to hesitate at the idea of riding a motorcycle as most girls would have, but she had not. Instead she had climbed on with the ghost of a smile on her face, and had taken everything in with awe as they drove. She occasionally asked questions and he felt like he needed to answer them, to tell her everything that he could about his world.

The *halwa pur*i shop had been around for years, and as he sat there he recalled another time when it had been a permanent breakfast spot for him and Fahad. They would come here after their many nights out, and he had always found comfort in the noise around him. He had felt like he could drown himself in it and be whoever he chose to be. Here, people came to buy or sell cheap clothes or other artifacts and they barely looked twice at you. He did know that they obviously did talk about how someone from the upper class had decided to slum it with them, but apart from that, the *bazaar* was like a safe haven. Nobody expected anything of him here.

"Do you have any siblings?" He was brought out of his reverie by the sound of Seher's voice. They had been talking ever since they had sat down, only stopping when the food had arrived. She had gazed at it with longing and he had felt guilty about her obvious lack of nutrition in the past, but had quickly disregarded that thought, choosing instead, to find comfort in the fact that he was helping her now, even if he was completely terrified at the idea. But it somehow felt right; giving this one girl a chance at happiness. To him, it was like a chance to redeem himself, even if it did mean going against his parents. He would worry about that in a while, not now.

"Nope," he answered at last, putting down his cup of tea. "I'm an only child. You?"

"I have a brother and sister back at the village," she said slowly. He noticed that her expression became slightly distant as she mentioned them.

"Do you miss them already?" he asked with a chuckle, and she looked back incredulously at him.

"God, no," she replied, smiling slightly. "I don't know what kind of person that makes me. But I don't miss that place or them right now. I know I'll miss my sister eventually, but right now I just want to get away from it all even thought I don't know how."

He understood every word that she had said. "I understand," he answered quietly as she looked up at him over her tea. "And since I did say I'd help, I intend on keeping that promise." The words had tumbled out of his mouth too fast, he realized. A part of him was warning him about the promise he had made to this strange girl over a phone call, a promise that he had no idea how to keep.

But another part had basked in the memory of her voice long after she had hung up. Her voice had been a mixture of sweet and rough, he had noted as he had driven through the dark roads to the park. It had been like one of those songs that you listened to once and never got out of your head. The fact that it had sounded like that while she had probably been scared out of her mind had made him want to get to her as soon as possible.

Seher stared down at the table for a minute before looking up, her eyebrows creased. "I never intended on asking anyone for help," she said. "Especially not…" she trailed off.

"Someone like me?" He raised an eyebrow, and she settled back in her chair, crossing her arms.

"You can't exactly blame me," she said. "I mean the people you work for are the reason people like me are in this mess."

Ahmed nodded before realizing what she had said. "The people I work for?"

She sighed before taking a sip from her tea, her expression relaxing slightly. "The politician you came to my village with," she said and he almost started to laugh. "You do seem different though."

"He's my father," he said and then laughed at the horrified expression on her face. He was enjoying himself now, he realized. Despite her having judged him and assuming he was as bad as his father, he found that he did not mind her questions or assumptions. He wanted to prove her wrong, and the expression that was now covering her face was priceless.

"Oh," she said and then paused as if trying to decide what to say before she opened her mouth. "It is true though."

Ahmed watched her sipping her tea wordlessly and then nodded. "It is true. But like I said, I intend on helping." Seher smiled and then put her cup down. She had drank her tea in under five minutes, not bothering to hold the saucer as she sipped. His mother would have been appalled, he noted, feeling the corners of his mouth turn up slightly.

"You really do seem different," she said and then added. "Would your father mind?"

A bitter taste settled upon his tongue then, but he spoke past it. "My father is in enough trouble of his own to mind what I do right now." She nodded and seemed to struggle to decide whether to probe further, before deciding against it.

He had been ignoring all of his calls ever since he had slipped out of the house, but he knew that both his father and grandfather would have been livid at finding out that he was not there when it was time to say their goodbyes to the other guests. Ahmed had slipped out unnoticed, quietly taking his motorcycle from the back of the house, and driving out after telling the guards to tell his parents that he would be back soon, both of whom had been too preoccupied to notice at the time. He would take care of all that later, he told himself as he watched Seher finish off the last of her *halwa puri*. She looked as if she had eaten to her heart's content, and he smiled as she sighed in satisfaction before leaning back in her chair and peering at him. It was strange, he thought as he looked back at her. She seemed at ease now, as if she knew things were going to be okay. Or perhaps the village had gotten so repelling that anywhere else seemed like a good alternative.

"Do you think you would like to study Art?" he asked her at last.

Seher looked back at him, her lips a thin line and her eyes slightly wide. The sunlight that fell on them made the brown in them turn lighter, and he caught another flash of what he had seen back in the village. It had dimmed slightly as she had gazed around the city and marveled at the people, but he knew that it would always be there, just as some part of himself would always resent himself and the world around him. "Study it?" She asked at last and he nodded.

She did not answer for several moments, and he was just starting to think that she never would when she leaned forward in her chair. "That's what I've always wanted to do," she admitted, and then hesitated for a second before continuing. "I wanted to make a living out of it, but then some things happened and I haven't drawn for years. That day was the first after a long time." She looked down then, as if surprised that she had told him that piece of information. He was too, at the fact that she had chosen to share some details of her life in the village with him.

"That did not look too bad for someone who hasn't drawn in a while," he commented, and she smiled as he paid the boy who had been serving him for years now. "Have a good day," he said and the boy winked at him. Ahmed was reminded yet again of the many times he had come her with his friend. Casual conversations with the staff had always been a part of their routine.

Seher was gazing at a shop displaying clothes right across from where they were standing when his phone rang. It was his mother. Ahmed paused, gazing at the screen as her name flashed across it. Now was probably a good idea to answer, he thought with a sigh, preparing himself for the onslaught of questions. He would stand his ground. After considering his options, and deciding that it would probably be better to prepare her before she actually saw Seher, he put the phone to his ear.

"Hello?' There was a pause at the other end, and he pictured his mother pacing in their living room after finding out that he had not come home the previous night, while his father slept in.

"Where are you?" Her voice was heavy with exhaustion, and he almost felt sorry for delivering the news about Seher but gritted his teeth. He would help her in any way he could.

"I'm with a friend," he told her. Telling her that he was in the middle of a *bazaar* in the old city would not help anyone, he told himself. He also did not want to be reminded of just how prejudiced his parents were, he knew that already.

"Of course you are," she sighed and he rolled his eyes, knowing exactly what kind of friend she had assumed he was with. "Ahmed, we only asked you for one favor. Just for a little while, at least pretend you care what happens to this family." He bit his tongue, resisting the urge to tell her that there really was no family left. The word was a shell now, hollow on the inside. Nobody except his father and grandfather even wanted to preserve the family's political legacy.

"I do care," he heard himself saying, as he looked over at Seher who was looking curiously back at him. "That's why I need you to listen. It will help dad too." The plan had formed in his head as he had been driving, slowly taking form as they had sat and talked over breakfast. If his parents were to be convinced to help Seher, they needed to think it would help them too. His father never did anything for anyone useless he knew that he would get something out of it, and since they were all desperate to save his name, it would not take much convincing to show them that helping Seher was a good idea. Ahmed did not want to admit it, but he knew that he would not be able to do anything for her on his own. He needed them for this.

#

Minutes after he had hung up, he was standing behind Seher as she gazed at the different colors of shawls on display, a few paces away from where they had had breakfast. He watched her as she ran her hand over the soft fabric and felt something shift in his chest. He could still see the hard determination and resentment in her eyes but for a moment there was something else there, a spark of joy, and he was glad he had played a part in bringing it there. He had realized by now that she was strong, stronger than she knew at least. Leaving a family was no easy task after all. But she had done that, to make something of herself. He found himself wishing for her strength but knew deep down that he would never have it.

They did not talk much on the drive back and Ahmed was grateful for that because it allowed him to think. Seher continued to stare at the people and sights that they passed, taking everything in with wide eyes, and he wondered just how bad her situation had been back at

Zaleemabad. He would not ask though, just help in any small way that he could. It felt good, as if he had been given a second chance after letting that girl die in the street upon seeing her moments after she had been raped.

But as they weaved through traffic now, the city having completely woken up around them, Ahmed's mind drifted to his father again. Was it really necessary to tell him about Seher at that moment? After all, his mother would be the one who would actually have to make the calls anyway, telling Raza Khan would only complicate things right now. He had other things to worry about now in any case. The fact that he was not telling his father had nothing to do with him knowing how he would react to the news of his son getting involved in the life of a girl from a village that he barely knew, Ahmed told himself as he swerved in and out of traffic. He would worry about his father's reaction when the time came.

He imagined his mother sitting in the living room waiting to get this meeting over with, and exhaled. She had relented after a while, agreeing to do what she could to help Seher get into *NCA*. Her NGO could use a good cover story, he had told her in a low voice so Seher did not hear, and that at last, had been what had made her listen. She had admitted that they could use this as a way to boost his father's popularity, and it would not cost that much either, just a couple of calls.

She had always been that way, he thought to himself, easy to convince, easy to please. At least it was easy for his father; Ahmed had not really had that chance yet until today. His father could sway her towards anything with just a few words and she, in her desperation for a perfect world where her family was happy, would agree. He had always resented his father for that, for taking advantage of that weakness of hers to get what he desired. But it had helped him today and he would be lying if he said he was not glad for it. Despite their unusual relationship, she had agreed to help. He had not liked the way she had referred to Seher as 'uncultured', or the way she had talked about how it would be an inconvenience having her stay at their house but an inconvenience they would bear for a while, but had bit his tongue, knowing it was more than what he could expect from his mother.

They soon emerged onto the wider roads of Gulberg, with huge printed billboards and buildings on either side. There had always been a perceptible difference between the people of inner Lahore and here. They were in more of a hurry here, more impatient. The very air was thrumming with life, the cars and their occupants brimming with barely contained energy. The music that was being played in all of them reached them as a collection of beats, slamming against their eardrums as they drove on.

He could tell that Seher had not heard anything like that before, and smiled slightly as the bass seemed to reverberate through her whole body. This was one of the reasons he loved this city, he decided. No matter what time of day it was, even if it was ten in the morning, it was always bursting with life and energy and music. The air was clearer now, the fog having dissolved a while ago, and the sun had come out. But it was still chilly, and he shivered slightly as it brushed his face. They had stopped at a traffic light and his hands were frozen on the handlebars. Behind him, Seher was gazing at the few trees that bordered the road, their leaves slowly rustling as the cars swept by them.

"Is it like this every day?" she asked him at last, motioning towards the throng of cars that was slowly moving forward.

"Always," he replied, turning around slightly. "You should see it at night."

Her eyes glazed over for a minute before she answered. "I did once. With my family. It was beautiful." The traffic began to move again and he turned around, almost glad for the excuse of not having to respond to her. He imagined that day had meant a lot to her, and it sickened him to know that he could not think of a single family outing that he still clung to like that, a memory of being out with his parents and actually enjoying himself.

It was not for a lack of trips of course. While Seher's idea of a family outing had been a trip to Lahore, his had been trips to London and New York. Strolling down Oxford Street in the summer had been a yearly ritual, and winters in New York had been the only way he had spent his Decembers. But there had never been a single moment where the three of them had been out together, and when they were, his father would barely be there, a phone pressed to his ear or clutched in front of him as he typed furiously away. His mother had never complained, the promise of endless summer sales making up for her husband's lack of attention. She had always loved the summers in London, and they would return to Pakistan with double the luggage they had taken with them.

After a while, he had stopped caring if his parents barely talked to each other or to him on those trips. He would go off with friends while his mother sought out her own. Everyone was in London during the summer, it seemed. His mind drifted again to the friends that he had made at Oxford then, to Irene and he wondered what she was up. But he quickly realized that he did not care at that particular moment. The days and nights that they had spent together were a distant memory now, and the very idea that he had hoped to hear her voice the previous night felt absurd when Seher's grip tightened around him as they sped over a speedbump. He was finally doing something that made sense.

They were near his house now, he realized. It was only a couple minutes away, and he was surprised to find his heart beating slightly faster. He had known that Seher would eventually see his hose, he tried to silently will himself to calm down. It was not a big deal. Surely she had to have guessed already that since he represented the class she despised, he would be living like them too, not that he wanted to.

But it was a big deal, he noted as her arms twitched around his waist, the only indication that she had seen the house looming ahead with its red walls gleaming in the golden sunlight.

"Wow, what does your father even do exactly?" He sensed the resentment in her voice just as the words left her mouth, and did not bother to call her out on it as they turned onto the narrow, familiar road. The redbrick stood tall over the surrounding houses and the barriers that cordoned off the rest of the city had never seemed more useless and pretentious to him.

"He's an MNA,' he told her. "Or hoping to be one anyway." They weaved between the barriers, and he nodded at the guards that stood outside the gleaming black gate.

The only sign of shock Seher showed at this new piece of information was a small gasp that she quickly covered up, having just realized why he had been at her village that day, and he sighed with relief when she made no further comment. Somehow it felt important that her opinion of him did not change after he told her about his father, the very symbol of a breed of people she so obviously despised.

"I'll vote for him," she joked, and he grinned.

"I wouldn't." She rolled her eyes.

"I wouldn't have either. I just thought it was the polite thing to say." They were laughing when the gate opened, and he drove down the familiar path towards the back of the house. Seher took in the rolling green lawns with the evergreen trees and fountains without a word. When her gaze fell on the cluster of black SUV's parked in front, he could feel the embarrassment washing over him in waves. He wished they had not been there that day.

The sight of the round infinity pool at the back almost made him apologize to her, but he stopped himself. What would he be apologizing for exactly? Where would he begin? They silently made their way back to the front after he had parked his motorcycle and they had clambered off, Seher tugging at the end of her *dupatta*.

"My mother knows about you." He tried to sound casual, confident.

"Okay," was all she said, her gaze travelling over the freshly cut grass in the lawn, and then returning to his own. He suddenly felt small standing there in front of the grand oak front doors of his house.

Chapter 14

Seher

As her gaze travelled over the huge red brick mansion in front of her, she was reminded of her mother. Her childhood might have been spent in a small mud house in the village but that did not mean that the house was something out of the blue for her; she had grown up imagining herself in another place. Her mind reeled with memories of simpler times spent by her mother's side at night, falling asleep to the sound of her voice as she told her stories about 'other people', people who lived far away but seemed so near and led lives that sounded fascinating and impossible, and yet she yearned for them.

She gulped in a breath of cool air as she remembered herself hanging on to her mother's every word as she spoke about the wealthy class of people who dwelled in the mansions in the city. She did not know back then how much of it was true because her mother had never actually been inside one herself, she had only heard conversations of people who had gone to work there from their village and shared gossip about the scandalous lives of the wealthy elite class of Lahore. She remembered how one of her mother's friends had gone to work there with her husband and every month, they would return and tell them about how easy it was there, how the *Begum Sahiba* they worked for went out wearing whatever she pleased, and how she often smoked expensive cigarettes, not caring what people might say. They would also tell them about the extravagant dinner parties that were held in their house almost every week, and how they always seemed to have an endless supply of food and drinks.

 Her mother's stories at night had been her version of fairytales, and Seher had grown up imagining a life inside one of those mansions, a life where she had been born into money and beautiful clothes and dinner parties. The house she had imagined for herself looked so much like the one in front of her that she nearly gasped out loud.

 Standing tall at the end of a driveway that stretched on for miles, it resembled an old fortress with its towering walls that ran around the parameter. The golden rays of the afternoon sun were reflected by the huge French windows, and the lawn went on for miles in every direction. She let a small gasp escape her lips as she noticed the beautiful fountain bubbling in the center. Her mouth had already gone dry after the sight of the blue swimming pool that she had seen a minute ago, but she tried her best not to appear fazed.

As they stood in front of the oak front doors, her resolve returned and she stood up taller, stiffer. She was reminded yet again of the fact that the man next to her and the people inside that house had everything while she and countless others like her were stuck in sickening situations, that they led lives they did not deserve. A glance in Ahmed's direction told her that he was embarrassed too, no doubt remembering the mud houses he had seen in her village. She let the wave of satisfaction wash over her at his expression, knowing it made her petty, and not caring in the slightest.

"My mother knows about you." Ahmed's tone was tentative, soft.

"Okay," she said simply as he pushed the doors open.

They stepped into the foyer, and as the doors slammed behind them, she felt as if she were a little girl again, lost in one of her daydreams about a better life in a better place. It was warm inside and she immediately attributed it to central heating, a luxury she had only dreamed about. Ahmed looked awkwardly back at her, and placed his keys in a bowl on a table with a beautiful flower arrangement, before nodding his head to the right.

"She should be in there," he said slowly. "Don't worry about anything she might say. They hate having me as a child if that helps."

"It doesn't," she said simply but she could not help thinking why Ahmed's parents could possibly hate having him as their child. He looked like the kind of boy anyone would want to know and talk to, and seeing as they were not short on money either, she could not figure out exactly what would possibly drive his parents to be unhappy.

She had wondered the same thing earlier when he had mentioned that his father would hate to know where he was. But a further analysis of that statement had only caused her to resent his father before even meeting him. But she had pushed those thoughts away as quickly as they had come.

A voice inside her whispered that these people were helping her, that she was so close to escaping everything that she resented them for, and that the boy standing next to her had no obligation towards her, but was making sure she got to a better life after one brief encounter throughout which she had not said a word to him. A sudden image of herself drawing by the cotton field, and him slipping his phone number in her lap with a few words flashed inside her mind, and she allowed herself a faint smile.

He had been nothing but kind ever since she had met him, she told herself, remembering that she had had her first meal in days that day, and it had been because of this boy.

"We're not as bad as you think." He had read her mind, it seemed, and she could not help the small smile that curved its way onto her mouth. "At least I'm not." Ahmed shrugged and then she was overcome with shame. Shame at herself for thinking like her mother would, like everyone back at her village did. She despised them all for their intrusiveness and uncalled for judgments from the bottom of her heart and yet here she was, doing the exact same thing.

But she was saved from answering as they entered another room, this one lined with beige sofas, and Seher could only imagine how soft they would be. The rug placed in the center looked like it was soft as clouds, and the low table in front of the sofas would have made her sister swoon. Ahmed cleared his throat, and she realized that he was motioning forward, towards a woman who could only be his mother.

She could feel her throat going dry as her gaze settled on her, and she debated whether it was more appropriate to move forward or to say *salaam* from where she was. Her mother's stories had not prepared her for how the rich and powerful handled greetings. The woman in front of her sat with an air of complete and utter calm about her; and yet it felt as if she could undo her with a single withering stare.

Seher noticed her hair first, the dark auburn reminded her of someone she had seen on television once. Her perfectly plucked eyebrows and ruby red lips were enough to make her glance self-consciously down at herself, and she was suddenly aware of her dusty complexion and chapped lips, but chose to stand tall and smile. After all, that was what these people did when they had something to be ashamed of.

"*Assalamalaikum*," she said as Ahmed's mother got up to greet them with a smile of her own. The smile was thin, her lips barely moving, and yet Sehr felt as if it was the most she would get out of her. The woman was surveying her slowly now, and she had to remind herself yet again not to shrink away from her.

"*Walikumasalam, beta*," she said. "I hope he didn't drive too fast." Seher stood motionless as she lightly kissed both her cheeks before moving abruptly away. "This one's always going too fast, and on that motorcycle too. I've told him to slow down, but will he listen?"

Ahmed had stiffened at his mother's words, and was standing with his arms crossed against the wall.

"Oh no, he drove perfectly," she laughed, having no idea why she suddenly wanted to explain further. Ahmed's mother patted the sofa next to her. "There was a lot of traffic so he really couldn't go fast."

"The traffic!" his mother exclaimed. "Yes, of course." She looked over at Ahmed as he came and sat down opposite them. Seher noticed how his gaze kept shifting between her and his mother, and began to wonder what he had told her about her. He looked somehow different now, more on edge, and he kept looking around as if expecting someone else to walk into the room.

She remembered how he had told her not to worry about anything his mother might say, and now she was beginning to understand why. She would not let anything get to her, she decided in that moment. She would only think about the end result.

"You have a beautiful house," she heard herself saying after a moment.

#

Ten minutes later, they were still sitting in the living room, and Seher had come to the conclusion that there was clearly a lot of tension between Ahmed and his mother. She had been polite to her ever since she had come, but somehow it felt like every time she spoke to her, it was due to a huge effort on her part, that she would rather be doing anything than talking to a girl from a village that she had never heard of. But she chose to ignore it. A tea service had been brought in, and Seher had gazed in wonder at the trolley for a minute before quickly recovering and accepting the cup of tea that was offered to her. She knew there was something wrong in the way she was holding the cup, because Ahmed's mother had raised her eyebrow more than once in the past two minutes.

"So Ahmed tells me you've given your matriculation exams?" she asked her and Seher nodded quickly before speaking, her heartbeat quickening.

"Yes, ma'am," she said. "I finished in the first division actually." Her voice broke a little as she remembered how her mother had sat her down the day she had told her. "I could not continue after that though."

"She's very good at sketching," Ahmed spoke from across the table, his mouth was curved into a thin line, and she suddenly wondered why he was so willing to help her, why he wanted his mother to know she deserved it. She had been wondering for a while now, but had not come up with anything.

"That is a very valuable skill," Mrs. Raza Khan smiled, and then put her cup down. "My

NGO could actually get you admitted into a nice Art college like *NCA*." Seher did not tell her that she had never heard the name of the college before but allowed herself to smile, imagining herself in a classroom full of other people, learning something she already loved, or would come to love again.

"Thank you so much." The words were tumbling out of her mouth before she could stop herself, and she knew that they were aimed at both Ahmed and his mother. Mrs. Raza reached over to pat her on the shoulder before quickly retracting her hand. "If I could do anything in return I would." She had felt the sharp need to say those words as soon as she had walked in, and was relieved that they were finally out. She did not want these people to think that she was a leech or some pathetic girl looking for a break or somewhere to live for free.

"That's no problem, *beta*," Ahmed's mother smiled a little before continuing. "You won't have to wait long either. We'll have you taking your inter exams in a few months, and then you can consider yourself a part of the *NCA* student body. They have a special agreement with our organization so it will not be a problem."

The organization she talked about definitely sounded like a charity, she decided. Seher had always hated that sort of thing, but now it seemed like the only way. She would never allow herself to be in this position again. She smiled slowly; she had wanted to take the inter exams for a whole year now. At least she had before her village had managed to trample all hope for another life.

"We will need to get in touch with your parents though."

The words sent a jolt down her spine. Her blood ran cold in her veins, and she was trembling before she knew it. A picture of her mother and father sitting over the stove in the courtyard back in the village flashed before her eyelids, and she blinked. She could just imagine what they would be thinking right now.

A girl who had run away from the village would never be welcomed back or looked favorably upon. She would never be married and she would forever be a disgrace, whatever the circumstances might have been. She imagined Arshad looking for her out in the streets and shivered, knowing what would await her if she ever made it back, her whole body began to ache at the thought of his hands on her, and then she was trying not to think about what had occurred just a few hours ago against the banyan tree.

"They will be furious with me if they know where I am," she said at last. Mrs. Raza nodded as if she understood, but did not say anything and Seher knew she would be made to tell someone soon. There was a certain way these people worked, and from what she knew they liked doing things their way.

"You have to tell someone, Seher," Ahmed said softly, tentatively. She noticed how his mother's eyes narrowed when he spoke to her.

"I'll call Rabia," she said at last. "She's a friend. My parents don't have a phone."

Ahmed seemed to visibly relax, and his mother smiled as if she was glad she did not have to push harder. "You can stay here as long as it takes, *beta*," she said.

"Thank you."

Mrs. Raza then reached into a drawer next to her and pulled out a small phone. Seher's mouth opened slightly, but she shut it quickly. Did they really keep a spare phone lying around like that? "You can use this. It already has a SIM so you don't have to worry about that."

She took it with trembling hands, her fingers lightly brushing the sides. The phone was like the one Hamid had back home, but lighter. She felt a sudden thrill at the thought of finally having something that her brother did not, and she noticed Ahmed smiling as he watched her holding the device and quickly looked away, biting back her smile. She would not let them see the little girl from the village that would always live inside her.

A part of her hated that she had to accept the phone from them, but she reminded herself that it was all so she could never be in a situation where she had to depend on someone else in the long-run, that was what all this was for anyway.

"Don't worry; you will not have to go back. We're happy to have you here." His mother was smiling at her again.

"Thank you," she replied again.

Seher felt as if there might be a double meaning attached to those words, as if she might actually be doing them a favor by staying at their house too, but she chose not to dwell on it as she was shown out of the living room and up a flight of stairs.

She tried not to let her awe show on her face at the magnificent chandelier that hung overhead, or the polished hardwood floor that was so clean she could almost see her reflection in it as she walked. She noticed again how Ahmed's eyes kept darting around as they walked, as if he was afraid of something popping out of the corners. Or maybe he was afraid of running into his father, she thought to herself. Had he even told his father?

They reached the first floor landing, and he excused himself as his mother opened the door to her room. "Just let us know if you need anything," she said. "We have lunch at 2. It'll probably just be you and me though." She sighed. "Ahmed barely eats at home."

Seher smiled and nodded in thanks, too shocked by the sight of the room to say anything out loud. The door closed behind Mrs. Raza and she exhaled, walking farther inside. The worn bag that dangled at her side suddenly looked smaller than it was, the extra set of clothes too dirty.

A king sized bed took up most of the room, and her eyes slowly travelled over the black silk sheets and the pillows that seemed to be filled with cotton as soft as clouds. Her heart ached for a minute at the thought of spending most of her life curled up on her cot back home, her back often feeling sore because of the hard plastic digging into it all night long.

The ache soon turned to anger again, anger at the whole world for giving so much to these people, and leaving her with nothing. She could not help but feel jealous of Ahmed. He was about as old as she was, but had grown up in a completely different world, one where his bed was comfortable and where it was made for him every day. She hated him for living in this mansion while she had to grow up inside a cramped mud-house with the weight of ridiculous rural norms pressing down upon her, containing her whereas he was free to do whatever he wished here.

She sat down on the bed and slowly ran her hand over the sheets, savoring the feeling of soft silk brushing through her fingers. For a moment she wished her sister was there. Zara would have loved being here, she realized. When they were children they had often talked about living in a palace like the ones in the stories they heard, oblivious to the harsh realities of life. Seher sighed as she pictured her sister now, alone with their parents and Hamid, and she felt a wave of guilt pass over her.

Her sister did not deserve to be stuck there after everything that she had been through. Zara was probably one of the few people she would do anything for, she realized to her own surprise, and at that moment she found herself thinking that even though some part of her would always resent her sister for putting up with what everyone said, for letting their village crush her spirit, she would still always have that ridiculous need to see her sister rising above it all, to help her achieve it. She then found herself silently vowing to help her after she had made a name for herself here, if she ever managed to do that.

An hour later she decided that it was time to shower and change. A maid had come in at some point and had left fresh clothes for her on the bed, and Seher had debated whether she wanted to wear the ones in her bag or these new ones. The answer had been obvious, and so her old clothes now lay forgotten in her bag in a corner of the room.

She padded into the bathroom, and felt her mouth opening in a silent gasp at the sight of the huge bathtub in the corner. She instantly recognized it because of all the stories she had heard but it had still taken her breath away. The mere idea that people actually bathed in that huge tub and washed themselves with fruit smelling liquids that came in different bottles baffled her. Back in her village, they only got a bucket and a bar of hard soap, a packet of shampoo when they got lucky which was usually only when someone was getting married.

So she sat there in the tub for about forty minutes, letting the lukewarm water roll around her body, feeling it brush against her, and it was the best bath of her life. The water eased her sore muscles, washed away the dirt and grime and even managed to make her forget about Arshad's hands on her for a while.

It felt as if her mind was at ease for the first time in years. She did not have to worry about leaving enough water for her siblings; she supposed nobody had to worry about that sort of thing here. She also would not have to worry about embarrassing her father or soon to be husband; she was free. Her mind had drifted to how the next few months of her life were going to be and she smiled.

She was finally going to be independent, something more.

When she came out of the bathroom, it had felt like a weight had been lifted from her shoulders, and she was a completely new person. Thoughts about her village had started to fade away, and she vowed only to look forward from that point. She just needed to do one more thing now, and then she would be able to breathe ven more freely.

Her fingers hovered over the keypad of the phone that Ahmed's mother had given her and she considered once again just tossing the phone aside. But a voice inside her head insisted she needed this as much as her family did. She needed them to know where she was, that she was alright and was not coming back at least for a while. Her parents' faces flashed in front of her eyes again, and their voices rang dully in her ears as she began to dial the number.

Her father at least would be genuinely worried about her safety as well, she thought. He might be angry, but he would also want his daughter to be alright, while her mother and brother would only be thinking of how they had to explain her disappearance to Arshad. She would talk to him soon, she decided. A picture of Zara lying on her cot in the courtyard flashed before her eyelids and she blinked. Despite their strained and changed relationship now and her need to please everyone around her, she knew she at least loved her and genuinely wanted her happy.

"Hello?" She was jolted out of her thoughts by the sound her friend's voice. She imagined her sitting by the fire in her own courtyard, and smiled. Her husband must be out of the house given the time of day.

"Rabia, it's Seher," she said, barely able to keep the excitement out of her voice. There was silence on the other side for a moment and then her friend was almost screaming, her words tumbling over one and other.

"Seher?! Are you okay? Where are you? Hamid came here yesterday looking for you. And Arshad just left. They're looking for you! Arshad was so angry…. Your wedding, it's…"

"There is not going to be a wedding." Finally saying the words out loud felt like utter bliss, and she felt the weight of each word leaving her as it fell from her lips.

'What?" Shock oozed from her friend's voice. "What do you mean? Seher, I'm worried about you. They're going to kill you if you don't come back. You have no idea how angry they are. Your wedding is in two days. I think he'll still marry you but he's very angry."

He was angry? She almost laughed out loud, almost. She could barely feel the bruise on her arm anymore, but in that moment it was as if a phantom hand had clamped down upon it, squeezing slowly. She had to blink thrice in order to get rid of the feeling. "I'm not marrying that animal, Rabia," she said slowly, enunciating each word. "I'm in Lahore."

"You…" Rabia paused for a moment as if making sure she had heard right. "You're in Lahore? What? How?"

So Seher told everything, starting from the day in the cotton field; it felt so long ago now. The day she had unknowingly met a strange boy from the city who seemed to want to help her. She told her how she had barely thought about him and his offer for days after that, until that night when Arshad had come for dinner, and then the previous night. That had changed everything. She told her friend what had happened and she listened in silence, occasionally sucking in a breath as she described how Arshad had made a fool of her in front of his friends and had hit her as they watched, laughing.

She told her that she had had enough and that she could not stomach the thought of staying in the village another day. The words sounded absurd as they left her mouth; the way she had just left sounded like a farfetched, and yet perfect story. Rabia listened in silence, not saying a word until the very end when Seher stopped to take a breath.

"Seher," she said slowly. "This is… so good. You're going to be an artist like..." she paused and Seher laughed softly. 'Like one of those girls in the dramas…who draw and paint…" She stopped and then they were both silent, each lost in her own thoughts for a minute.

Seher felt a single tear roll down her cheek slowly, moving past her cheekbone and then her chin. It all sounded so good when it was said out loud but she knew it would not be easy. She knew what she had sacrificed to get here, and no matter how much she resented them, her parents' disappointment and anger seemed to resonate within her at that moment.

Then Rabia was talking again and she realized how much she had needed to hear her say the words. "You're going to be amazing, Seher. They will be angry but this is worth it. Your freedom is worth everything. Don't make the same mistake I did. What they make us do here."

She was referring to her marriage of course, and Seher realized then that she owed it to herself and the rest of the girls in her village to do this, to make it in this new world. She would prove that a girl could do anything she wanted, that spending money on their education was never a waste, that it was something they were owed. She would show Arshad that she could not be pushed around the way he had imagined, that she could be independent and earn. She would not look back now.

"I'll miss you," she said at last.

"I'll miss you too," her friend laughed. "Just think of me when you go to that fancy college and make new friends."

Friends in this world seemed like a strange concept to her. It was hard to be friends with people you would always despise and resent. A small voice reminded her that everyone was different, that making judgments based on generalized ideas was what her parents and the rest of the village excelled at.

"Are you sure you can trust them though?" Rabia was saying. "This boy… you know after everything." Seher smiled, feeling stronger than she had in months.

"I'm not," she admitted. "Never again."

Chapter 15

Ahmed

The wooden desk was all that sat between Raza Ali Khan and his son, and yet Ahmed felt as if there was an ocean separating them. The tension in the room was thick to say the least, and he could almost feel it curling like smoke around them. The lone glass of whiskey that sat in front of his father seemed to be staring at him, mocking him silently, its contents almost gone.

His father had drank in silence as he had spoken, looking at him over the rim, his eyebrows creased the whole while. The stress from the last couple of days was clear on his face. After feeling jumpy the past two hours, wondering when his father would come outside, he had decided that the talk with him was inevitable, so it was better to get it out of the way now rather than later.

"A girl from a village." His father spoke at last, drawing out each syllable.

"Yes," he replied. "Her name is Seher and she is really good at Art." He had spent the last five minutes explaining how this could benefit him and his party, and his father had listened in silence.

"A village." Raza Ali Khan was having trouble grasping the idea of a girl from a village being inside his house at that very moment, and it was showing. His hands were clamped tightly over the desk; they were visibly shaking now, and Ahmed could see a vein pulsing on his temple as he reached forward for the glass, seemed to think better of it and leaned back in his chair. "She's in my house?"

Ahmed remembered how his father had always insisted on the help inside the house being from the city, claiming that the only kind of people the villages had were uncivilized savages. They had thus had to dismiss countless maids and cooks sent to them by the agency. It had always made his blood boil seeing his father talk like that.

"Her name is Seher and she needs help. I promised her." Ahmed repeated, gritting his teeth.

His father, clearly having decided the remaining whiskey could not wait, reached over and sipped from the glass, draining it completely. "So while my political career is in the process of going down the drain, you have gone and brought a leech into my house."

Ahmed stiffened. He had known his father would not take kindly to his idea, he never did, but he had promised himself he would do this, he had to.

"Dad," he said, his voice level only because he knew what an argument right now would mean. "This could be used as part of your campaign…" His father cut him off.

"My campaign," he said, leaning over the table slightly, his eyes bulging. "My campaign has gone to hell. While you were off running around the city like an *awaaragard*, my name was formally put in the ECL. I can't campaign. They've tried everything, but we're out." Each word was uttered with such contempt and resentment that for a moment he actually felt sorry for the man sitting across from him. The party was what his father and grandfather had sacrificed everything, including their family for, and they had pulled all the strings they possibly could for this election. To see all that go to waste had to be painful.

"I'm sorry about that," he said in what he hoped was a sympathetic tone.

"Like hell you are," his father sneered, leaning back in his chair. His eyes drifted to the ceiling, and Ahmed noticed how unfocused they were. Turned towards the light, the shadows under them were clearer and he could easily see the redness around his father's pupils. "Do whatever you want then." He knew he was referring to Seher now. "I suppose letting some savage from the village leech off our money is what my life has come to now." He was slurring his words, and Ahmed wondered just how much he had had to drink in the past few hours, but he chose not to ask. He also knew that he should defend Seher, explain that she did not want any of their money, just a decent life, but something stopped him, and he wanted to punch himself for letting it.

"Thank you," he said instead. "She'll be gone in a few months." But Raza Ali Khan was already fast asleep, The warm sunlight that streamed in through the huge window cast his father in a warm orange light, and he was suddenly reminded of the amount of times he had spent sitting at this very table when he was a little boy, waiting for him to be done with his work so they could go outside.

Ahmed's father had always put politics before family, and had spent more time greasing palms than with his son so he wondered what he would do now. His mother had molded herself according to her husband's love for his work, and he wondered how this would affect her. For someone who put self-preservation above everything else, this change had to be a monumental one.

The office felt eerily silent as he made his way across the room to the door, looking back only to glance at the sleeping man for a second. The man had spent every ounce of energy he had trying to restore his father's party to its former glory, only to be forced aside due to his own carelessness. He could only imagine how his grandfather would be feeling right now. He had a feeling that the man already had a counter plan of action in motion, probably having been prepared to see his son being investigated by the feds. He would never be entangled in the same web as his son though, at least not visibly. The old man knew how to cover his tracks.

The door shut softly behind Ahmed, and he sighed as the sound resonated inside him for a minute before his phone buzzed. Already having some idea of who it could be, he breathed out slowly.

We've come up with a plan. We need to meet.

Ahmed slid the phone back into his pocket without opening the message.

His mother was waiting at the bottom of the stairs with one of her signature expressions on her face, lips pinched inward into a line and eyebrows raised slightly. He expected this was going to be about Seher. She had talked to her calmly, almost pleasantly and he was almost sure that Seher had not caught on to the slight air of pride in her tone, or if she had, she had not said anything of it and he was glad. His mother had watched her take the phone with a knowing expression on her face, as if she had expected her to take it with a smile, thus adding to her earlier observation of her being here to take advantage of their money. He had ignored it.

"He doesn't have a problem with it," he said to her by way of greeting. His mother sighed.

"The poor man is distraught," she said. "I'll make the call though, and she can start studying for her inter exams right away. I suppose we will have to provide the books too?"

"Yes," he answered and when his mother did not say anything, he continued. "It's not as if we are short on money."

"No," she crossed her arms. "But your father is facing a problem, or were you too focused on your charity project to notice?"

"He told me," he said simply. He wanted to tell her to stop referring to Seher as a charity project, like she had been for a while now, but contained himself. After all, he needed her to make this work. His mother knew the right people who would make sure Seher ended up at *NCA,* which meant she could help him redeem himself as well. "This will work in his favor too," was all he said, before walking into the dining room where lunch would be served. His mother followed him and soon after they heard footsteps coming down the stairs.

Seher walked in uncertainly at first but then, noticing him smiling from the end of the table, seemed to relax visibly. She was not wearing her clothes from before anymore, and looked calmer somehow. Her hair was damp, he noticed. Her eyes seemed brighter, the hazel in them catching the light.

He was glad that she had come down to eat with them. Somehow it made eating with his mother a lot more bearable, and he could not explain why seeing as he had only just met her. But he simply could not bear the thought of having a meal with his mother alone at that moment. After everything that had happened in the last seventy two hours, the very thought seemed ridiculous.

He knew he still resented her for putting up with all of his father's ideas, he resented himself for that too. But seeing her sit there and defend him was too much, not to mention the fact that the only thing the both of them seemed to have in common was his father. She would go to any length to defend the man who was responsible for her social status.

In a way, he was just as bad as them, he knew that. He also knew that he was using his mother and her connections for Seher while resenting her in his mind. He was also pretending to keep all of his emotions in in order to get something done, and that made him a hypocrite as well seeing as he judged his parents for doing the same. But he pushed all that aside as lunch was brought onto the table. His mother had ordered sushi from *Fujiyama*, and he watched as Seher looked on in fascination as the plates were unloaded in front of her. The look, however vanished as his mother turned to her.

"It is fish, *beta*. You might find it bland compared to what you're used to but..." she laughed, and Seher narrowed her eyes. "Just try it, why don't you?"

Ahmed's lips quirked up as Seher squared her shoulders. "I don't mind really," she said with a small smile of her own. "It looks delicious." He noticed how even though she had conjured an air of solid defiance and pride about her, she waited until they had both started eating before she did, noting how he held the chopsticks in his fingers and then imitating him. His mother raised an eyebrow, but did not say a word.

They were silent as they ate, Seher looking down at her plate the whole time as well as his mother, each lost in her own thoughts. Ahmed found himself to be calmer now that they had formally decided to help Seher, and he could feel the image of the girl from the street slowly erasing from his mind at last, replaced by a small scrap of hope, hope for doing better, changing the county in a small way. His mother was talking now, glancing at him now and then as if to confirm that he was still here. He did not blame her, being at the dinner table for meals was a rarity for him due to the kind of relationship he had with his parents. But now, knowing he was doing something on his own despite the way his father treated people, it felt easier.

Seher would stay with them for a while and prepare for her inter exams while maintaining a portfolio that would get her into *NCA* where she would be given complete financial aid. His mother would take care of all the paperwork, so all she needed to worry about right now was studying and coming up with a unique mixture of sketches. She would live with them until she could move into the hostel at the college, and someone would be talking to her parents soon.

Seher had balked at the idea of someone meeting her parents, but when his mother had told her that technically since she was over eighteen, she had no legal obligation to return to her house if she did not wish to, she had relaxed slightly. His mother had told her that talking to them was just a social call they had to make, and that they would try to convince her parents that this was best for her, but she had not looked convinced at that. Nonetheless, she had nodded with a small smile.

The sound of a phone ringing in the living room drew his mother out of her chair, and she moved quickly out of the room, muttering something about the press and his father. She had said that people were eager to know the details about the investigation, and so far three news channels had had to be turned away from their house that day. The fact that his father was deemed unfit to compete in the upcoming elections had raised many questions about their party in general.

"Your family will understand eventually," he said, needing to get his mind off politics. Seher looked up at him from her plate and slowly shook her head, an unreadable expression taking over her features. He noticed how her hair looked cleaner, the golden light from outside turning it a soft brown.

"They won't," she said. "You don't know the kind of people they are. They'll be very angry, especially since my wedding was supposed to be tomorrow."

"Tomorrow?" he asked. "Wow, poor guy. *Bechara.*" It had been meant to be a joke really. Ahmed had figured that things had to have been really bad for her to leave her village like that. But he had wanted to lighten the mood in the room after the tense conversation with his mother about her future and then her parents. Clearly it was the wrong thing to say because Seher narrowed her eyes, and glared at him. He was shocked at the venom in her voice when she spoke.

"He is far from being a *bechara*," her voice hardened even more. "And he doesn't deserve to even be with a woman." She did not say anymore ,but at that moment Ahmed was glad he had gone to Zaleemabad with his father when he had. He decided not to push her to say more, after all he had a pretty good idea what she had meant. There really was more to her than she let on. But then again, that made two of them.

"Well," he backtracked. "At least you're out of that place. I'm still living my nightmare."

She did not say anything for a while and he was starting to think she would not answer, but then she gazed back at him, chewing slowly. "What's your father like?"

He paused, taking a sip of water, debating how much he wanted her to know. He could feel the shame growing inside him again, knowing he was the son of a man who thrived on coning others. "He's a crook," he started, and she rolled her eyes before motioning for him to go on. "He cheats people to get what he wants, and he expects me to do the same."

"But you're not old enough to be a politician," she put it more like a question.

"I was not old enough to know my father is a con and live with the guilt of being related to him either, but there you have it." Seher nodded carefully.

"Most of us have to grow up too soon," she said. "I just did not think it would be the same for you too." He knew what she meant. To her and others, he was just the son of a wealthy politician who had everything handed to him and had nothing to complain about.

"It is actually," he said. "And now they want me to replace my father in the election race." He had hoped that saying it out loud would change the reality somehow, make him think of a way to say no, but nothing happened.

She picked up the nearly full glass of water in front of her and gazed into it before she spoke. "So why don't you do it?"

The faces of his father and grandfather flashed before his eyes, and he shook his head. "I can't be like them. I already can't bear being part of a family that lives on other people's money, but actually representing them is ten times worse."

He could hear his mother's frantic voice over the phone outside, no doubt trying to keep someone quiet on the other end, or talking to his grandfather about their next step. Seher was looking at him with a thoughtful expression on her face, the glass of water forgotten in front of her. He could almost feel the tension that had suddenly engulfed them both. Her voice was solemn when she spoke.

"So don't be like them. Be different."

Chapter 16

Seher

It had now been a week since she had arrived at the huge red brick house in the city, a week since she had left her village, the home she had known her whole life. Lahore was different to say the least, with its deafening noise and overcrowded roads. She had gone outside once over the past week to purchase new clothes, courtesy of Ahmed's mother, who had said it was all part of her financial aid at the Arts college that she was going to get into. Seher had not missed the look of disapproval on her face as she had handed her the wad of cash.

Going outside had been strange. She had gone with one of the maids that worked at the Khan residence, and they had gone to the market in a rickshaw. The city had gone by them in a blur of colour and sound, and she had caught the maid staring at her as she had stuck her head out of the vehicle for a second, just to let the air wash over her face. She did not mind the noise or the traffic or the people, all she cared about was that she was out of that small, cramped village that had been suffocating her for so long until now. The music blaring from all the different cars around them had been like a balm to her ears, and the blur of green and grey and brown on all sides had been a welcome sight. She had been in complete awe as she had chosen different clothes for herself, the maid nodding approvingly from the side as she handed the cash over to pay for them. Seher felt the energy of the city buzz through her on her way back to the house, laden with shopping bags.

Ahmed had knocked at her door the previous night to tell her that his mother had talked to her parents herself, and she had felt the blood draining from her face at the words. He had tried to soften the blow, she recalled with a faint smile. But it had not worked on her.

Her parents had been furious to say the least, she had gathered that much on her own. Her mother had started talking about sending her back immediately, that they were being ridiculed in the village, and that her wedding had been postponed already. She had then gotten her brother and fiancé on the phone and Arshad had been livid as well.

He, as well as Hamid had started to spew about honor and respect right then. Ahmed had told her that Arshad had even gone as far as to sound worried about her safety in the village. That revelation had made her scoff to herself.

She would show them all, she promised herself as Ahmed's mother had told her that it would be okay, with contempt in her gaze the next day. She would show them what she was capable of, what a woman desperate for an escape and a thirst to prove herself could actually accomplish. Ahmed had said that her father had expressed a desire to talk to her, that he would call soon. She had not allowed herself to think much on that, or to hope.

So she had slowly began teaching herself the ways of the people of the city; how they talked and how they dressed, even going so far as to try to learn a few words and phrases in the English language from the television set in her room. She would note down whatever she found interesting in a small notebook, and then memorize the words. A sketchbook and set of pencils had been bought for her, and she had started to fill the pages with drawings and sketches. Ahmed had called them beautiful.

They had started talking more now; over meals and outside in the lawn right before night set in. She believed if there was a term for this arrangement, it would be friendship. But she was not ready to acknowledge that yet, especially considering the fact that she would leave soon. He had not brought up his father or political career after that first day, and she had not asked him anything either, choosing instead on completing her portfolio and studying. She had noticed that he spent a great deal of time outside the house but had not asked why.

Her inter board exams were in a few months and she had been studying religiously for them, pouring over the books that she had found in her room a day after she had arrived. Ahmed's mother had looked expectantly at her over the dinner table that day, and she had then murmured a stiff thank you, which had been answered with another thin-lipped smile. Seher had noticed that talking during meal times was something unheard of at the Khan house, at least between Ahmed and his mother.

His father had yet to make an appearance at the table. She had gathered that he took his meals in his office most of the time. Sometimes she would catch the servants talking about how he always seemed to be sleeping or rambling about nonsense these days. They said it was because he had been caught by the authorities, that he would be going to court one day to explain where he had gotten all his money from.

Seher had been delighted to hear that piece of news after her conversation with Ahmed that day at the table. But she soon realized that there was nothing to be happy for; the man would get away. She had heard Mrs. Raza Khan on the phone, and had caught the words, 'postpone' and 'price', a sure sign that the wealthy and powerful could worm their way out of anything.

  Ahmed had been hard to understand lately, only talking when he had to, and sometimes not being at the house for a full day at a time. She had wondered whether he had taken her advice, if he was actually doing something different, but had not been able to talk herself into asking. He avoided talking about his family altogether now and she had decided she would not bring up hers either. After all, the whole point of coming here had been to get away. They still talked outside in the lawn after dinner, just not about anything important. She still looked forward to the meetings but she would never admit that to anyone, not even herself.

  Seher had instead, chosen to burry herself in her studies and her drawings, dreaming quietly about the day that she would leave this house and start her own life. She knew that once she left the confines of this magnificent mansion, everything would change for her. Visions of crowded classrooms and fine clothing plagued her dreams, and she longed for the day when she could finally claim that life, the life that she had been owed for years now, but one people like Ahmed's father had stolen from her.

  It was almost time for lunch, she realized as her gaze drifted to the top of the screen. The phone had been another thing that she had spent her time on, slowly learning how the different applications worked and teaching herself how to use them. It had come easily to her. Rabia's number had been the first she had saved there followed by Ahmed's. Her fingers hovered over her friend's name now as she debated calling her. It had been a week since they had talked, a week since she had promised her friend that she would make a name for herself, and do it for all the girls of their village. She yearned to dial her number now, and tell her everything that had happened, to ask about Zara.

She had dialed before she could stop herself and could hear the phone ringing. Rabia picked up on the third ring. "Hello?"

"Rabi, it's me," she said, and was shocked at the amount of relief she had felt when she had heard her friend's voice. Her husband was probably outside at that moment too which was precisely why she had called, knowing that Rabia would not get in trouble this way.

"Seher?" Rabia shrieked over the line, and she smiled as she sank back onto the pillows, feeling her back relax against the headboard. "How are you? I've been trying to call the number you called from, but I think I lost it. Tell me everything!"

"I'm fine," she started. "I'm still living at his house, but I'll be able to go to college soon. I'm studying for the inter board exams right now. How are you?" They talked for what felt like ages, exchanging news, and telling each other what had happened over the past week. Seher told her everything, how she planned on leaving this house and neve looking back. She would forget her past completely and take everything she deserved. Rabia had sounded doubtful at first, but she was ecstatic when she heard about her being able to earn money after she graduated from *NCA*.

"I went to your house yesterday," Rabia said after a while, and Seher sucked in a breath; she wanted to know what had happened, and yet was trying to make herself feel indifferent.

"How are they?" she asked. "How's Zara?"

There was a pause at the other end before her friend spoke again. "Zara has gotten worse," she answered. "She just sits inside the whole day, and does not talk. Your mother said she just stares at the walls." The words were like knives slicing down her back, and Seher could feel a warm tear sliding down her cheek as she realized that even though she had found a way to get out on her own, her sister still needed her.

But she knew what would happen if she tried now. Rabia confirmed it a moment later. "Your father is angry. They've started mocking him outside saying how he could not even control his daughter." Her mind flashed to when Ahmed had told her father had wanted to talk to her and she blinked, he had not called yet.

She felt a dull ache in her chest as she asked. "Does he say anything to them? To the people who say that?" She knew the answer long before it came.

"He tries to laugh with them, saying if he ever finds you, he'll set you straight." Rabia's voice broke, and Seher could feel her heart shattering. "He says he'll marry you off to Arshad the minute he finds you." The words might have hung in the air for seconds or minutes, and she sat there, slowly feeling them sink in, leaving numbness throughout her body. Her head swam with memories, all at once as they came flooding back to her.

She saw her father taking her with him as he tended to the crops, and swinging her around in the mustard fields on his shoulders. She saw her father taking her out to play in the cotton fields where she would run till dusk. All that had stopped the minute he had put the village before her.

Rabia had started talking again, about how what she was doing was good for her, that she would do something better with her life. But Seher barely heard her over the roaring in her head. She could feel the blood rushing through her veins, and her heart thundering against her ribcage. She could feel moisture behind her eyes, and then on her face and at that moment, she wanted to scream at the whole world for taking so much from her.

She had known it all along, how she had sacrificed her life with her family for this one, but she had not stopped to think about how it would feel when she heard that her own father hated her, that he was willing to listen to people as they ridiculed him because of her, that he did not even think of her as his daughter anymore.

She sat there on the bed long after the call with Rabia ended, staring off into space and thinking about nothing and everything. She thought about how she could not afford to go back now, that she had to make it in this city, whatever it cost her. She had lost too much to go back at this point. Outside, the sun shone over the house, and as she watched its rays fall on to the lush green lawns of the house with its large pool and driveway full of cars, she summoned ice in her veins. As the minutes ticked by, she tucked her village away in her heart, vowing not to think about it, or the life that she had there for a long time.

When the maid came to summon her for lunch, she smiled politely at her and followed her out of the room, down the winding staircase and into the exquisite dining room where Ahmed's mother was sitting, her neck glittering with pearls. She must be going out right after lunch then, to one of the many meetings that were now held in order to somehow secure their family's political name. She suspected that it was what Ahmed was busy with too, but was not sure. She wondered yet again if he was still doing what they told him to do, but did not ask.

Chapter 17

Ahmed

The music was a dull roar in the back of his head as he struggled across the dance floor to the makeshift bar at the far end of room. He could spot some familiar faces, some of Lahore's finest, seated there, chatting away over glasses that were either full or on their way to being full. He realized with a jolt how long it had been since he had come to one of these parties. These people had been his friends once, they bonded over the mutual need to see and be seen.

He smiled as his gaze travelled around the manicured lawn, picking out familiar faces, old flames, and others who had clearly just gotten in. A young boy dressed in a GAP hoodie and jeans was eagerly looking at a fair skinned model in a skimpy black dress, and Ahmed almost laughed when the boy's mouth fell open as she turned and blew him a kiss. He had to be new.

The place was crowded with bankers, businessmen and models, all after the same thing, connections and freedom. Everyone wanted to have someone at their beck and call, someone who could save them if they ever got caught doing something they shouldn't be. Parties like these were the perfect place for that, he realized. They were something you had shared together, something sacred that bonded you together.

Freedom was another thing people sought here, a chance to be who they were, to escape from a controlling wife, or if you were lucky enough, an escape from the world with your wife. He realized that people looked to these as a way to get away from a world that they did not choose, and into one that let them be who they were underneath the layers of polite smiles and handshakes; greedy, self-centered vultures.

"Thought you died, man." The voice had come from right next to him, and yet it seemed as if it had come from miles away. The familiar sent of Versace Eros engulfed him as he looked up from the untouched glass of scotch in his hand, and suddenly he was staring at a tall, lean man of about his age, his eyes bloodshot, and a wide smile stretching across his face.

"And I thought you finally started working for the Russians."

They hugged, and Ahmed felt an overwhelming wave of nostalgia sweep over him as he looked back at his friend.

He had chosen to wear a polo shirt tonight and the very sight of him brought memories flooding back, getting stoned together and driving through the city of Lahore, cursing their responsibilities and vowing to make the most of the money they had been born into. Fahad's smile was like it had always been, a promise that he knew things about you that you did not, and a conspiratorial gleam in his eyes told you that he would keep your secrets for as long as you wanted to. If you looked harder you would know that he would also go to any extreme with you in order to have a good time, to live life to the fullest.

"Where the hell have you been?" Ahmed knew that Fahad would ask him that sooner or later himself, considering the amount of calls ad texts that he had ignored, so he decided to ask first and avoid spilling about Seher. They were making their way over to the far wall now, the glass of scotch long forgotten on a low table. People were starting to get overenthusiastic on the dance floor now, less talkative and more eager, eager to move and to touch. The floor was a blur of sweaty bodies as they walked around it.

"Around," Fahad passed an arm around his shoulder and laughed one of those deep belching laughs of his. "Did as my father said for a while..." He started to sway a little, and Ahmed steadied him. "That did not work out so I decided it was time to go out. I came back a few days ago. Been waiting to run into you at one of these things."

Ahmed swayed a little now, the lights burning into his eyes. "Yeah, I haven't been to one of these in a while."

"Why? You didn't start politics did you?" Fahad was slurring his words slightly.

"Bro, do I even look like a politician to you?" He laughed and Fahad joined in, memories of days spent whining about how they were being pressured into a life they did not want washing over them.

They were just rounding a corner when another familiar voice called out behind them. "I thought I'd never see you two around here again." They turned, and Ahmed was hit with another wave of nostalgia as Fahad enthusiastically embraced another slightly shorter guy in a worn out leather jacket. They had met Amir about five years ago, and he had contacted him a few times after he had come back from Oxford. The guy was not exactly bright but he could get you a good bargain when you really needed a fix. Sure enough, he was already handing a small white pill to Fahad.

"Got you guys some ex," he was saying as he thumped Ahmed on the back with a huge grin on his face. "Pay me later." Fahad was smiling widely at him, and Ahmed realized they were both thinking the same thing. Amir charged everyone twice what it had cost him to get anything, but to some select few, he acted as if money was never an issue. He was hoping to make friends through this arrangement.

He was not from a rich or influential background as far as they knew, and yet managed to be at every single party thrown by Lahore's rich and famous. Ahmed suspected that Amir could beat his mother if it ever came down to a social climbing contest. In return, they acted as if he was one of them, all of the people he sold to. They called him up, pretending they wanted him over, and smiling and laughing as they held short, frivolous conversations with him, their minds already in another place.

Fahad was laughing at some sad excuse of a joke that Amir had cracked, looking over at Ahmed and winking. It was one of those discreet winks they shared when they were in the company of an outsider who, no matter how much he tried, would never be one of them. Amir smiled, clearly pleased that he had made them laugh. "Let me know if you guys need anything else," he said before moving away. When he was out of earshot, Fahad turned to him, and scoffed before picking up two glasses of water from a passing waiter and splitting the tiny pill in his hand into two.

"Cheers," he grinned, handing him a glass and the small white pill. "'Here's to the good days." They swallowed, and Ahmed smiled. It was good that he was here. He had needed this for a while now. He had been feeling on edge lately, and it had finally occurred to him that afternoon that he needed a break, from his father being distraught at the thought of not being able to run in the election, his grandfather who was determined to make sure his party survived, his conversation with Seher that kept playing in his head, everything.

They made their way around the huge lawn of the farmhouse, stopping here and there to make small talk with people they knew, and pretending they would absolutely love to do lunch or dinner next week. Fahad practically sped by everyone else. He would stop every now and then, and they would talk to old friends, laugh once or twice, crack a joke, and then casually walk off. That was how it had always been with him. He never gave anyone his full attention, and yet managed to make everyone feel like they were his top priority.

"So that ended pretty fast." They were standing a few paces away from the bar and listening to Shehzad, one of their friends from school talk about how his fling with some girl named Anita had ended. He called it a fling now, but they all recalled a time when he had been madly in love with Anita and the two of them had been inseparable.

"Dude, I always hated her anyway. You did yourself a favor breaking up." Fahad was saying and Ahmed remembered that they had all in fact hated Anita. The high pitched laugh of hers had been enough to make him want to leave every time she was near.

"Yeah," Shehzad answered with a grin. "I mean hey if she was unhappy that's her loss really. Her sister did it way better anyway." They burst out laughing. "Not that she would know about that." They laughed harder, and Fahad reached to pat him on the back.

"Dude, you're a legend." Fahad's voice held pride and fascination, and soon the others started to agree with him. When they had yet again moved away under the pretense of getting something to eat, Fahad turned to Ahmed with another one of his wide grins. "What he doesn't know is that she left him for me."

Ahmed was not sure if he had heard right. "What?" He stopped and turned around. The air seemed to be buzzing with electricity now, the music was amplified, and he could hear the sound of his own breathing in his head.

"Anita and I started going out while she was with him," Fahad laughed. "She complained so much about how utterly boring he was, and I sure as hell made it worth her while." He clasped his shoulder and Ahmed could feel the exact spot his fingers made contact with his shoulder, the only thing separating them from his sweat-soaked skin was the thin material of his shirt. "I had to end it though."

They were walking towards the opposite wall, and Ahmed cast his gaze around them, taking in the lights and the people. He could see thin trails of light coming out from the string of fairly lights along the walls. They danced around him, and he suddenly wanted to touch them. "Why?" He heard himself asking, his mind already a thousand miles away from Fahad.

"Commitment, bro." The voice came from far away, distant and dripping with the ghosts of memories he found himself drawing away from. "She wanted us to be long-term or something and that stuff isn't for me, you know? Live in the moment, right?"

"Live in the moment," he echoed. The words sounded foreign, and yet as familiar as his own name. He remembered how those words had been their moral code for a while. The air was cold as it touched his face, and he wished he could stay there forever to savor it as it caressed his skin with soft cool hands. Fahad had turned around, and they were floating towards the dance floor with its blinking lights and moving figures.

The music was like a second heartbeat, thumping inside his chest following a steady beat.

It was all he could hear now and he was glad. He did not want to hear what Fahad was saying as he moved a little farther away from him when they reached the lights. He did not care who he chatted up here only to toss them aside later. He just wanted to feel free. So he watched as Fahad smiled at someone else across the floor and then grabbed her hand, the girl smiling in return, and laughing as he whispered something to her.

All around him, he saw everyone who was anyone in Lahore, moving in sync or drinking whiskey that had been especially flown in for this party. They ate as if they were the only ones in the world and tonight was the last day of their lives, their bloodshot eyes and painted smiles telling a million beautiful lies.

Soon, he was one of them. He soared above the dance floor, his feet barely brushing the ground. He could reach up and touch the blinking lights if he jumped high enough, and brush his fingers along the multicolored trails that they left in the air. He had no idea who he was dancing with, only that they were moving so fast that the others were a blur, the bodies melting into a blend of colours. He had not seen her face and he was happy that way, just moving with the music and her as she threw her hands up in the air, and he let his hands go wherever they pleased.

He felt as if they had been dancing for eons, surrendering themselves to the beat. His mind was blank for the first time in ages, and he was happy. This felt good, he realized. She was facing him now, and her hands left burning trails on his skin whenever she touched him. He then found himself needing to see her face, to know that he had truly escaped from the life his grandfather had laid out for him. Taking his eyes off the blinking lights above, he finally allowed himself to look.

Seher's face stared back at him.

He recoiled in horror, and winced when she tried to touch his arm. She was wearing the clothes she had worn when they had first met in the village, a dark orange shirt and a white *shalwar,* with a maroon *dupatta.* She was shaking her head at him, her mouth drawn into a frown and her hands clenched at her sides, angry at the way he had chosen to spend tonight with these people, people who had everything and acted as if they were entitled to it.

She looked around at everyone laughing around them, and then at the ones far away eating shrimp out of cocktail glasses. He knew she was thinking of her family, of herself and how she had been made to live, while he enjoyed all this.

He was moving away from her now, too sick with his own self to look at her. But she followed him as he made his way across the lawn, the blades of grass digging into his shoes as he ran. Every time he looked over his shoulder, he saw her slowly walking and shaking her head at him with an ice cold expression on her face. She was disappointed in him and he knew it. He was part of the very crowd she despised with all her heart, and she had thought he was different, that he could be different.

The lawn looked to be endless, stretching as far as he could see with tall stone walls bordering it from all sides. The lights at his side seemed to be following him, mocking him as he ran, and they chased after him; a thin ribbon of gold. He felt as if he had been running for years, the grass a soft blanket beneath him. It had to end somewhere, he realized. It had to. All he had to do was find his car.

But the lawn stretched on forever, and he could see trees in the distance too. Seher's face was still there when he looked over his shoulder, and he started to run faster. He flew over the lawn towards the grove of trees, and only stopped when he reached a tall oak, its trunk so wide that he was sure it could fit four people standing with their backs around it.

He leaned against the tree and let the trunk dig into his skin, feeling it make contact with his back. He was breathing fast, and if he concentrated he could see the clouds of air as they were expelled from his mouth. He was shivering too, but did not know whether it was from the cold. With trembling fingers, he reached into his pocket and drew out a single cigarette and a lighter.

Laughter floated towards him on the cold breeze and he sighed, sinking down to his knees against the oak tree. His spine was already starting to ache, and he could tell that it would be a rough night as he inhaled the smoke. It burned him and he welcomed it, savoring it, as it reached the very core of his being. The wind rustled the leaves of the tree above him and he looked up. The sky, an endless expanse of black was punctuated with thin brown branches, and they moved slowly in the wind as he sat there.

Ahmed closed his eyes for a second and breathed out. He knew if he opened them, he would see the tiny rings of smoke as they left his lips, only to be carried off to some unknown place. As he sat there with his back against the tree, he felt himself drifting farther away from the present, into the dark recesses of his mind that he had tried so hard to escape from over the past week.

A face began to form behind his eyelids, one he had almost been successful at chasing away because of how he had helped Seher. It was back, the girl's steely glare was the same as it had always been, and her eyes still held that look of defiance in them. He could see her hair too, matted around her shoulders and soaked with blood, sweat and tears.

Sighing, he got to his feet. There was a throng of people making its way to the driveway at the far end and he joined them, not bothering to see if Fahad or Shehzad were there. He wanted nothing to do with them. He had come here thinking he could be one of them again, part of a crowd who thrived on faked conversation and friendships, who lived on what was not theirs, not caring about where it all came from, and realized that he could never go back now.

"Be different." Her words echoed in his mind as he walked slowly over to the line of cars. He found Amir standing next to his beat up Suzuki, and smiled as he waved him over after taking one look at him, a genuine smile void of any self-entitlement taking over his features. He grinned back as he opened the passenger side door, and helped his trembling form inside.

Chapter 18

Seher

The sketch was almost done, and she smiled when she realized that this would mark the end of her portfolio. Unconsciously, she had managed to show the journey of a girl through the many sketches that lined the thick book. They started off with a girl struggling to escape the cramped space she had grown up in, went on to show her losing all hope, becoming a shell of her former self, and then showed her transformation. By the end, she was a fierce, independent woman, free of the chains that had held her back, capable of doing anything that she desired.

She had given up so much to get here and it showed in a couple of her sketches, in the way the girl's eyes were hollow sometimes, or the way she gazed at her surroundings as if reminiscing some minute detail about her past life.

It showed in the shape of her mouth sometimes as it turned down at the sides in some sketches, and in her smile as well, how it never reached her eyes. By the end however, the girl that stared back at her from the page was someone completely different, someone she almost did not recognize.

She stared ahead with a sort of steely determination in her eyes that made chills run down Seher's back. The girl looked like she could conquer the world with no regard for how she did it or how she did it, as if she was willing to do whatever it took to get to her rightful place in the world. She both admired and feared her.

Leaning back against the headboard, she took one final look at her completed drawing and sighed. This was it then. Her portfolio was complete, and now the only thing standing between her and going to the Arts College were the exams that she needed to clear. Those would take another two months and then she would be out of this house and on her own.

Her mind drifted back to her village then, to her sister who was probably in worse shape now and suddenly she yearned to feel her arms around her, to tell her that it was going to be okay and that she would make things right for her. She imagined her father working alone in the fields at that moment, trying to avoid people's stares and whispers, to ignore their snickers as he walked past them. Seher's mind flashed back yet again to the day Ahmed had told her that he had wanted to speak to her but she quickly dismissed that thought, remembering what Rabia had told her during their last phone call.

"So it's done?"

She was jolted out of her thoughts by the sound of Ahmed's voice. "The door was open, and my mom wanted to know if you were hungry," he clarified, stepping further into the room. He was dressed to go out, in a brown leather jacket and black pants, his hair combed back. Seher noticed that he was staring at the sketchbook that was open to the last page on the bed in front of her.

"It's done," she answered. They had not spoken much over the last month, only exchanging a few words over the table now and then. He had started spending a lot more time outside, and Seher was almost sure that he had been seeing his grandfather. Sometimes they would have meetings at the house, and Ahmed's mother would look overly on edge that day, claiming that time was of the essence. She had not asked any questions.

"That one looks great," he said pointing to the last sketch of the girl with the steely, determined eyes. "She looks a lot like you." The words were carelessly thrown into the air, but she found that she had needed to hear them, that someone else thought she looked stronger too.

"Thank you," she said slowly, trying to think of a way to draw the conversation forward.

She would not admit it out loud, but she had missed talking to him out in the lawn after meals.

Ahmed was looking around the room now, at the different piles of books that were strewn around it, and at her notes scattered around her on the bed. She caught a small smile on his face and was surprised to feel herself smiling too, as if seeing him smile without much trace of that self-loathing she had seen earlier had somehow made her want to do the same.

"You look like you're going out somewhere," she observed, motioning to his hair and clothes. Ahmed looked surprised at the gesture, but quickly met her gaze. He looked better with his eyes twinkling, and a trace of a dimple in his left cheek.

"I am," he smiled. "My grandfather wants to go over some things today." He paused as if waiting for her to ask another question, but continued when she did not. "I did what you said, I'm being different, trying at least."

Seher could not explain the emotion that passed over her at that moment, at hearing him say those words. She had wanted him to be different from what his father and grandfather were, from the people she had grown to despise. But she had not let herself believe that he actually would try, that his need to be different would be enough to make him try. "You're running in the election then?" She asked, her heartbeat quickening.

He nodded. "I am, and if I somehow manage to win, it will be on my own terms." He waited for her to say something, and a lump formed in her throat. The weight of her resentment towards him and his family was crushing down on her and yet she felt like she needed to shove it aside, at least for him.

"That's great!" Her voice cracked at the end, and then as a full smile spread across Ahmed's face, guilt bloomed in her chest. "I'll vote for you." The words brought on a real smile to her own face as she remembered the first day they had talked about his family, and he laughed, crossing his arms.

"Yeah, just like you were going to vote for my dad, right?" There was humor in his tone, and she laughed.

"Hey, I mean it this time."

"Of course you do," Ahmed looked down at her. "So, should I tell my mom you're coming?"

"Yeah," she nodded before getting up from the bed. "I'm coming." But just as she was reaching for the doorknob, Ahmed right behind her, her phone began to buzz on the bedside table. He saw the screen first, his lip curling into a frown.

"You were expecting a call?" he asked, arching an eyebrow. "It's some number."

"No, I wasn't," she replied. Rabia would never call her at that time. She reached for the phone. The number that was flashing across the screen was only too familiar, and her heart started to pound. It was Hamid's. Ahmed was looking at her curiously, and for some reason she wanted him to stay next to her as she answered, not knowing if it were Hamid or Arshad on the phone, and not letting herself believe it could be her father. She sat down, sliding her finger across the screen before putting the pone to her ear.

"Hello?" Her heart started to pound in her chest at the voice. It was not Hamid or Arshad, it was too soft and low to be either of them. Her palms started to sweat as she sat there, not believing her ears. "Hello?" Her father's voice floated towards her over the line, soft and sweet and she basked in it, welcoming the wave of nostalgia as it crashed down upon her, and she almost forgot to answer, allowing herself to be swept up in the moment, to imagine that her father was right next to her and telling her that it was all going to be okay.

"*Assalamalaikum, abba.*" Her voice was small, sounding miles away. Ahmed's eyes went wide as he heard the words fall from her lips. There was a pause on the other end, and she imagined her father sitting in their courtyard on his cot, the phone clutched in worn, tired hands as he spoke. She waited for the blow to come, for him to shout at her and tell her that she had disgraced his name and that he would never forgive her, trying to brace herself, but knowing that no amount of time could prepare her to hear those words from his mouth. That was the whole reason why she had not spoken to him yet, even though she yearned to hear his voice.

"My daughter." The words were like a salve on aching wounds as they reached her ears and she squeezed her eyes shut, not wanting to let a single tear slip, especially not while Ahmed was in the room. "How are you?"

Sweet relief flooded through her at the words, and she almost let out a sob, not knowing how much she had needed to hear them.

"I... I'm okay," she started. "I'm fine. I'm going to take my inter exams soon." Despite his words a moment ago, it felt as if there was an ocean between them. Her father did not speak for a few seconds.

"I never wanted you not to study more, my child," he said. "The money..." He couldn't finish, and Seher wished she were by his side.

"I know," she said at last.

"Arshad won't marry you now," her father said, his voice slightly more even. "You've tarnished his name. And mine." Although the words were cruel, she could not detect a shred of cruelty in them. It was a fact that her father had uttered, one that she already knew. Her heart was racing, begging her to speak the words that she had been keeping in for so long. Whenever she had said them to her mother, she had been made to stop talking, to 'think of her family.'

"I never wanted to marry him, *abba*." The words tumbled out of her in a rush, and she realized that she was crying, her tears sliding down her face in slow rivulets. Her father was quiet for a few seconds.

"I know," he sighed; a long sigh that was cut off at the end as her father coughed. "I know you didn't. Your mother told me. But the village, it…" He trailed off, the words dangling in the air. Seher sat there watching the door close as Ahmed left the room, shooting her a small smile over his shoulder, letting her know that he was outside.

Perhaps it was that smile that made her utter the next few words, words she had never dreamed she would say to her father because she was sure he would not pay heed to them. She knew he loved her, he always had. But the shackles binding him to the village had made him into a completely different person. But his voice had changed something in her, and she desperately wanted him to know that she would never have purposely hurt him.

"He hurt me, *abba*," she said, the words feeling like razor blades down her own back. She closed her eyes again, as images from that night flooded her mind. She was not sure when she would be able to completely erase those memories. "The night I left. He and his friends pinned me against a tree, and he beat me." Her father sucked in a breath on the other side, and she felt a simmering rage inside her, not entirely at him, boiling inside her. "Before that as well when he came to talk about the dowry."

She fell silent then, needing to hear her father's next words, needing to know that he did not blame her. Despite all her earlier thoughts about the village and escaping from it, she knew now that even if she did get away, she did not want her father to hate her for it.

Memories of being pressed against his chest on summer nights when they would sleep outside in the courtyard flashed in her mind, and she let another sob wrack her body. She had never shared much of a relationship with her mother, that had always been Zara. But with her father it was different. Losing him would be different.

"You should have told me," her father said at last, and she realized that his voice was shaking with barely controlled anger. At that moment she barely even recognized it, the few words were filled with so much rage and bitterness that she almost wished she had not told him. Almost. A larger part was glad that she had, and gladder still that he was angry. She knew it was not entirely his fault, but a small part of her did blame him for not being there for her, for making her feel like she could not talk to him about what had been going on.

"I wanted to," she said instead, choosing to keep her words in yet again. There was no point now, seeing as she was not even there anymore.

"I know why you didn't," her father replied, his tone softening. "I'm sorry." The words hung in the air between them, uttered in the heat of the moment, but Seher knew that he had meant them. Her blood had stilled now, and she felt as if her veins had turned to ice. She was having trouble swallowing.

"I know, *abba*," she choked out.

The line went silent then, each of them was lost in their own thoughts. Seher was imagining running into her father's arms after all of this was over, not bound by any norm. She imagined showing him her degree after she had completed her studies, and him finally sweeping her in his arms again and placing a kiss on her forehead.

"Zara wanted me to tell you she misses you," he said at last, breaking the spell. Seher smiled, imagining how close she was to finally achieving what she had come for. She would soon be able to help her sister as well, to talk to her at least.

"I miss her too," she said, and paused before continuing. "How's *amma*? And Hamid?"

"Your mother is…" he trailed off. "The same. But she will be okay eventually, like me."

Seher scoffed at the absurdity of the statement. Her mother was probably mourning the loss of another daughter to scandal. She already treated Zara like she were a burden and that she had gone through some world-ending tragedy because of her miscarriage and divorce. She could only imagine what she must think of her now. She also noted how her father had not mentioned Hamid.

She wanted to ask him about Hamid and whether he still talked to Arshad. They were friends after all, and the news of his sister shaming their family and his friend like that had to have rattled him, which was probably why her mother had not called either. But she could not get the words out.

"How are you, *abba*?" she asked instead, sinking back against the headboard.

"I'm surviving, *beta*." And suddenly her father sounded ten years older to her, his voice frail and thin. "I'm getting old and it's obvious now. Come visit me soon, won't you?'

#

Long after she had hung up, after promising that she would come see him as soon as she could, Seher sat on the bed contemplating everything her father had said. She had never thought about how old her father was, birthdays not being a concept she was very familiar with, especially birthdays for grownups.

She knew that her father was not as young as he had used to be, seeing as he now always looked to be in need of help carrying the heavy sacks of flours, and would come home earlier in the evenings claiming he had gotten tired. Streaks of grey had started appearing in his hair some years ago, and lately his joints had been hurting him. She only hoped that the trip to the city had proved to be fruitful for him.

When she at last got up from the bed and started walking towards the door, it was as if a weight had been lifted from her chest, a weight she had not even known she was still carrying, but one her father's words had gotten rid of. She could feel a bounce in her step as she walked, a flush in her cheeks and a smile, a real one on her lips.

Chapter 19

Ahmed

"You look happy today," Ahmed observed as he walked into the living room. Seher was seated on the couch, a thick book open on her lap, and a pen between her teeth as she read over the text carefully. Her dark brown hair was pulled away from her face and rested on top of her head, soft tendrils escaping to frame her face. She looked at peace.

"I am," she smiled at him, looking up from the book. "I just have one more exam to go and then I'll be done." Her eyes were practically shining, and Ahmed felt his own heart lifting at the idea of her being genuinely happy, and not seeing the haunting look in her eyes that had been there for so long.

"Oh so you're going to be leaving me soon," he winked at her and when her cheeks flushed, he felt another feeling overcome him, one he had not known he could feel. The words had meant to be a joke, but the meaning behind them was true. He had gotten so used to seeing her around the house that it now almost seemed natural to come home to her studying at the table or in the living room, while his mother did her best to get out of being in the same room. They had started talking more now despite his busy routine that was plagued with meetings. He took all his meals at home, and they would have long conversations at the table while his mother tried her best to ignore it all. He knew she would be glad once Seher left; happy to be rid of the girl from the village, and to have another good deed in her husband's name.

"As if you won't be busy enough," Seher finally answered, her eyes twinkling. "You know, being different and changing things." That was true; he had been trying, and he had to admit that it felt good. His grandfather had been reluctant and was still skeptical of the new route the campaign was going. But he knew that the old man was desperate, and having Ahmed finally take charge had pleased him.

They had refocused all of their work towards social welfare, even going so far as to change their slogan. Ahmed had also floated several ideas of establishing platforms that would help people like Seher out, a foundation that would cater to girls like her with big dreams, as well as several others to make sure the people outside in the streets got what they deserved. His grandfather had said that it would be expensive, but had relented in the end. Ahmed knew it was because he had no other choice but to listen to him.

"Not busy enough for you," he said at last, deliberating whether to tell her about the foundation. She looked away then and he decided that he wanted to tell her, just so she would know that he really had changed, so she would keep in touch. Would she keep in touch? His mind told him that she would, she had to after everything they had been through.

"I'm flattered," she answered after a moment, looking back at him, her eyes locking onto his. He noticed how quickly she had blended into his world, adapting to their way of speaking and dressing. Ahmed did not know how to feel about the fact that she had not worn the clothes she had brought from the village in weeks. The book closed with a snap, and she got up, slowly running her hands through her hair so that it tumbled down her shoulders in soft brown waves. "How's everything with your father now?"

"My father can barely see straight these days," he replied with a laugh. "So I'd say not good, but at least this means more room for me to be who I want to be." It was true. Raza Ali Khan had drunk his way through the past month, not bothering to ask how everything was going with the campaign. He had barely even left the house, and Ahmed knew it had to be because of the charges against him. Everyone knew that he was a dead man walking. Any day now, they would have enough evidence against him, and it did not matter how many palms they greased. The new inquiry committee was filled with people who he had managed to make enemies of, and it had finally caught up with him. He would be lying if he said that he did not feel the least bit sorry for him. Seeing everything you had worked for slip out of your grasp like that had to take a toll on you.

Seher laughed and he joined in. "At least something good came out of it," she said. "You finally stepped up." He smiled, the corners of his mouth lifting.

"Don't be modest now," he told her. "You played a part in that too."

'Of course," she smiled back, but he noticed that she looked away quickly. She was so modest, he realized. She had no idea how much she had impacted him, and she would never know how grateful he was.

"Is lunch ready?" she asked after a few seconds and he blinked, realizing that he had been gazing at her face intently as she stood there framed by the light streaming in from outside. It turned her hair a light brown, and her eyes had specks of gold in them. They were filled with light now, a new kind of determination and something else that he could not place. Lately, he had taken to going to her room to tell her when lunch or dinner was ready instead of the maid. His mother had been appalled, considering the fact that she had always needed to send the help multiple times to call him from his room, but now it looked as if he was always ready to come down.

"It is. Let's go," he said at last, tearing his eyes away from her. "That is if you can spare a few minutes for us common folk from your books." Seher rolled her eyes, starting towards the door.

"And give your mother another reason to hate me? I don't think so."

Ahmed chuckled, the sound sounding foreign to his own ears. "She does not hate you." When she looked back incredulously at him, he let out a laugh. "Okay yeah, she does."

They were both laughing as they entered the dining room, Seher gently elbowing him as they sat down. He noticed his mother's mouth press into a thin line, but chose to ignore it. Somehow it had become easier to tolerate her pretentious uptightness now. Maybe it was the fact that he was doing something on his own or the knowledge of actually doing something that counted but he was starting to feel like he could start building a relationship with her despite their differences.

She clearly could not help the way she was; the need for self-preservation and security had been embedded in her, and it was too late to change the way she saw the rest of the world. But he was willing to see whether it got better with time.

"Your father won't be joining us today," she said to him by way of greeting. It was a fact that she repeated at every mealtime, as if the repetition would make it sound like it was not common for her husband to miss meals with the family. He nodded, not bothering to voice the thought. They ate in silence, the only sound being the clatter of the knives and forks. They were having steak that day, and Seher was shoveling hers into her mouth with another one of those faint smiles that he had grown to love over the past few weeks.

"This is good," he said at last, motioning to his plate. Food was perhaps the safest subject to start a conversation about in the house. His mother beamed at him over her glass of water.

"It's the new chef," she told him. "He knows all kinds of things and he used to work at Marriott." Her voice oozed with pride as she told him about what had clearly been a great accomplishment for her, to secure a chef from one of the most prestigious hotels in the country certainly was something to brag about at the next party she went to.

"He's good," he said simply. Seher was looking off into the distance with an unreadable expression on her face, and he thought that she must be thinking about how the man was probably from a place like her village, forced to work to make ends meet by serving a class of people who lived in mansions, while his family lived in a one-room house. "I started work on the foundation I was telling you about," he said in an attempt to change topics. "You'll have the details by next month."

His mother would have a significant part to play in the inauguration because of all her connections. She nodded; a barely perceptible nod that was directed in Seher's direction, she was still looking off in the distance with that far-away look in her eyes.

"Good," his mother smiled at him, a tightlipped smile that did not reach her eyes. Ahmed sighed, reaching for his glass of water. His phone buzzed in his pocket then, and he took it out to see Fahad's name on the screen. He had been calling him ever since that night when they had run into each other at the party, and Ahmed had ignored him each time. He had thought long and hard the next day about the kind of person he had been when he was with Fahad, and had found that no matter how hard he tried. He could not be that person anymore.

He had changed, and the idea of going around and living each day with no thoughts about consequences was ridiculous. In a way, Fahad, Shehzad and everyone else there were just like their parents; the people from whom they claimed to escape at their parties and outings. They drifted through life, wrecking and manipulating wherever they went, not waiting for the dust to settle from their mistakes and when it did settle, they would no longer be near. His friends lied and cheated their way through life, just like their parents.

The phone kept ringing and Seher and his mother were looking curiously at him now, the latter going as far as to raise an eyebrow. "It's Fahad," he said at last. His mother simply nodded, clearly glad that he had not answered. He knew she had picked up on the fact that he was no longer spending time with his old friends and that she was happy about it.

"Oh," she said, nonchalantly as if she had not spent the majority of her years glaring and sneering whenever he mentioned his former friend. "Have you heard from your other friends though? From university."

He knew that a bunch of people had gone away to England to study the year he had, he had been instructed to remain in contact with them and get on friendly terms, but he had not. Instead, he had turned to reinventing himself, choosing to forge new friendships. An image of Irene and himself sitting on her front steps, cigarettes dangling from their mouths as the others laughed and drank and danced around them popped in his head and he smiled.

"Not really," he told his mother. "I haven't really been in touch with them." Mrs. Raza Khan frowned, clearly displeased.

"I wanted to host a dinner for them, make sure they're still on your side. We need them you know." Seher was smirking at him from across the table and he rolled his eyes, not bothering to hide his own smile. His mother would never change.

#

His father's office was barely recognizable, the hardwood desk that Raza Khan had always kept immaculate and insisted nobody else touch, was now littered with folders, papers and three empty glasses. The wood was stained in various places, and the tottering pile of books that was always on the right side of the table had collapsed. The books were lying in a jumbled mess, their covers peaking over one another. The blinds had been drawn so no sunlight streamed in, and the electric fire in the corner burned merrily, but was clearly not enough to get rid of the chill in the room.

His grandfather sat on his left, a cup of tea in front of him while his father occupied the chair behind the desk, both with serious expressions on their faces. The two men looked more alike than ever in that moment, with their receding hairlines and tired eyes. Raza Khan had more bags under his eyes than ever before, and his father looked no better with his worry lines and sallow cheeks.

They had decided on meeting one last time before his father had to leave; the charges were concrete against him now. They had managed to get his name out of the ECL for a while on the grounds of an important family emergency, and a huge bribe that would only manage to keep them quiet for a while before the case was brought forward again. He needed to leave within the next few days, at least for some time. The party was Ahmed's now, he realized as he looked around at the men who had criticized his every move up until then.

"These numbers look good," his grandfather said at last. They were looking at the results of a survey that had been conducted to judge their chances of winning the election race. He knew these polls were not reliable, but so far it looked like they had a good chance. The turnout to his campaign events had been great so far; he supposed people really were desperate for a change, and they were not doing too badly in the other constituencies either. The news of his father being a fraud had been quickly replaced by the fact that the party now had young blood, and that he wanted to do things differently.

"They do," his father agreed, looking over at Ahmed. "You seem to be doing a good job." Ahmed would have done anything to hear those words from his mouth a few years ago. But now he nodded solemnly, his face the picture of seriousness.

"Thank you," he said. "We have another rally tomorrow." It would be in front of the Lahore Fort, and they were hoping for another great turnout. He was supposed to make a speech there and he was not going to admit it, but he felt nervous and exhilarated about it at the same time.

"I know," his father answered, an unreadable expression crossing his face. "They told me about it." He looked at his own father for a second before turning his gaze back to his son. "You have nothing to worry about. They already think you're the answer to their problems."

Ahmed knew that most of the youth was on his side, that they were glad someone this young was to be an MNA, but a part of him had never thought his father would say the words as well. Raza Ali Khan was sipping from his cup of tea, and as he locked eyes with his son, there was a faint gleam there. Ahmed gazed back and nodded, the back of his eyelids suddenly felt damp, and he blinked.

"How is Sarah? Is she still here?" His father asked and Ahmed clenched his fists at his side. It seemed that as if despite everything he had lost, his father still thought Seher was an inconvenience, not worth his time.

"Seher,' Ahmed corrected him. "And she is." He felt a wave of sadness sweep through him at the realization that she would not be thee for long, but he pushed that thought aside as his father and grandfather looked back at him. His grandfather had taken the news of him helping her better than his father had, choosing to believe that it might bring some good to their name after all. Perhaps he had seen the bigger picture after all.

Raza Ali Khan nodded slowly after a few seconds, his eyes drooping slightly, probably because of the fact that there was nothing he could say or do to change things whether it was with his son or his career. It was over.

"Good." The word hung in the air between the three men, and the silence stretched on as they sat. Outside, it had begun to rain and Ahmed heard the sound faintly through the closed glass windows, it was slow at first but then it rose to a crescendo, hammering against the roof. He imagined Seher downstairs in her room with her books. She would want to go outside, and stand under the shade of the veranda. For some reason she liked to watch one particular elm tree at the edge of their lawn. It would always bend against the ruthless wind, refusing to let itself be knocked over. He stood up at last.

"I'll see you tomorrow then" Ahmed said to his grandfather who nodded quickly.

"You will." Exhaustion dripped from his voice and Ahmed almost told him that his party would not die out after all, that it was in good hands. But one more look at those beady eyes had him turning the handle of the door quickly. The eyes might have looked tired, but he knew what lurked beneath, what would always lurk there; hunger, pride and the need to control.

Chapter 20

Seher

The sun had finally come out after a week of rain showers and the city almost looked magical, bathed in hues of gold and orange. Seher had been looking out into the distance from her window for a while, trying to burn the view of the garden beyond into her memory. The fountain in the center was gurgling quietly and as she watched, a lone pigeon flew overhead. She had not seen a pigeon in a while, since most days the sky was dotted with crows and sparrows.

The bird stayed perched on one of the branches of a tree below for a while, before flapping its wings and taking off again, and she realized how similar she and the pigeon were, moving from one place to another and never settling. Perhaps she would settle down after she had found a decent way to earn a living, but for now it certainly felt as if she was constantly moving and not able to call any place her home.

She had first left her village in hopes of starting a new life for herself in the city, to come and stay in this large house that had started to feel more like a home lately, only to leave it for a hostel where she would stay for four years before leaving that too. Seher sighed. At least she was finally about to start her life on her own; that had to count for something. The day was almost here.

Smiling faintly to herself, she drew the curtain close and walked back over to the bed. It was still early in the day and she imagined that lunch would not be ready for a while now. That gave her enough time to make the call.

The phone in her hand felt like it weighed a ton as she stared down at it. By now she had learned everything about it, and she could not help but feel proud of herself for that. She could speak English almost fluently though she still had trouble sometimes; Ahmed had been a huge help, correcting her grammar, always with one of those warm smiles of his.

The phone's applications however were easy to use. She had been taking pictures of all her sketches and sometimes of the view outside her window at dawn when the rest of the house was asleep. She wanted to remember these moments, these quiet minutes that she had to herself before the day actually began. Seher imagined herself scrolling through the memories later, and could not help but want to capture each one. There were a few selfies with Ahmed in there as well, ones he had taken while trying to explain how the front camera worked. Her favorite was one he had taken of them out in the lawn one day, his eyes sparkling in amusement as she tried to knock the phone out of his hand.

She began to scroll through the pictures, trying to imagine what her sister would have said if she saw them, or Rabia. They would have both been happy for her; but Rabia would want to come here herself, Seher thought with a smile. She would have loved this place and the crystal clear pool outside. She had often found herself standing at the edge of it, and wondered when the family even used it, if they did use it at all.

The water had remained undisturbed ever since she had gotten there. She supposed it was because everyone was too busy trying to make sure Ahmed's father did not lose his political career, while the man himself had taken to keeping himself locked in his office the whole day apart from the occasional interview. She doubted he even knew there was another person living in the house.

Glancing down at the screen again, she realized that someone would be there any minute to call her down. She was just about to get up from the bed when the small device began to buzz in her hand. Rabia's name flashed across the screen, and her heart leaped at the thought of hearing her friend's voice. "Hello?" she smiled into the phone.

"Seher, thank God you picked up." Rabia's voice sounded urgent. "Are you alone?'

"Yeah, of course," she replied, a little curious now. "How are you? I was just thinking about you."

"I'm… I'm okay." Her voice cracked. 'Listen, I need to tell you something important. Arshad was here the other day, and Hamid as well. They found out where you live, and they want to see you."

It was as if the world had stooped turning and she was losing air. She could feel the chills going down her back at the mere mention of Arshad's name. She had not had a good relationship with her brother for years now, so it was obvious whose side he would be on, not to mention the warped idea of honor held by the people of her village. Her heart had started to beat a mile a minute, and she could feel her forehead breaking into a sweat.

"They… they want to come here?" The words tumbled out of her mouth. "How do they even know the address?"

Rabia was quiet for a minute; an excruciatingly long minute that made Seher realize the answer even before she heard it. It was enough to make her sink back against her pillows. She felt as if something had crumpled inside her.

"He came here. Arshad. They've been spending time together these days, him and Tahir. Tahir's gotten worse, Seher..." Rabia paused for a minute. "I didn't know what else to do. He asked me and he kept asking. He wouldn't stop...."

Seher could not keep up with the rest of the conversation, and she did not remember exactly when the maid had at last knocked on her door, or when she had ended the call without a word. She had quietly made her way downstairs into the now familiar dining room, and had taken her place at the table. Her father's face was flashing in front of her eyes and she could feel her throat going dry as anger and grief shot through her veins.

He had been happy for her, had more or less given her his blessing that day on the phone, and they had even talked once more after that. Not once had he mentioned anything about her brother or Arshad. Seher's heart sank as she realized that her father had not been able to get her brother in line, or to stand up for her in front of Arshad. If he had, they would not have dared think about coming. The world was spinning around her, and she struggled to keep her face neutral.

Mrs. Raza was there, her face painted with a heavy layer of makeup, while a thick emerald necklace glistened around her neck. Seher internally rolled her eyes, the woman clearly felt the need to flaunt her wealth in her own house as well. But she smiled politely at her before reaching for the bottle of water that was placed in front of her. The smile quickly faded as her father's comforting voice echoed in her head. She wanted to scream.

"Seher, *beta*, you look like you just saw a ghost. Is everything okay?" The words seemed to be causing Ahmed's mother physical pain as she uttered them while glancing at the opposite end of the table where her son sat. She shook her head.

"I'm fine, auntie. Thank you." Mrs. Raza looked taken aback by her choice of words but quickly covered it up with a small smile. It was clear that she was surprised that the girl from the village was using phrases like thank you now. It was more than that too. Ever since Seher had started to study and pay attention to the norms and values of the people of the city, Ahmed's mother had looked upon her with silent fascination. She had picked up on so many things so fast that sometimes it was hard to even tell that she was not from there, and Seher knew that drove her crazy.

"That has to be a lie," Ahmed spoke from the other end of the table, and she finally forced herself to look at him.

His mother rolled her eyes, just as she had all the other times Ahmed had tried to start a conversation in front of her. He was wearing a black polo shirt and navy jeans, a contrast from the black kurtas he had started to wear lately. She supposed they were reserved for public appearances with his grandfather. Then again, she would not know anything about those because she barely watched the news, choosing instead to occupy herself with her books.

He was smiling slightly, and she realized how different he looked compared to when she had first seen him. He still had that look of self-loathing about him, but it looked as if it was buried deeper now. The smile reached his eyes.

"Not really," she said and realized that they were the first words she had said to him that day. His smile widened and he shook his head, while his mother continued to eat her steamed rice and vegetables without a word. Ahmed glanced at her again and nodded slowly, as if understanding that it was something she did not want to talk about in front of his mother. She hated that he understood.

He shook his head slightly before motioning towards the window that looked out upon the lawn, signaling that they could talk outside after lunch, and she was nodding her head before she could stop herself.

"Your father might join us for dinner today," Ahmed's mother said after a while, looking up from her plate at her son.

"Really?" he laughed. "It's kind of pointless now, isn't it?" She tried to focus on her food, but when his mother spoke next, Seher could not help but stop and listen.

"Ahmed, please don't make this time any harder," she was saying. "You've managed to turn things in his favor and he is happy with you. We're going to be okay." Seher could practically hear the woman smiling through her words, and she wondered exactly what it was that Ahmed had done to make things better for his father. Had he and his grandfather managed to bribe the right people and set things right for his family? Who knew how many people he had deceived and wronged to do that? A part of her knew that Ahmed would never do that but she did not know what to think at the moment, considering how her own father had managed to let her down after everything that had happened.

"I did not do it for him," she heard him say and instinctively looked up. He was looking right at her as the words left his mouth, and his mother was gazing at him with an expression of deadly calm on her face, occasionally looking over at her as if to see whether she was listening.

"Ahmed," she sighed. "He is your father."

"Yes, and he had the power to change things out there." He motioned outside, beyond the windows of the dining room. The sun was still casting its golden light over the green grass of the garden, and the red brick walls looked as if they were glowing. But Seher knew he was talking about the city beyond the walls of their house.

"You never seemed to care about all that before when you were out doing God knows what all night with those friends of yours," Mrs. Raza said coldly and Seher, at last nodded encouragingly at him, needing him to know that she understood.

"I did," her son stared right at her. "You just never noticed."

#

The air around them was cold, the sun having vanished minutes earlier, and Seher felt as if it were biting into her skin. It was one of those days in the middle of winder when you could not think of being outside without a sweater or a shawl. The house had always been warm inside but now, she found herself wrapping the pale pink shawl she had gotten a week ago tightly around herself.

The smog would settle in soon, and she shivered at the very thought of it- that, and what possibly lay ahead for her. Ahmed had not pushed her to speak yet and she was grateful for that. He had just been walking silently next to her, and they had unconsciously made their way to the back of the house where the pool lay, glistening under the wide sky.

"Don't you ever use this thing?" she heard herself asking. Ahmed stopped next to her.

"We do," he answered. "But it is winter so the water needs to be heated before we get inside and that takes a while, so I never really bothered and my father well, prefers to stay away from it these days." She wanted to know how they could possibly heat all of the water in the pool at once, but stopped herself from asking.

"I think he prefers to stay away from everyone these days," she said and he laughed. The sound was unlike any she had heard before, simple and pure. She had heard him laugh before but this was different, as if he was not stopping himself from genuinely laughing. She hated to admit it but she was glad for it.

"Yeah, well," he said after he had stopped. "He'll be back to his old self once he realizes I've managed to do his job for him." When she did not answer, he continued. "I did what you wanted, and I think I might actually be helping people."

She turned to look at him when she heard the words. "What did you do?"

"There is a trust that is going to help women and children in the rural areas- the villages." She considered telling him that she knew what rural meant but stopped herself, trying to wrap her head around what he was saying. "So it will provide aid to them, start education and vocational schemes, that sort of thing. We're also working on a sort of shelter for women wanting to get out of abusive marriages and households, and a foundation that would help them gain financial independence."

Each word touched her heart as he uttered it. She thought of Zara and her heart broke a little more. When she thought about all of the things she had thought about this boy at first, she was only left with a numb sensation in her heart, and a dizzying feeling in her head.

"That's… that's amazing," she managed to say. Her voice sounded thick.

"I know there are a lot more problems out there,' Ahmed said, looking at the red walls that surrounded the house. "But I thought this was a good start."

"It is," she smiled at him and he smiled back, a smile that reached his eyes and caused his cheeks to dip slightly. He looked as if he had conquered the whole world at that moment.

"So what was up with you in there?" he said after a few moments, dipping his head towards the house. "You seemed more moody than usual." She knew he was teasing, but could not help but feel like it was true. She had not talked to him or returned any of his attempts to start a conversation in the past couple of days so it must have looked that way.

"My brother and fiancé are coming." Ahmed turned to look at her fully now, his eyes wide.

"What? Here?" he asked, his voice steady but with a hint of urgency in it.

"Yes."

"How do they even know where the house is? The address?"

"My friend," she replied. She could feel her voice trembling and warmth behind her eyelids again. She had tried to hold it in all through lunch and then as he had talked, but now she could feel her life slipping from beneath her fingers. "Her husband knows Arshad and he made her tell. They're coming today."

He was silent for a minute, and they just stood there, gazing out at the water, its surface opaque now because of the cold that was settling in. The trees bordering it whistled and she shivered.

"Okay," he said finally. "Let them come. We'll talk to them. My mother will." If his mind had drifted to her father and why he had not stopped it, he did not let on and she was grateful.

"You don't understand these people, Ahmed." She turned around, her cheeks stained with tears. "They want me back. Back there, and to marry that animal, and after this it's going to be even worse…"

She trailed off, her head swimming with memories. She had managed to keep them at bay for a month, but now they came rushing back, crashing on top of one another; Arshad pushing her up against the wall of her house, his nails digging into her skin and his breath fanning her face, his large hand gripping her arm and pulling her behind the banyan tree on that street behind the school at their village. She shook her head, trying to shake off the feeling of his hands on her.

"Seher." Ahmed was next to her. She could feel him standing in front of her, his hands on her shoulders, unsure what to do. She realized she was shaking. "They won't take you away. I won't let them."

She could feel Arshad dragging her behind the tree and pressing himself up against her, his hands holding her still. She was crying now, and it was getting hard to breathe. She imagined her father again, talking to her over the phone and telling her that he wanted her to be happy, and the tears came faster, spilling down her cheeks and onto Ahmed's shoulder. He had started to rub circles into her back, and she both hated and loved him for it.

Chapter 21

Ahmed

Her whole body was trembling in his arms, and he had no idea what to say or do to make her feel better, only that he really wanted her to feel better; better and safe in his house. He wanted her to know that nothing could happen to her here, and that they would not be able to take her away.

It was obvious that she was remembering some terrible day back in her village and he doubted she wanted to talk about it, but he wanted her to know that she could count on him to protect her from them. If they came here to take her, he would talk to them and send them away, fight them if he had to.

"I'll send them away," he said to her before reaching for her hand. She flinched for a second and then looked at him, moving a step away. Ahmed could not help the lump that formed in his throat at the movement, but he decided to ignore it. She was probably thinking of her past in the village, and something that her fiancé had done, and it was natural for her to not want to be touched by anyone at that time.

"I can't go back there," she said, her voice steadier than he had imagined it would be. She had stopped crying by now, and he was glad.

"You won't have to," he promised. "I'll talk to them."

"You don't understand…" she began, her voice still steady, but her face was ash white.

"Seher," he said and she stiffened, as if hearing her own name rattled her. "Your father is not with them, that's a good sign. It makes it easier to send them away. I promise you'll be safe." Each word felt like an oath as it left his mouth and when she looked back at him, her eyes hard and yet filled with doubt, he reached over and tucked a loose strand of hair behind her ear. She flinched, but did not move away, and he felt relief inside.

"Okay." The word echoed around them as they stood gazing down into the pool. Ahmed's mind raced as he thought about all the possible outcomes of the day. There had to be a way. He would think of one.

They began making their way back to the house, and he was already thinking about whether his father needed to know about this predicament or not. He would certainly not be happy about it, but then again the man owed him for the way he had brought his party back into a good light, and bought him some time as well. He felt as if his mother would not care as long as they got rid of the disturbance quickly, she had taken to cooperating lately. But he would talk to Seher's brother and fiancé outside, he decided. There was no need to bring them into the house near her anyway.

He would tell them that she was well taken care of, and he would make sure that she was safe. He could not explain the feeling that had settled in his chest as soon as she had mentioned them taking her away, but he was sure that if they did, he would not be able to live with himself. She had such a long way to go, and such potential too, he thought to himself, as they neared the front steps. But he also knew that those were not the only reasons that he wanted her to stay.

They had just reached the front door when she turned to him, her face completely free of tears now. "Thank you."

She was looking at him with an intense look in her eyes, and at that moment she reminded him of the sun. He knew he needed to look away simply because of the intensity of the gaze, but he also knew that he did not want to. There was something in that look that made him want to keep looking at her until she looked away. His heart swelled at her words, not because of what she had said; he had never really expected or wanted gratitude, but just the way she had said them. In that moment she looked more exposed than she ever had, it was as if she was letting him see the real, broken, yet somehow fearless woman behind all those barriers. She looked vulnerable, but he also knew she was perhaps the strongest person he would ever meet.

"Don't mention it." It felt as if an eternity had passed between her words and his. She was still looking at him, and smiled a little at his answer before nodding slowly. Her eyes had a strange look in them, determined and yet sad, as if she was trying to decide something quietly. A minute passed and she blinked, motioning to the door.

"Your mother won't appreciate this," she said with a little laugh and he chuckled, silently wishing he could draw that sound from her again. Maybe he would later. They did have some time after all before she had to leave, and it was not as if they would never see each other again...

"Don't worry about her," he said and meant it. He would make sure both his parents helped her. He had made a promise after all. They stood in the entryway, and he noticed her gaze shift to the huge crystal chandelier overhead before moving to the twin set of stairs leading to the upper floors. A shadow passed over her face but was gone so fast that he was sure he had imagined it.

"When will they be here, did she say?" he asked her, referring to her friend from the village.

Sher shook her head. "She didn't," she replied. "But it will take at least three hours or more because they will have to change buses and then find their way here too."

"The busses take that long?" He remembered that it had taken them only an hour and a half to get to Zaleemabad for his father's campaign. That day seemed so long ago now. Seher shook her head.

"They do." At his surprised expression, she added. "We don't all have cars that go as fast as yours without stopping, you know?"

"Touché," he smiled at her, and she blinked. Of course she did not know what that meant, he scolded himself and backtracked. "It means…" But Seher was already making her way up the stairs.

"I need to shower!" She called down and he sighed before shaking his head. She had come such a long way; she was clearly no longer just a girl from some village anymore and knew almost all of the ways of the city. He remembered how quickly she had started to learn and adapt to their ways, and smiled as he walked into the living room where his mother was sitting on the couch, a cup of green tea on the table next to her and a magazine open on her lap, while her phone buzzed repeatedly next to her.

"Are you not going to get that?"

Mrs. Raza Ali Khan looked up at the sound of her son's voice, and placed a bookmark in her magazine; it was a page with a picture of a leading Hollywood actress and some man she was supposedly having an affair with, clearly her husband's present status had not changed the gossip junkie within his mother.

"It's probably that reporter from *The News*," she said absentmindedly, taking a sip of her tea. "He's been hounding me for two days now for a statement about the new foundation." She did not mention the exchange from lunch and he was not surprised, talking about problems was never how they handled things. Sweeping things under the rug was more their forte after all.

'The foundation as in the shelter?' Ahmed asked just to be sure he had heard right. His mother nodded.

"Why aren't you giving them one then?" His mother had always been quick to give her two cents about any topic, even when it did not concern her, so it was a surprise to see her refraining from it now.

"He wants to know what inspired it and I am not going to confirm your outrageous statement about some leach from who-knows-where making you see the light." Her words were ice cold, and he could feel the weight of each one striking him one after another. Of course she would still think she was a leach, even after all this time. Seher had been nothing but polite to her, taking all of her sarcasm in stride and not saying a word, and here she was refusing to acknowledge her.

"She is nothing like what you think she is," he sighed and his mother rolled her eyes.

"Do you think I don't know what's going on here? She asked. "I know what she's doing to you, and I know you've let her take control of you."

"She hasn't taken control of me!" he answered, his heart sinking with the realization that despite everything he had done or achieved, things between him and his mother could not change. "Is it so hard for you to understand that I genuinely want to be different?" His mother watched him for a moment before answering.

"Different from your father?" she asked incredulously. "The man who has ensured you get the best of everything, who made sure this family lived comfortably?" She was looking at him with an unreadable expression, and Ahmed was sure that it was disappointment.

"Yes," he answered, and his mother stood up.

"Ahmed," she said. "I know it might seem like the right thing to do, but you need to understand…"

He looked back at her, the woman who had brought him up for all these years and yet one who seemed so far away now, but then again she had always been far away, lost in this new world that the Khan family had allowed her to enter and one she refused to let go of, even if it meant living a lie.

"You're afraid of people realizing your son has started mixing with questionable people again?" Ahmed asked slowly, knowing the answer already. His parents had always had a set idea of the kind of people he was allowed to talk to and be friends with ever since he was a little boy and he had adhered to those rules until ninth grade. That had been the year everything had changed, when he had met Fahad and the others. His mother nodded.

"We need to present a certain front," she told him as if he did not know already. "We need to be careful who we are seen with, Ahmed, and helping her is fine, but telling people you have allowed her to get so close…"

"I have let her get so close," he cut his mother off, his throat burning with the words. "She has changed me and I'm glad she did." When his mother tried to interrupt, he continued. "You may not like her but I... I feel like she's better than all of us. She does not use people like we do, and she does not pretend to be something she's not. She deserves so much, and I want to give it to her. If she inspired something good, people should know about it." He had a feeling the words would make no difference to his mother, but he had needed to say them.

For a minute that seemed to stretch on for an eternity, Mrs. Raza Khan looked on at her son who was miles away from her. He had changed ever since that girl had come, and she needed to admit that to herself. He smiled and laughed more than he had before, and he did not have that air of self-hatred about him as he always had. She was glad for that of course, but a small part of her broke in that moment as she sensed that things would be different now.

Her husband, the man who had made sure she lived within the safety of such a well-crafted world where stability and security was guaranteed, would no longer be able to protect her. She felt strangely exposed in that moment as she felt those layers of protection coming off, and the inevitability of an unknown future took form. The man who had ensured she got all her work done and yearly shopping sprees as well as the prestigious position in society was no longer an integral part of his own political party, and the one who had replaced him was her son, with whom she already had a rocky relationship. If she was to feel secure again, she had to fix that.

"Okay," she said at last. "I will tell them about Seher; that she... made this possible."

"Thank you," Ahmed answered slowly, knowing that his mother hated this new arrangement, but choosing not to say more on the subject.

His mother smiled at him, a small smile that reached her eyes and made them sparkle in the light that was streaming in from outside. He did not know what had just happened or why she had suddenly just agreed, but he decided he did not want to know. There were more important things to do.

"I need to talk to dad," he said as his mother picked up her magazine again, her manicured hands gripping the covers tightly, as if she was holding on to a lifeline.

"He's in his office," she told him without looking at him. "Ask him if he got my message earlier about the interview with *Geo*." He nodded even though he knew she could not see him, and started for his father's study. He knew his father had been avoiding the media lately; the old man had been cooped up in his room for days, only showing his face for meetings with his grandfather.

To his surprise, the door to the study was open, and he walked in to see Raza Ali Khan seated behind his mahogany desk, a phone pressed to his ear and a pen twisting in his right hand, a sore contrast to how he had been the past few days. He looked healthier too, his eyes less bloodshot than usual and his complexation slightly less ghastly. A shadow crossed over his face when he saw Ahmed standing in the doorway.

"To what do I owe this pleasure?" he said, after placing the phone back on the desk. Despite, the worry and exhaustion that had been gripping the man lately, he sounded relatively better than he had in days.

Closing the door softly behind him, he made his way to the chair he had so often occupied, mostly right after he had gotten in some kind of trouble, only for his father to bail him out before delivering the lecture that would always stress on him bringing shame to the family name. The desk was less cluttered now, he noticed; the only items present being a laptop and a stack of newspapers on the side. Ahmed clasped his hands together on the smooth hardwood surface.

"Congratulations," he began, choosing to ignore his father's earlier greeting. There was no point quipping about it now. When he got no response, he continued. "On the results of the polls. We seem to be doing pretty well."

A brisk nod was the answer. "They will have all the evidence they need soon," his father said, looking directly at him. Ahmed could not help but gaze at those brown eyes whose approval he had sought since he had been a boy, and he felt a pang of pity for his father. "I will have to leave in a couple days." Ahmed nodded; clearly there was a limit to the amount of bribes you could offer to the people leading the investigation.

He wanted to tell his father that it was what he got for all the dirty deeds he had been doing for years, for the people he had hurt, for the money he had accumulated through means that was never legal. He had been covering up his tracks quite well over the years, but things were bound to catch up with him one day. Instead, he just nodded.

Raza Khan was leaning back in his chair so the light from the golden sun outside shone directly on his hair, hair that had now turned a dull shade of grey, even white in some places. "They will be investigating everyone for a while now, and it's better to be away from all that. For me." Ahmed knew what he wanted to say, that it was a good thing people were finally being forced to take responsibility for their actions, but he stared back at his father as he continued. "I don't know when

I'll be able to return but for now, it's all in your hands."

"I'll do my best," he found himself saying and his father smiled, a rare smile that he did not usually bestow on anyone. He was suddenly reminded of the day before his rally in front of the Lahore Fort, when his father had at last acknowledged that he was doing a good job.

"I know you will," he said. "Your mother told me about the shelter idea you came up with, and I think it has potential." He knew his father liked the idea for all the wrong reasons, one of them being that it meant good publicity, but he smiled back.

"Thank you. They are going to start working on it soon." His father nodded and they sat in silence for what might have been hours or minutes, each lost in his own thoughts. Ahmed was thinking about how he had been ready to finally tell his father exactly what he thought of him, he had been for a while now. He wanted to step out of his shadow on his own, and do something that was completely his, to show his father that he was a better person than him and the rest. But he had not been able to go through with it in the end, he realized, and now instead of that familiar throb of self-loathing that echoed inside him, he felt nothing.

His father knew, he thought to himself. On some level he knew that Ahmed was a better person than he was, and that he could do a lot more than he thought. He had realized that now, and he was willing to leave the country and let him take over, and just the fact that he had finally come to realize this was enough to make him consider letting the past go. He had what he wanted now after all.

Seher had played a huge part in that, and he realized that he was smiling now. She had managed to make him see that he did not have to continue hating himself and the world for what his family had done. Instead, he could be the change himself. He imagined her looking at him over the dinner table with those deep hazel eyes of hers, and her dark brown hair falling in loose curls around her shoulders. He thought about that morning, and how she had cried in his arms and he had wanted to do anything to make things right for her.

"I need a favor," he said, perhaps for the first time in his life. The words felt foreign and dry as they left his mouth, but he was glad that he had said them.

Chapter 22

Seher

She did not know what kind of deal Ahmed had made with his father or whether he had even agreed. It was now almost time for Arshad and Hamid to arrive, and she was trying not to panic at the thought of not having seen Ahmed since their encounter outside. Her breaths came fast and ragged as she waited in the living room alone. Mrs. Raza had not been there when she had come down after showering about an hour ago and that was a first.

A lifestyle magazine lay open on the coffee table along with a half empty cup of green tea. Her mind brimmed with questions as she clenched and unclenched her fists in her lap, a habit she had picked up from her mother. Had he talked to his mother too? Why wasn't he here yet? Had his father agreed to help? She knew she would be indebted to Ahmed if today went well, after al he would make it possible for her to have a chance at a better life.

Ahmed was a good person, she decided. He had to be the only man who had not disappointed her yet, and that said a lot about his character. Her own father had chosen the customs and opinions of others before his daughter in the end, and her brother had slowly started to realize that the benefits this society offered him for being a man were worth more than his love for his sister. He had allowed them to be the driving force behind his actions and she barely even recognized him now.

Arshad had been the most recent one, she thought. She had never liked him and had never thought that she could love him either, but she had also never thought that he would be the one to drive her out of her village. In some twisted way, she was grateful to him for that. But it did not change anything he had done, she told herself. A man who was supposed to protect her, with whom she was expected to spend the rest of her life with had made her completely lose faith in the opposite gender. She hated him for that, for making her doubt Ahmed as she had more times than once, for making her believe she could not trust him.

"My father will help." She was jolted out of her thoughts by Ahmed's voice and she nearly winced, remembering what she had been thinking about. "He says chances are that they will agree to letting you stay here in exchange for money, and he will talk to them about that…" He hesitated before correcting himself. "Your fiancé."

She sat there and let his words sink in for a minute before answering. "They won't listen, and they'll want to talk to me too." She shuddered involuntarily at the thought of being in a room with Arshad again.

"So let them talk," Ahmed looked at her and smiled. "It will be in this house, and they can't take you anywhere without me knowing." She smiled back and sighed. Maybe this would work after all.

"My brother isn't going to make this easy," she sighed. "Neither will Arshad." Ahmed appeared to struggle to decide something for a minute before sitting down next to her on the couch, their legs barely touching. She fought the instinct to move away.

"I won't make this easy for them either then." His smile was so genuine that it nearly broke her heart.

"Okay," she nodded.

"We will give them enough to drive them away," Ahmed continued. "My dad has enough money that he needs to get rid of so that won't be a problem, and he also says that these people will do anything if it means money for them and their families so this should work." He stood up then and looked over his shoulder at her, the hint of a smile on his lips. "I'm going to look for my father." She watched wordlessly as he retreated from the room.

There were so many things that were wrong with what he had just said, she realized. Just the idea of them paying her family for her made her sick to her stomach. It was like putting a price on her, and the very idea made her want to hurl. Referring to them as "these people" and making it sound like they were that desperate made her want to scream that she had been one of them too.

The fact that she was different was another story. But it made him sound like the conceited rich boy she had first assumed that he was. But she bit her tongue as she imagined finally being free of the shackles that had held her back for so long.

It was not even about just money, she thought. They would feel betrayed and dishonored, and that was something money might not be able to fix. She was supposed to be their pride after all. There was no telling how far they were willing to go to satisfy their own egos.

She knew that she did not want to be completely cut off from them. They were family after all, and she wanted to keep them all in her life, except Arshad. She knew she would still miss her father even after everything he had done, and so she found herself hoping that he had at least tried to talk some sense into her brother and fiancé. Seher waited in silence as the minutes ticked by. She wondered silently about where Ahmed's mother was or whether his father would come downstairs. That latter was answered soon enough.

She heard him before she saw him, the footsteps being quick and heavy on the stairs and then outside the living room. The door that led to the entryway opened, and her breath hitched in her throat. She did not know what she had been expecting, but this had definitely not been it. A tall man of about 6'3, perhaps with a bald patch and wide set, intimidating dark eyes had been a few of the characteristics that her mind had come to associate with Ahmed's father, but now, standing a few feet away from her, he was completely different.

He was shorter than she had pictured him for starters, with thinning salt and pepper hair, and a mustache that she could just about picture him twirling when he was deep in thought about something. Sallow cheeks and a droopy mouth adorned his face and from the dampness of his hair, she could only guess that he had only just showered.

She was surprised to see that he looked like a worn out rag doll in his immaculate blue suit that had quite possibly been tailored especially for him. Perhaps it was the slight redness of his eyes or the way his shoulders hung back in a resigned fashion that gave her that impression, but the man certainly did not look like someone who was capable of stealing from the people of his country and using people for his own personal gain.

"*Assalamalaikum*," she instinctively stood up as she spoke and the man nodded before his lips stretched into a smile. It had to be causing him a lot of effort because it was gone after a second. Ahmed's father clasped her hand politely, and nodded to the sofa before sitting down across from her in a chair

"Ahmed has told me so much about you," he started and she was surprised to hear that his voice was soft. But then again, she realized. That was what these people were good at; pretending to be one thing when they were the complete opposite. "I'm glad we were able to help you."

She knew he was not, but nodded. "He has been so kind," she said. "Your wife too, and I'm really grateful." Something twisted in her stomach as she said those words. However, this seemed to please him because he smiled again and nodded.

"I'm happy you are getting along fine, *beta*. He told me about your family…" He paused, searching for the right word. "Situation. But we will take care of that too."

"Thank you," she said and then added, her voice trembling. "They're not so easy to talk to though."

Raza Khan smiled at her again. "I know," he said, a hint of understanding in his voice, and Seher began to understand how people found it so easy to believe him. "Ahmed is outside talking to them now and if there is any trouble or if they want to talk inside, we will know." His words chilled her bones.

"What?" she gasped, unable to comprehend the words. She had wondered where Ahmed was, but she had not for a second thought that they could be here already, and that he could be talking to them at that moment. The world was sliding under her feet and the room began to spin in front of her for a moment, her mind brimming with a thousand thoughts, a thousand possibilities. "Where are they?" she whispered, and Ahmed's father looked back at her. Was that concern on his face? She doubted it.

"They had just pulled up at the gate when I came in," he explained. "We thought it would be better if Ahmed talked to them outside first."

Seher could feel her palms beginning to sweat, and her heart felt like it was about to beat out of her chest any minute. Her mind reeled with possibilities. What were they saying outside? Had they agreed to what Ahmed had said? Was Arshad there? A small part of her, a part she did not want to acknowledge, began to fear for Ahmed's wellbeing. Arshad would lose his mind when he saw him. After all, to him it would just look like she was with another man, and never mind any explanations; a man's ego and pride blocked the way to his mind in the village. She could only imagine what they must think of her.

"*Beta*, it will be alright," Raza Khan was saying in what she assumed was supposed to be a soothing voice. Another part of her began to loathe him and his son for simply deciding on the best course of action without consulting her. It was her family after all. But she pushed those thoughts out of her mind.

"They might get physical," she said, trying to explain just how extreme the situation could get. A look of contempt passed over the man's face, and she was almost sure she knew what he was thinking. Villagers, uncultured, unrefined…

"I'm sure it will be fine," he replied instead. "Besides, Ahmed is quite fond of you so I'm sure he will handle it. He does not want them to take you away at all." An unreadable expression passed over his face, but she was almost sure she saw a flicker of displeasure flash in his eyes, though it was gone instantly. She sat there and let his words play over in her head, struggling to come up with a suitable answer while her heart continued to race.

She was almost glad when a knock sounded at the door, signaling the entrance of an ashen-faced manservant. "Sir, they want to see *baaji* before they leave." It took Seher a moment to realize that he had referred to her.

Ahmed's father shifted his gaze to her for a second before saying. "Bring them in then." The man nodded, his expression doubtful as he exited the room in a hurry. She barely had time to gather her thoughts before the door opened again and he came back, followed by three other men. Instinctively, she got to her feet.

The three men entered slowly, as if knowing the gravity of the situation they were in. Ahmed was in the front and Seher noticed that his hair, usually combed back, was now a tangled mess at the top of his head. He had probably been running his fingers through it. His eyes were impossible to read as he walked over and stood next to her, clearly trying to decide whether it was a good idea to sit down. She could see both Hamid and Arshad stiffen at the gesture.

Slowly, she let her gaze drift over to the two men. They had halted as soon as they had entered, and she noticed her brother looking around the room, clearly trying not to show the fact that he was impressed by the grand crystal chandelier or the white rug that was placed in the middle of the room, the rug that made you feel like you were walking on clouds. He was looking at the sofa now, his eyes taking in the fine cushions. Despite their differences, she knew her brother, and she could tell when he was impressed but did not want to show it. A part of her was happy at the thought of him knowing she was living here instead of the dump they had shared back home.

Then, she let herself look at Arshad. He had the same look of suppressed jealousy and enchantment in his eyes, she decided as she watched him taking in the exquisite painting on the wall and then the electric fireplace under the mantle.

She was surprised to see that he still looked the same as she remembered him; she did not know what she had expected but she had not counted on him looking like the same man she had left. His hair, still the same dark curls and his eyes the same dark ones that had stared into her soul as his hands had raked all over her. Every nerve in her body was telling her to look away now, to hide, but another part of her, a more rational part was pushing her to stare back into those soulless eyes, to not let him or anyone have power over her again.

"*Assalamalaikum*," Arshad said into the silence that now reigned in the room. Hamid was looking at her too, his face completely blank.

"*Walikumasalam*," she replied, trying not to think about that day behind the banyan tree. The memories were resurfacing now, or perhaps they had never really gone away; they were trying to push past the wall she had constructed in her mind. But she forced them back as she locked eyes with Hamid. "How are you? How is *amma*?"

The words had been an effort to get out, but she realized then that she really did want to know how he was, how her parents were and Zara as well. God, she missed her sister.

"Good," her brother answered. "*Amma* is sick though." When she did not respond he continued. "Of course you would not care." She had not responded because her gaze had darted to Ahmed instinctively. He was still standing next to her, watching the other two men through narrowed eyes, and when their gazes locked, something passed through his that made her heart stop beating for an instant.

She blinked, feeling moisture behind her eyelids and whether it was because of Hamid's words or from what had just transpired between herself and Ahmed, she did not know. But she nodded to the man standing next to her, letting him know that she was okay and that he could leave the room if he wanted to. As he cast one last glance at her and then at his father, signaling to him that it was better for them to talk privately for a while, she wondered how it was that a simple nod from her had managed to convey so much to him.

"I'll be right outside," he murmured leaning towards her ear, and she stood still as he brushed past the other two men who were now bristling. Arshad's eyes were raking over her entire body, his gaze as hard as ice. She knew what was going through his mind, it had to have hurt him to see her with another man.

He was looking straight into her eyes, and she stared right back, not willing to show that a part of her was still in their village behind that tree, struggling to escape from under his grip as his nails dug into her hair, forcing her face towards him.

"I do care," she said to her brother when the door had closed. "You know that too." She was referring to the days when she had stayed up waiting for her mother, father and brother to come home from work with a pot of tea ready for them on the days when thy did not have anything to cook, and plates of gravy and chapattis when they had.

"*Abba* is dying," Hamid said coldly. "He does not have long, and *amma* just stays in bed all day." An icy stillness settled in her heart at the words, something she was sure Hamid had known would happen. She could tell what he was doing of course. He knew that he could not take her with him, so instilling guilt within her was the next best alternative. But she had to know.

"What happened to him?" She hated the tremor in her voice as the words left her mouth.

"You left him." Arshad was talking now, and she could feel the hair rising at the back of her neck from his voice alone, but she did not break eye contact with him. "You left him, made a joke out of him and it cost him his health. You put yourself before him and look what came out of it." She wanted to scream at him, tell him that she had talked to her father on the phone and that he had understood. But the words refused to come out.

"I didn't do it on purpose," she shot back instead. "That village was suffocating me and you all saw it. I never wanted him to get sick." She was looking at her brother now. "None of you stood by me through it, through…" She wanted to say 'through what he did', and the words were right at the tip of her tongue.

"The village was suffocating you?" Arshad laughed, and Hamid was shaking his head. "Who taught you that word, these rich city people?" He came closer, and she balled her fists at her sides. Did Hamid even know the kind of man Arshad really was? Of course he did not, she realized. Even if he did, he would never stand against him after his sister had tainted his name.

"You are supposed to be my wife." He enunciated each word slowly, making sure it hit her as hard as he intended. "You are supposed to be at home. With me. Do you realize what you did to your name? To mine?"

"Your name?" she retorted, and silently applauded herself for not backing down. "You deserve to be stoned after what you did." She could still see herself against that tree with him hovering over her, the bruises he had left on her arms starting to throb.

Hamid was looking at her through half-lidded eyes and it was then that she realized that he knew, he had to know what had happened or he would not be so calm right then. He had to know what Arshad had done to her, but he was not going to do anything about it. She waited for the betrayal and disappointment to seep in, and for the grief and tears to come at the realization of her brother being at peace with the fact that her fiancé had beaten and almost raped her. But nothing came.

"I am allowed to do as I please to put you in your place." Arshad screamed and she shuddered involuntarily. "You disobeyed me, and I am permitted to punish you as I see fit. I was merely doing my duty." His words rushed at her, and she let them sink in, reveling in the eerie calm that they brought. He no longer made her feel helpless, or afraid, and his words no longer caused her to tremble.

"When was the last time you read the book?" she asked, laughing now, referring to the Holy Book. There was silence in the room, and she looked at Hamid. "You can keep trying to use religion to justify your own twisted mentality, but I'm glad I won't be around to see or hear of it."

Arshad was laughing at her now. "You've let all this," he waved his arm around the room. "Cloud your judgement, but you will see sense eventually, and when you do, the only thing you will have to come back to will be our village. I won't forgive you then even if you kiss the ground I walk on. "

"I won't be coming back," she said slowly, more to herself than to him. She was picturing her father, lying sick in bed and her mother next to him. She imagined them talking about her, blaming her for leaving and not wondering why, or whether they should have stood up for her. "I'm done with that village. And you."

"You're making a huge mistake, Seher," her brother said, using her name for the first time since he had come. "These people will spit you out soon and you will not have anyone."

"People like you deserve no one," Arshad put in. "You know you can't be what they are even if you try reading their books, and studying and behaving the way they let their girls do. Sooner or later, you will know your place and then it will be too late. You can still earn forgiveness." His last words sent a shudder down her spine and she shook her head. She wanted to see him and men like him be punished, to be taught never to treat another woman the way he had treated her, to be locked up for using religion as a tool.

"You'll see," she said simply, her mind already far away from the room she was in. She watched with eyes that were now glossed over as the two men continued to talk, trying to hit a nerve, threatening her and in the end, when all else failed, cutting all ties with her. She watched in silence as they walked out, leaving her alone with tear stained cheeks and a clear conscience.

Ahmed walked back in minutes later and she allowed him to talk to her in that sweet, gentle voice that he had been using with her for a while, to look at her as if she was a miracle from God, and to promise her that he would make sure she stayed safe here in this city, knowing that it was a lie.

#

She was sure the suitcase felt much heavier than it actually was as she dragged it out into the hallway, her palms sweating under the effort. Golden sunlight was pouring onto the slanted lettering on the newly-purchased leather bag, making sure the letters stood out. Her eyes drifted to the silver watch dangling from her wrist and she realized that she only had five more minutes if she wanted to make it in time for the orientation.

"I never thought August would come so soon." She knew the voice before she turned around, her heart fluttering just like it had recently taken to doing every time she heard his voice. But, just like every other time, she ignored it.

"I guess this is it," she said. He was wearing one of his usual black shirts, his hair carefully combed away from his face, leaving his eyes completely exposed. Without meaning to, she looked into them; they had always been filled with cold, unyielding hatred before, but now they shone as he looked at her. She could no longer see a trace of that all-consuming self-loathing there. She wished she could say the same for herself.

"I still don't understand why you won't let me drop you off," Ahmed was saying. They were standing a few inches apart on the first floor landing, his hand reaching for the handle of her suitcase. The gesture moved something inside her. "It's almost as if you're embarrassed to be seen with me." He bumped her shoulder gently and she laughed.

"People would see you as soon as you stepped out of the car," she replied, turning away from him and making her way downstairs. He followed. "You wouldn't want them getting the wrong idea." He was quiet after that, and she almost hated herself for the words that she had uttered, knowing the truth that they alluded to, the truth of his feelings towards her, feelings he had been making obvious over the past few weeks.

He did not say anything until they had reached the front door where Ahmed's mother was waiting for them, his father had left the country some weeks ago, had run away from the mess he had made and left his son to clean up. She shook her head knowing she did not need to think about him. She was finally getting out of here after all this time.

"*Allah Hafiz*, aunty," she said as Mrs. Raza Khan wrapped her arms around her. She could feel her wince as her hand brushed her back, no doubt still not appreciating being embraced like that by a girl from a village. But Seher chose to ignore it as she pulled away and smiled. The sunlight was reflected in the dainty diamonds that adorned the other woman's neck.

"Take care of yourself," the woman said and she nodded. "Stay in touch. I'm sure Ahmed won't leave you alone now so I'll probably be seeing you again soon." She cast a look at her son who was standing a few paces away, and smiled.

"I'm sure," Seher replied. She could almost taste the lie on her own tongue.

"The bags are all in." Ahmed had come up next to her now.

"Thank you."

"Don't mention it," he replied. "You deserve this."

'I'm not so sure," she said, wanting to have a few more minutes on the steps, a few paces away from the car that would take her away from there, away from a place she had come close to calling home.

"You finished your portfolio and your exams, first division at that, in just a few months," Ahmed told her, pride lacing each word. He turned to her, and she trembled a little as he placed his hands on her shoulders, compelling her to look at him. "I think you do."

She could hear the distant roar of other cars as they sped by outside, the rustle of the leaves as they were stirred by a breeze, and the honk of the taxi she would be taking. She knew the rest of the world awaited her, knew that once she left this house, she would be completely on her own in the world with no one to hold on to, no one who believed in her. Alone.

"You don't hate yourself anymore," she said, her voice coming out thicker than she had imagined. Ahmed smiled at her, a smile that she had come to associate with him alone. It told you that he was completely at ease in that moment, that he was glad to be with you, and that he knew the very next minute had the potential to be magical. It was real, he was real, free from the demons that had been holding him back all these years.

"I don't," he told her. "Thank you for that." She allowed herself a smile too, letting herself enjoy that one moment with him, of knowing that she had made a difference in his life and he had made one in hers. They had both helped each other out of something only they could understand, and it was a connection they would share forever, even if they never saw each other again.

"Don't mention it," she repeated his words, and started to walk towards the car parked a few paces away. The breeze that had felt warm a few minutes ago was now cold against her skin.

"I'll see you again," Ahmed said as she started to get into the taxi. When she looked back, she could barely make him out. He was standing directly in the path of the harsh afternoon sun now, illuminated by it. She found it impossible to make eye contact as the car began to slowly back out of the driveway. Seher nodded silently, already a hundred miles away from him.

Epilogue

The city buzzed with life around her, the blistering heat failing to vanquish the electric energy that flowed through the atmosphere. Music reached her ears, a mixture of beats all blended into one, and the sun reflected off the sleek, luxurious cars that that stopped at the red light next to her own car. She rolled her eyes as a woman with a baby in her arms knocked on her window, asking for spare change.

The dirty, worn *dupatta* that covered the beggar's head might have been red at some point and the skin around her face supple. However, now she was gazing into hollow eyes surrounded by parched, brown skin that reminded her of paper. The baby was fast asleep on her shoulder, wrapped in a hideous blue blanket despite the heat. Seher glanced down at the phone in her lap. She was late.

"Could you please hurry up?" The driver glanced back at her, an expression of irritation crossing his face. This was the third time she had asked him to speed up. Traffic was worse than usual today, and they had been stuck at the stoplight for about ten minutes now.

"We will be there soon, madam," he replied, his words coming out more clipped than he had meant them to. After all, she was his main source of income.

Seher sank back against the leather seat of the car and allowed herself a gulp of air, the smell of leather always calmed her down. She glanced out of the window yet again at the tall structures around her that looked as if they might touching the sky, the radiant sun reflected in their glass windows. There had been a time when they had intimidated her, a time when she had felt like the smallest person alive as she walked inside one of them. Now however, she felt as if there was nowhere else she would rather be. This city, with its tall buildings, fast cars and fine food was exactly where she wanted to be.

News of her father's death had reached her the previous year, breaking her heart along-with any connection she might have had to the village she had grown up in. There was nothing there for her now, she had realized that day with tears streaming down her face as her sister cried to her over the phone. Zara had refused to come to the city, choosing instead to stay and support their family in their time of need. The two had argued and Seher had not heard from her ever since.

Several phone calls had been planned on her part with an intention to fix things, but none of them had come to pass.

The traffic had begun to move at last, and she breathed a sigh of relief when she realized that she would not be late after all. She needed this meeting to go well. Architecture was a tough field of employment but it paid good money, she thought to herself. It also made sure she did not lose her house in Gulberg or the many designer clothes that now hung in her closet.

Her mind drifted off to the dinner she was supposed to attend that night, it was an exclusive party being thrown by one of her company's many clients in order to celebrate the opening of their hotel. She would have to get her hair done right after the meeting if she wanted to get there on time.

Her phone buzzed in her lap then and she slid her finger across the screen to read the message, the name of the sender sending a wave of nostalgia and memories through her as it always had. It was Rabia asking if she was doing okay. The two barely talked now, only conversing about once a month to check on each other. Seher could not help the small sigh that escaped her lips at her friend's poor grammar. She would learn someday, she decided. Typing out a quick reply, one she had no doubt Rabia would spend an hour trying to understand, she looked around her. Seher tried not to let the familiar nervous sensation take over her as they pulled up in front of her office. She took one minute, as was her habit to look at herself in a small compact mirror that she had now taken to carrying around. Her lips were painted a deep shade of red and her hair was perfectly in place, pinned away from her face. A gold chain dangled from her neck.

The glass doors slid open upon her arrival, and she breathed in the smell of cleaning liquids mixed with jasmine and lavender. She was where she belonged now. Hiking the strap of her new leather purse up over her shoulder, she made her way towards the line of elevators on the side. A pile of newspapers sat on a table next to them and she picked one up, absentmindedly reading over the headlines. 'AHMED RAZA KHAN, VOICE OF THE YOUTH TO SPEAK AT ANNUAL WOMEN'S ENTREPROURIAL CONFERENCE.'

The picture that accompanied the headline was of a man she barely recognized, sallow cheeks, hollow eyes and a mouth that was pressed into a frown. A shiver ran down her spine as she realized that what she saw in his eyes was pain, still raw and true, even after five years.

Printed in Great Britain
by Amazon